MW00676210

GOOD MEN

A NOVEL BY

JEFF PUTNAM

BASKERVILLE
PUBLISHERS, LTD
DALLAS · NEW YORK · DUBLIN

BASKERVILLE Publishers, Ltd.
7540 LBJ/Suite 125, Dallas, TX 75251-1008

Library of Congress Catalog Card Number: 92-070842
ISBN: 0-9627509-7-2

Manufactured in the United States of America
First Printing

ONE

All summer long dad saw us off after breakfast in his bathrobe. Good thing people with bathrobes on are always in the family. Even the men I knew in Dudbury could have said something about my father's taste: inch-wide, shiny stripes of blue and the kind of tan that could have been off-white once.

An Andover man would have told the true story until the whole school knew: huge balls that chased each other whenever he crossed his legs or hung there when his knot got loose. He'd only flashed them twice in front of me but I never stopped worrying about the next time, when someone besides Tom or me might see.

I'd had my response ready since winter term of last year when a guy from Greenwich had said he might drop in on me during spring break but didn't say when. "He was a Shakespearean actor, for chrissakes. Haven't you ever been in a dressing room?"

My father and I never went anywhere together these days. When we were still on good terms—last summer before my grades arrived—he'd taken me to some ballgames. Even then I was walking ahead. Oh, he was no one to be ashamed of when he was tweedy, and he didn't try to put his arm around me in public, but I'd known what he was going to find in a certain manila envelope from the school and if I'd acted as if I thought I was good enough to be his pal he'd have been twice as bloodthirsty when my true worth came out.

When my grades came this summer they were even worse and the reports about my conduct sounded desperate.

"I'm not wasting another penny on him," he told my mother. "If he goes back there to make fools of us for another year, you can foot the bill."

My mother didn't say anything. At this point she often said, "I don't want to start an argument." Whenever we were all together she would try to stop the arguments. Nothing could ever shut up my father, and I was always good for an infuriating reply. Tom took my mother's side, but he could seldom do it openly.

Tom was my younger brother, we were only a year apart, but it was obvious that we were on different paths in life. The gulf between us was really an ocean. Tom was a plodder with home-run power and I was supposed to be a genius who was attracted to bad company.

My father thought I had an unhealthy interest in the seamy side of life. The only seams I cared about were the ones in girls' clothes, and it's true, I was very interested in the ones with work to do.

Actually, Tom was smart as hell, but he'd never done anything in school to tip off his teachers and my parents gave him a pat on the back whenever he rose to a B or a B+. Anyway, my father didn't give a damn about Tom's grades. He was happy as long as my brother wasn't hanging out with the kids who wanted to work on cars for the rest of their lives.

Tom was a great athlete, one of the best baseball players our town ever produced. My dad's idea was that Tom would get a baseball scholarship to some shitty school in California or the Southwest—one of those giant universities famous for its sports programs and the size and short hair of its students.

My father was a baseball fanatic. If it weren't for baseball he'd still have been doing Shakespeare or hanging out with his old-time radio and vaudeville friends at the Lambs or calling horseraces or hobnobbing with First Ladies. The only position he held now was President of the Dudbury Babe Ruth League, which said it all about him. Or maybe not. The only reason they made him President, in my opinion, was so he'd stop having fistfights with the managers.

First thing at breakfast, before my mother even brought him his orange juice, he had the paper open to the sports page and was talking baseball to Tom. I was a good pitcher and knew as much about baseball as Tom, but I was on the other side of my father's paper. Tom would look over and ask what I thought, but the paper never came down when I replied. Sometimes Tom would relay my opinions to my father, but if my father had any comment it was because he chose to treat my opinions as if they were Tom's.

It was great to have a job to go to after breakfast. I'd done summer jobs from the time I was ten. I'd had a newspaper route and I'd mowed lawns. Then I branched out into the gardening business and really cleaned up because Dudbury, Connecticut is famous for its rich people. Even the not-so-rich people, such as my family, the Bancrofts, were sure to have a little land.

Dudbury was still "the country" and New York was "a good commute," which meant an hour playing bridge or swaying in the bar car for my dad's friends. He'd been one of them when he was going to New York to look for work and ended up at the Lambs Club playing bridge all day, and maybe poker. It was poker that kept him going when he was a Shakespearian actor.

There was no way to prove it but I was sure my dad sat over breakfast in our war room in his bathrobe till the last possible minute, till he was wild with yard fantasies and plots concerning undelivered mail.

Tom and I both had full-time summer jobs so there was no way he could give us baseball practice all afternoon. Back in my Little League days, before I was old enough to work, he'd take time off from the Lambs to get me to pitch to him. In May and June—even in September and October—

he'd be waiting for me when I got home from school. He
had put in a regulation mound and a home plate right on our
front lawn. True, there was a hill behind our house, the only
level ground was in front. Still, I hated the looks the neighbors gave us. He'd catch me for hours, sometimes, down on
one knee. He wasn't dumb enough to try to squat at his age,
but even on one knee I wondered how he could take it. I was
too young to know what a fanatic was.

At supper during the summer there was bound to be an
argument. My father didn't have a paper to read and there I
was to the left of him looking down at my food. By supper
he'd usually had one or two martinis, and booze made him
want to talk. When he couldn't ignore me even baseball was
something he didn't want to talk about. With the rest of us
shifting in our chairs and my mother's eyes wide as an owl's
with what looked like fear but was really anger—*I* was all he
wanted to talk about. He'd hold off as long as he could,
though, weak from the booze though he was. Then he'd look
me in the eye and pounce. The only time Papa Owl ever
looked me full in the face was when he was ready for some
mousing.

For instance, during soup or salad Tom might have been
asking me about my date the night before. Where we went,
who we saw, innocent stuff. I'd tell him about all the things
we'd done and I'd feel my father's eyes on me. The corner
of my right eye was incredibly keen.

"Sounds to me as if you blew a week's earnings in one
night."

"So what if I did?"

"Don't answer me like that! You know why I don't like
to see you out till all hours throwing your money away. Ha!
Because your mother will be the one to pay for your good
times. You're supposed to be saving your money for school
expenses and you know it."

"Let's not have another argument, John. It was such a
lovely day."

"Look, mom's only paying the tuition, right? If I want

4

to live it up a little this summer, why shouldn't I? I'm willing to make up for it at P.A. by cutting back. You always wanted me to live like a monk when I was up there, anyway." P.A. (for Phillips Academy) was what we students called school besides "Andover."

"Gordon, that goes for you, too." Suffering was in her voice. Neither of us wanted to see what her face was like.

"I never told you how to live at school or what to do with your leisure time. I just wanted you to do enough work to justify the whopping tuition we were paying. Was it such a great sacrifice to hit the books a few hours each day?"

There's no point in going on. My father had me dead to rights. But our argument was sure to last until the ice cream because I couldn't admit to being the worthless person he thought I was. I was forced to find some good in the way I spent my last year at Andover or my parents would have nothing to hope for.

All the weightlifting had made a change in me, dad couldn't deny that. But my new musculature did nothing for his morale. I was proud of the fact that I'd read all the available books of W. Somerset Maugham in one year. Only a couple of them were assigned reading—*A Moon and Sixpence, Of Human Bondage*. When I tried *The Razor's Edge* on my own, I was hooked.

Explaining Maugham as an addiction hadn't convinced my parents. Then it dawned on me that I was reading so much Maugham because I wanted to be a writer. This made sense to my mother even though she didn't approve. My father thought he knew what I was up to and was furious.

"You're just trying to make your laziness respectable. Anyway, everyone's a writer, don't you know that? Only one in a million ever gets published. Skid row is full of writers. You'll be right down there with 'em if you don't listen to me. Put these silly ideas of writing out of your head and get to work on your assignments!"

"But writing is a big part of my assignments, except in

math. If I'd only learned to write in junior high my grades would have been higher all along."

"Then make it a sideline and try to improve. But don't go telling yourself that because you want to become a writer your schoolwork isn't important. If you don't know anything, what will you have to write about?"

"My experiences . . . "

"Life behind bars? Life in the gutter? Who'll want to read about it?"

This was the most civilized argument I had with my dad all summer. It started at supper but we ended in the living room where we'd had our heart-to-hearters before I became an Andover boy. From the beginning all of my talks with my father became lectures at some point, but I'd long ago learned how to pacify him—then goad him to new heights of rage before I gave him what he wanted again. There was an art to talking to my father.

We had four talks in the living room the summer before my senior year. One was almost fatal. That was when he jumped me on the sofa. I can't remember what I said (I think it was, "So what?"). Next thing I knew he was kneeling on me and trying to cave my face in. I think he did, too—the left side. As soon as the swelling was down I had a long look in the bathroom mirror, holding my mother's "beauty mirror" at an angle to get the side view. My left cheek was hollower and the cheekbone had been raised an inch. If my mother hadn't rushed in screaming he'd have left me looking like Carmen Basilio. Don't worry, he didn't get off me for mom's sake. He was worried about the neighbors who might have thought he was beating her. Fortunately, because of the way I'd spent my upper year, I knew enough about boxing to clinch and keep him from killing me. It was our only hug all summer, which isn't as weird as the fact that it was a real hug. There was a fleeting closeness in spite of the strain.

Having my father explode was a relief. I knew he was going through hell on my account, but what could I do about

6

it if he wouldn't listen to reason? At different times in different ways I'd told him to keep out of my affairs and let the school treat me like any other boy. But ever since I first got in trouble my lower (sophomore) year he started firing off letters to the Dean of Students, the Assistant Dean of Students, my English teacher, the head of the Music Department (I gave up the French horn my lower year and took up singing), the Choir Director (who was also my voice coach), the head of the sports program (who didn't know me that well since I'd never been a star athlete in spite of my supposed potential in baseball), and in the year to come there would be piles of letters to Dr. Bellini and my housemaster, who were the only people who would have time to reply.

At least he had sense enough not to write the Headmaster. Out of nearly 800 guys I doubt if the Headmaster had looked more than 10 in the eye, and I hadn't been favored. A letter from my father would have been the ultimate embarrassment.

Making all these important people aware of me was a lousy way to inspire me to work harder, but my father couldn't get that through his head. These people became so interested in what I was doing that I started making promises right and left to keep them off my back.

It's easy to exaggerate when you're making promises. I exaggerated about what I was willing to do to improve my performance in class (or at rehearsals, or on the playing fields, and everywhere else I was being watched). Then I defaulted on my promises one by one. I panicked. I couldn't get anything right. Teachers would tell me stuff and it would go right over my head. I was the problem child, right? Whatever I tried to do I fell on my face. I found that the only way I could compete with the other boys was not to study at all. When I went to class unprepared and faked my oral responses and pulled a fair grade on the weeklies, the other guys respected me. Some thought I was a genius in idiot's clothing.

What all my teachers and my father couldn't understand

was that I needed less competition, not more—easier, not tougher. Andover men were smart. You were up against guys who knew three languages and were doing advanced calculus in 9th grade. Certain geniuses were well-liked and well-connected socially. If guys like this had a low opinion of your brains they could give you the complex of your life. They could pick on you with such insight that you had no reply. Once you'd lost confidence in your ability to think you weren't good for much at a place like Andover. You might get a few laughs mumbling and shuffling, but not for too long. Our geniuses could find a new clown and get tired of him almost simultaneously. Since playing the clown could brand you for life, the school was full of guys pretending to be absentminded about intentionally dumb behavior, suffering for a smile.

The way I saw it I was holding my own against the others. No one ever saw my light on in the middle of the night. If the choice was between handing in some homework and flunking out of school, maybe I would scrawl something during the breakfast and hand it in. During the evening study hours, however, I never did anything but lift weights with the intellectuals. My dedication made my detractors think twice before making a snide remark to my face. Sure, I got some shitty grades, and my father and I became enemies for life my upper year, but I'll always be glad I lifted those weights.

I should explain that a junior at Phillips Academy Andover was just a ninth-grader. A lower middler was a sophomore, and an upper middler was what the high schools called a junior. Seniors were just seniors and no one could see anything wrong with that. To call "junior" someone who's already in 11th grade might be hard to take, and nobody would want to be "sophomoric." Still, I think the school made the changes so that nobody would get the idea that Andover was anything like a high school. The guys at school never said anything but "lower" or "upper" to refer to each other ("He's only a lower."). At the time it sounded normal to me, but looking back I find it strange.

The school and its traditions had snowed my father from the time he brought me up for my admission interview. From his expression you'd have thought he was Balboa at the big moment. The campus was beautiful, but so big that I remember feeling lost and wondering how I would fit in. Of course when all the kids arrived your private world became more important than all the brick facilities. The landscaping and gardening vanished. Clothes and faces were all that mattered. Who was with whom and their shoes.

A lot of boys completed ninth grade in a junior high school and became lower preps. I'd been one of them. It was a bad break, having to be accepted by a lot of guys who knew each other. New lowers nosed around a lot trying to know the right people. Still, I was glad none of the old boys had known me as a ninth grader. I was no rock in my early days as a lower, either. My picture in the address book made me crawl with shame by the end of the year. I went from 5' 9", 135 lbs., to 6' 3", 185 in nine months.

I'd been warned by my father that he'd gotten his growth late, so during my first days at Andover I wasn't worried that I'd never grow, but it was a relief when I could see it happening. If the food had been better I might have become the biggest kid in the school and never had any social problems, but I wasn't thinking of my diet at the time. Nature was doing a great job. I was stepping on the scales each day and in front of every mirror I could find.

From my first day away at school I knew that my father would never understand what was really going on. How could I expect him to when the teachers didn't? Social acceptance was everything. To be included, to be "one of the boys," and not "out of it," to be a "good man" and not a "weeny," "flit," "fairy," "grind," or "clod"—these concerns crowded out the homework in our heads. Who was sitting next to you at commons? Who was walking with you from class to class? Everyone waited to see before they'd try to know you. It made no difference who you *were* if you were with the wrong people. But if you ate with football players or walked to class with one, the other football players would talk to you, or at least nod. (It was a sign of weakness for football players to be talkative.)

Our code was cruel—a lot worse than anything I see in the army now. The rules were stricter and there was less fraternizing between ranks. Weenies never sat with football players. Weenies never *spoke* to football players. If a weeny had told a football player that a car was about to run him down, the football player would have ignored him. But if a football player wanted to know something from a weeny— or what would be more likely, from a grind—he asked. As soon as he had his answer he was on his way.

The story of Rennie Rutledge would illustrate what was going on. Rutledge was one of the biggest men at Dudbury junior high. He went to Andover while I stayed at the school in town, but I never forgot all his achievements and when I found I'd be going to Andover I thought a lot about Rutledge.

Before he got his growth Rutledge and I had been good friends. I learned how to play chess from him and we played a lot of Scrabble because big words had meant a lot in the seventh grade. But in eighth grade he cut me. He'd got so big he could look right over my head and he never seemed to have a reason to look down. He was a hall monitor—a big honor for an eighth-grader. I was a nobody. Considering that I'd been the best pitcher in my age-group before growth was a factor, I wasn't even much of a pitcher any more. A lot of the guys were throwing harder than I could and I was relying more and more on fancy stuff.

It sounds stupid, but the shower-room was the most important place in the school. Pubic hair meant everything to us kids. Kids would be talking about other things but they'd always check to see how much you had. My miserable fringe was a source of great shame. I'd have given anything to be able to avoid the shower-room after sports, but the coaches made sure everyone cleaned up. They weren't concerned if some of us were crawling with shame. I used to fantasize going to school on another continent—in China, for example, where the people might not be much bigger than I was and were notoriously unhairy.

When I got to Andover I was still insecure about my shower-room appearances and wishing I were bigger. Maybe that's why I dropped Rennie Rutledge's name to some important men in my dorm.

"I'm a friend of Rennie Rutledge. From the same home town."

I was hoping they wouldn't let on to Rutledge that I'd dropped his name. Imagine how shocked I was when one of them said, "That's nice to know. Rutledge has a friend."

I kept my eyes open in commons to see who Rutledge sat with. It was amazing. He'd sit at a table full of guys that had to be nobodies and even *they* would start rushing their food. Cutting in commons could be more callous: sometimes guys would get up and take another seat to avoid sitting with someone who wasn't "in." Sometimes they would get up, dump their trays and go hungry rather than suffer the embarrassment.

I decided to sit with Rutledge and find out what had ruined his personality. Right away I could tell he was starved for someone to talk to. He put his hand over my wrist the way you try to detain somebody. This was the hand I was eating with—there was a fork in it! His eyes were rolling. It must have embarrassed him to talk to someone who had known him in his glory. I felt sorry for him, but I was a little glad to see him like this because of the way he'd cut me in the halls of our junior high.

What Rutledge told me terrified me more than his appearance. Jokes! The kind you could find in the magazines my mother got, or others that I'd already seen in *Playboy* (along with all the other kids in the school). Maybe a good comedian could have gotten away with an act like this. No. Good comedians always knew when to try new material or pack it in. Rutledge was no comedian. He was in agony—dying for a laugh. You couldn't laugh at a dying man.

After seeing what had happened to Rutledge I stayed in the background my lower year. Easy, because I was too small to be a good athlete, and you had to be an athlete to be accepted. Oh, there were a handful of intellectuals who were "in" because they could use their wits to cut other guys to pieces. (We called it "slashing.") Unless you were talking with your roomie or someone you trusted, the important thing in speaking to a classmate was to find words that hurt. Whatever they call it in the future, Andover will always have slashing. The intense competition, the pressure to get into a good college, the pressure from home, the need to have the respect of your classmates as well as your teachers to count for a damn—all these things will always be the same.

It's time to admit I volunteered for the army right after my Andover experience so I could learn to enjoy playing my French horn and maybe keep my sanity. One of the guys in my unit volunteered to play his clarinet and keep from flunking out of Yale. Maybe he's crazy but he swears he got it from someone in the know that Andover and Exeter are going to admit girls next year. I'm laughing it off. They don't have anything as subtle as slashing in the army but Allgauer is enough like my former classmates to know that it destroys me to think that what made it hell for me at Andover is going to be changed now that I'm gone. As much as I hated my years at the school Allgauer knows I still think it's the best in the country and am proud to have gone there. Hard to understand.

Girls had been a big part of my problem at Andover. When I was fully grown I found that horniness had been building over the three years I'd been wanting to be a man. I was so horny that I would see the drawing of a tit in the margin of a book and have to find someplace to masturbate. I was a menace around books. In the stacks of the library any thumb-dark book could be counted on to contain some hot parts. Medical books aroused me. So did Rabelais—in French. Photography journals were sure to send me zooming to the john.

Things would have been a lot worse my upper year if I'd had more opportunity. Or better. I'd have been thrown out for sure if I'd lived in Gill's dorm. His housemaster's wife was a notorious slut. I saw her up close just once when I went over to see Gill and I began to believe the stories I'd heard about her being gangbanged by some guys on the football team.

All the housemasters had apartments on the ground floor of the dorms and she was standing by her door. She looked at me hard as I went by and I kept looking back until my head was completely turned around. She had me mesmerized. Just before I took the stairs to the dorm rooms she put out her tongue and tilted the tip back until it touched her upper lip. I thought I was going to come on the spot. I'd never seen anything so sexy in my life, and Sheila Burke had already let me look inside her with a flashlight.

I knew I'd never have a chance with that housemaster's wife. She was teasing. Even though her husband had been way across campus teaching a class, she could only have trusted the guys in her dorm. But it was hell to forget the way she had looked with her tongue sticking out. God, I don't know how any of the guys in that dorm got any work done.

There was only one other faculty wife who was decent to look at, but she walked around as if she were carrying a big Bible against her chest. The other forty-eight or so were the rattiest-looking women I'd ever seen in my life. I won't say they put their noses in the air when we were around, but they seemed to be holding their breath, afraid to sniff. Believe it or not, Andover guys didn't smell all that bad because we had a shower every day after sports and aftershave was almost as important symbolically as the brandy and cigars we were denied. No, these wives were just trying to look superior and they couldn't bring if off. Half of them were pregnant and more pimplyfaced than some of our guys. Types you could find in the markets with curlers in their hair wearing something like a smock with little flowers in the design. Only teachers with washed-out wives could get hired, or else teachers with wives who weren't half bad had sense enough not to apply.

Our guys thought about sex a lot more than the preppies I've read about. We thought of sex continually. A few of the older teachers had daughters who would look back at you, and these girls were a big topic at the start of the fall term. Before long, though, they wouldn't be looking back any more and we'd be talking about the girls last summer. By the spring term our minds were so degenerate that we'd be telling each other what we thought about when we were jerking off.

The way we thought about girls was just one more thing my father didn't understand about my school. He didn't care what happened over the summer but during the school year my sperm production was supposed to fall off while my thoughts turned from tits to Homer. He wouldn't have cared if my dick fell off if I could be assured of a place on the high honor roll. Surprising, because he went to a lot of trouble to educate me sexually.

I had a Ph.D. in sex when I entered the seventh grade, but it was worthless because a few precious pubic hairs were all I could muster to indicate that someday I might be able to practice what I preached. You had to hunt for them, and under my arms and on my face you'd have had to use a magnifying glass to find anything but dirt in my pores. Actually, I was rather proud of my blackheads and whiteheads because they made me like other kids, at least on the surface. Down between my legs I was a disaster.

I'd suffered plenty of humiliation in junior high school but none of the girls had seen me naked. I'd been much too careful to let that happen. However, I had two friends in the seventh grade who already had big dicks and could jack off. We did it in the dark when we were sleeping over at each other's houses. These guys would put the light on to show me the sperm on their hands, but I always came up empty. Once when I pulled too hard too long my anemic dick swelled up till it looked like a red pepper. I think the guys might have been impressed with the swelling, but because my dick was different than theirs and couldn't produce any sperm it made them uneasy. Maybe they thought I was going to turn into a queer. Thanks to my father, though, even though I couldn't do anything I could talk more knowledgeably about girls than anyone in my class. Guys would ask me a dumb question and I'd come back at them with a lecture. Even the ones who'd had some experience were willing to learn from me to find out how to patch things up and get some more.

Until I got to know some Abbot girls (Abbot was in Andover, too—our sister school) I had no idea that girls talked about sex, or even thought about it. My father hadn't told me everything. One Abbot girl I was seeing on weekends my lower year told me that girls in her dorm talked about sex a lot and looked at each other's bodies and talked about men's. She gave me such a scare that downtown on weekends when I saw her coming I'd change course at top speed and once I created a sensation among some old ladies in an antique store.

I idealized women, no doubt of it, but in my early days as a lower I could only take their naked bodies when I saw them in a magazine.

Summer changed all that. The summer between my lower and upper years was a big turning point. I even got laid, but I didn't do it right.

My father had explained everything about what organs were like, and how it was all right to put your tongue in a girl's mouth when you were kissing, and how a respectable number of people even licked each other's private parts. Normal people? Yes, my father assured me. The most respected and best-educated people went to bed at night and started licking each other "there."

It was great experience, but the first time I got laid I didn't get the hang of it right away. Oh, I had a boner that would have stopped the flight of angels, and it went right in, but nothing happened. The girl was a year younger than me, but she'd had a lot of experience. The look on her face made me deeply ashamed.

"Aren't you going to do anything?" she said.

Now she really had me. What else was there to do? That idiot father of mine, I thought, he's ruined me again. Here I was inside and it felt all right, but I was nowhere near an orgasm and this beautiful girl was in anguish.

I finally found the courage to ask what she wanted me to do.

"Well, move it around a little. You know. We don't have to do it if you don't like me."

Only a father like mine could have told me everything about sex and leave out the most important part: to screw a girl you were supposed to keep sliding the erect penis in and out. Up to then I'd thought of a woman's labia majora, labia minora, Ibiza and Formentera as the gates to paradise. Once inside Nature did the rest. Sure, I'd seen animals shoving it into each other, but they did it so fast I thought, ecstasy for a dog or a squirrel is a kind of spasm. Surely our species would have figured out a way to keep from jiggling like that and looking goggle-eyed.

In spite of my humiliation I was still rock-hard, and before long I'd forgotten my father and was doing a little cock-boxing with this poor girl for punching bag. The harder I hit her the more she seemed to like it. So this was the real thing: take that, take that, take that. My father had told me about sadomasochism, but he'd never hinted that it was at the bottom of everything.

Sports all over again. A one-sided fight. The girls wanted to see how tough you were the same as they did from the bleachers. On the playing fields they shouted "Rah!" "Hooray!" and in bed it was "Ooh!" "Aah!" For a guy on the track or swimming team they'd shout "Go!"

"Faster!," but for football players, "Stomp 'em!" "Kill 'em!" Sexual cheerleading was tame compared with that stuff. "More , , , More . . . " Sometimes even that simple word was too much for them. Give us an ooh, give as an ahh, give us an ugh.

Since the game was always rigged so that the woman was beaten to a pulp I didn't expect my partners to root for my organs as if a victory were at stake. School pride was undoubtedly more important, but even with the outcome never in doubt, sex was preoccupying me more and more and becoming more mysterious, and by the time I went back to Andover a senior it was the only game I wanted to play.

I'll give my father one thing. He never trained me to think of sex as a habit. After my education he clammed up about it and let me use my imagination. Everything else in life was supposed to be a habit, though, and my mother went right along. I had to look a certain way, my clothes had to look a certain way and hang in the closet just so, and my bed had to be made and I had to brush my teeth after meals and before I went to bed and when I woke up in the morning. Everything was meant to be a habit with us. With the right habits we'd go through life unscathed.

I wasn't the son they wanted. With me only bad habits were taking hold. Ever since I could hold a knife and fork I'd been told to use bread or another implement to push onto my fork the things I couldn't stab. Instead I used my thumb, especially when my mind was elsewhere. My hands were clean, there was nothing disgusting about it. I wasn't allowed to sit down at the table until I'd washed my hands. Chow-hound that I was, washing my hands before dinner became my only dependable good habit.

Sometimes I brushed my teeth like a fanatic and sometimes I forgot. Sometimes my room was neat as a pin, sometimes it was a shambles. Sometimes I remembered to use deodorant and sometimes I stank like a goat. My dad saw something sinister and unAmerican in the way I was turning out and my mother thought it was tragic.

I've had some minor complaints about my hygiene since those days, and there's no doubt that I've wasted a lot of time looking for things that wouldn't have been lost if I'd put them where they belonged, but all in all I'm glad I turned out the way I did. Good habits take the surprises out of life and people that try to enforce good habits are bores. You'd think my father would have learned something from all his failures, but every night, no matter what we were eating, in a voice weary with resignation or raised in rage, he could be counted on to say: "Don't push with your thumb!"

TWO

Jim Barton and I had decided to be roommates our senior year before we knew each other well. Unlike Jim I wasn't in with the athletes who started on the football, basketball or baseball teams. All my friends (except Gill) were intellectuals who were good at one minor sport: standouts in boxing, wrestling, lacrosse, or fencing—where there was a chance of really hurting someone.

Barton was captain of the boxing team, and he was always on the honor roll, but after an hour together talking over the summers we'd had I realized that Barton had a sentimental, puritanical side that hadn't emerged last year while we were running fartlicks together in the Cage or talking boxing after a match. I dated our friendship from our first long talk after the only match Jim had lost during his school career.

I'd been impressed by the way Jim didn't seem to care about losing, and figured he was drawn to me because of my reputation as a nihilist. I thought the reason we'd spent so much time talking about nothing important last year was out of respect for each other's despair. Trying to murder some kid during required athletics wasn't something you talked about. It was *de rigueur* to talk about the Saturday night movie or echo the latest witty comebacks while the bloody heap you'd left on a mat or a playing field was locked out of your eyes.

19

The chitchat while we unpacked and put our things away was what I'd expected until about a half hour before the scheduled evening meeting with our new housemaster, Ollie Sanborn (Oliver Francis). "Ollie" was too obvious and I'd already made up my mind to call him Sanborn.

"Barton, I'm not trying to tell you what happened with someone I wanted for a girlfriend . . . "

"Three girls, Gordon? You took advantage of three girls you didn't care about?"

He saw the terror in my eyes.

"Don't worry, I haven't converted." He was reading me just right.

"What gives, then?"

"You never told me what you did with women last year, and I liked you for it."

"I didn't know enough, Jim. I had too much respect for you to talk about where my finger had been. To be honest, the summer after my lower year was the first time I got laid and it was a disaster. In the sand trap of our country club . . . it still makes my flesh crawl . . . "

"You jumped her while she was trying to get out of a sandtrap?" At least Barton was someone who could allow curiosity to get the better of him.

"We'd gone there at night with beach towels and beer. It started all right once I figured out how my prick was supposed to move, but it ended with me spitting right in front of her and still spitting after I dropped her off."

"She made you physically sick?"

"I'm only going to tell you this because you're so naive about sex. Take it as a warning, Jim, and proof that I want to be honest in everything I tell you even if it makes me look as squeamish as you must be. I wasn't man enough to eat her, and I didn't get around to doing that with anyone this past summer, either. I'm still worried I might not have what it takes to be an irresistible lover. She was pretty and drenched in perfume and a year younger. She told me, 'You won't like it.' Maybe it was the power of suggestion . . . All last year while I was wondering if she'd ruined my life I was blaming her perfume, and the moon . . . "

"Never blame something like the moon. I'd say you were asking for it."

"It was shining on her behind and everything between her legs was dark and wild. First I had trouble finding my way . . . "

"All right, Bancroft."

"I'd have done better to take her on her back in bright light, like a doctor."

"That's what you've been doing this past summer?"

"What happened with those three girls was superficial compared to that moonlit sandtrap. I first saw her—I won't say her name, she might be trying to reform—when she came through the line where I was bagging groceries. I think she was wearing the same perfume. Then it was making me wild with desire."

Barton went down the hall to pee and do something about my head of steam.

"No more golf games . . . " he said, returning.

"She got to me through the produce manager. This was an older guy with a hot car. I could tell he was jealous."

"C'mon, it's time for the meeting. It'll be neat to find out who we've got in this dorm."

Room assignments came in the summer. All you could count on was having the roommate you wanted. The school administrators might have given some thought to the crowd they were putting together in a given dormitory. It was usually a mix of rocks and jocks, weenies and grinds, presided over by a pair of intellectuals who had a bedroom apiece and a common room besides. Bullsessions were held in the common rooms of intellectuals. The athletes who dominated the refectory had to knock and ask if they could join when they had something on their minds. Intellectuals were therefore the lords of the dorms.

When I saw Channing and Hobbs in Sanborn's living room I knew where the bullsessions were going to be this year and went on guard immediately to avoid saying something mundane. It would be hard to avoid cliches in front of Sanborn's pregnant wife, who was showing signs of wanting to like everyone.

Mrs. Sanborn reminded me of the pasty-faced sort of Englishwomen who might have welcomed people into bomb shelters during the Second World War, cheerful in spite of anemia. Much as we may have hated our training as gentlemen there wasn't one of us who didn't want her to sit down so he could bow to her instead of having to shake her hot blue hand. Sanborn was pumping away right beside her, pretending rumors about us had never reached him.

("Teasdale, is it?" What a joke.)

Because of my required visits to Dr. Bellini I was rumored to be insane, but I rarely did anything to give substance to the rumors. I was proud of my bad attitude but there were plenty of hints in my exploits that I was a regular guy in disguise. Teasdale, a star defensive guard, was rumored to have strung up feral cats outside his window in the junior dorm. No one would swear to having seen a cat hanging but Teasdale had always been content with the evil things that were said about him, which said even more. He might have been a guy who just wanted to be left alone, but that wouldn't come out until he left school and got national attention for his work as a humanitarian.

A lot of guys who roomed alone would be bouncing up to the stage of George Washington Hall on Prize Day while the rest of us were looking at each other, wondering how we could have been so wrong.

Farnham's father was a drunken journalist for a magazine I wasn't smart enough to read. Farnham wrote for the school paper and the literary magazine so a finished product in the mould was just a matter of time.

Thomson was another big, sinister football player like my friend Gill (who wasn't in my dorm this year). He'd made the varsity as a lower and had been friends with seniors who were like gods to the rest of us at the time. Thomson was huge, mean and smart. Since he was a Southern guy, having him deride you was like being cut to pieces by a dull knife.

A kid named Kingsley would be grinding away next door to us.

I won't name three pairs of introverts we had, types we'd have to get to know through a crack in their doors, though their names are what I remember best about them.

Mamelakis was the big surprise. Sanborn introduced him as a foreign student who would be rooming alone. The housemaster danced around in front of this foreign boy to prevent us finding out more on our own.

Proving that he was as dumb and kindly as we had all thought, Sanborn was trying to get us to say a few words about ourselves while his wife paraded her fetus to and fro distributing little plates of rabbit food.

" . . . Tell us where you come from, something about your family, your interests. Where you'd like to go to college. Mr. Mamelakis, I'd like you to lead off. Let me presume to say something about your origins before you do. Personally, I find it very exciting that Mr. Mamelakis comes to us from Athens. Gentlemen, I want you to do everything you can to make him feel welcome."

Sanborn clapped alone for a few seconds.

"Would you like to tell us more about your background, Demetrios?"

"Jim," said Mamelakis.

"Jim," said Sanborn, coloring. "You will find that Mr. Mamelakis . . . Jim . . . speaks better English than most of the rest of us."

"Of this entirely I am not sure," said Mamelakis through his nose, while Sanborn swung his head back like a donkey.

Being the butt of a joke by a foreigner made Sanborn laugh, and of course we all liked him more for that. Yet because he was someone who may have been unaccustomed to making other people feel so good about him, his laugh started to reach maniacal proportions and he had to cover his mouth with his tweed sleeve. This meant to us that he'd been nagged all his life about his disruptive laughter, and was another point in his favor.

"I am from Athens, it is true," said Mamelakis in a British accent, all business. "Though I spent most of my time on yachts, thanks to my father's business interests . . . "

Mamelakis would die in a scrimmage of some kind before he'd been here a week.

Sanborn was as shocked as the rest of us. "Your father is a shipowner?"

"Nothing like it. He goes where he has to . . . "

"A yacht salesman, then?"

"I'm honored that you're inclined to think so highly of my progenitor, but he's a worthless little man, if truth be told—a high-class gigolo."

He waited for the cheers and laughter to subside without cracking a smile. Mrs. Sanborn was giving our new hero the pink-eyed look of someone whose heart is slamming into her solar plexus, too frightened even to dribble.

"Thanks to my father putting down on so many laps of luxury a number of beautiful, well-bred, wealthy women have strong maternal feelings about me, and it was because of them that I was spoiled rotten and find myself among you in this beautiful, though somewhat primitive place, where I will dabble in American history and culture for a year before I'm off to Harvard to put the finishing touches on my image as playboy and gentleman scholar."

Sanborn was laughing again and his wife had caught on to the extent of placing her flat hands against her belly and blowing out her cheeks.

Mamelakis's opening remarks to his fellow seniors were all over the campus by the next day, but it turned out that the Greek wasn't someone who would let celebrity go to his head, and stumble trying to defend himself against wits even sharper than his. He had a taste of what some of our wags wanted to do with him and retreated into his studies for the rest of the year. Channing, a brilliant patrician, and

Hobbs, less brilliant, but undeniably genteel, protected him, and when the three of them were alone Mamelakis was rumored to have said something amusing from time to time.

After the rest of us had a go at describing our origins, aims and interests in the fewest possible words—some refused, citing the respect they had for Mamelakis—Sanborn told us that it was Mr. Kingsley's misfortune to have his eighteenth birthday coincide with "this, his first day back at school . . .

"But my wife has baked him a cake. The snacks you've just been offered are a concession to a healthy diet. Through the year we'll celebrate all your birthdays with a cake and a small party . . . "

"Kingsley is already eighteen?" was the question on our faces as I looked around. The thought that someone so insignificant could be that much older than Barton, for instance, who wouldn't be eighteen till April of next year . . .

We returned to the subject of birthday parties later with Channing and a couple of others outside our door.

Sanborn wasn't the only housemaster who wanted to celebrate birthdays this way, but housemasters who did were often held in contempt. My lower year a respected cynic from the senior class, a softspoken mean six-and-a-half foot Texan, had taken his birthday cake from his housemaster's wife, thanked everybody for it and gone upstairs, where he locked himself in his room and ate it all.

The Texan had been imitated and for all I know had been imitating someone himself. Anyway, we didn't admire the gesture because of the way it had hurt the housemaster's feelings, or the housemaster's wife's. We admired what the gesture had revealed about Harry Don (and those who followed him): "Regardless of what you think I am or want me to be, exemplified by my good fortune in going to school here and guaranteeing myself a good future, this is what I really am, and I'm not sorry . . . "

The men we most admired tried not to be obvious about their rebellious feelings. The knots of their ties would be loose, but not halfway down their shirtfronts. When their loafers began to disintegrate they bound them with surgical tape acquired gratis at the gym. Parents and teachers might talk about fads, unable to distinguish what we were doing from the penny loafers a size too large that had clopped through the halls of our junior high schools. The shoes we taped weren't falling apart, however. The point for most of us was to get more wear out of them at the school's expense.

Our conformity was only for the sake of cheapness or comfort, we had no truck with fads. And while outwardly respecting the rules, we seethed with desires and came up with countless plans to gratify them. The point was to sin as much as possible and just let Jesus bleed.

Not giving a damn was kind of an art with all of us. Take the phenomenon called a sonic boom that visited our part of the world from time to time. I could well imagine the townspeople coming out of their burrows to look at the sky or running somewhere to comfort their babies but our guys didn't even look out the window if they were in a bullsession, or get out of bed if it was the dead of night. Some of them were so inured to the idea of a bad outcome for the human race that they didn't even wake up any more.

No telling how many sonic booms I missed at night. The ceiling would have had to come down to stop me from having sweet dreams. My dreams were the high point of my time as an Andover boy. Anyway, they were until I met the girl this book is really about.

I'm stressing the ugliness of the men in my senior class to balance the unwarranted fondness that creeps in when we look back on hard times. Yes, we were awful people, but we weren't without a trace of human emotion. Regardless of the faces we pulled as we dragged around making our preschool appointments (saving our longest face for the photograph that would go in the address book) we were secretly pleased to see each other again and see the school again after a long summer away.

It was a beautiful place, marred only by a few modern

buildings, the new dorms, but they were beneath a treelined hill where no one ever saw them unless they had the misfortune to live there.

More than anything what I like to remember is walking around the campus, walking between the ivy-covered buildings from class to class. The bells were a pain in the ass sometimes, especially when some idiot was playing popular songs on them, but when they were ringing for no reason at all, or just giving you the hour, they could be beautiful—an echo of something old about the school that could never change.

While you were walking around it was easy to think of the thousands of boys who had come and gone to make their name in the world. Some alumni were famous. Humphrey Bogart went to my school (I was told) and got thrown out for pushing the manager of the Andover Inn (where all the visiting alumni stayed) into Rabbit Pond (a little dish of scum behind the inn). There was also a story that Mickey Cohen went to my school and got thrown out for trying to blow up all the buildings on the Main Quad, or at least for drawing up a plan and saying that's what he was going to do. Even with his connections the Main Quad would have been a tall order. Anyway, a few of our boys had gone on to become bigshots of some kind, so it wasn't hard to think that something might become of me, too. Let's face it, except for certain people, I loved my school.

Barton and I had lucked into a good small dorm. Barton wanted the smaller room and I had no objections. The big room had twice as many windows as Barton's and there was enough space for exercising and pacing.

There were drawbacks. Anyone who came to bullshit with Barton would have to do so in my room because I had the easy chairs. The second drawback was related to the first: if Sanborn came to the door, I'd be the first one to deal with him. That was stupid because Barton was respected by the faculty as a hard worker and a morally sound person, while I was considered a troublemaker capable of anything.

Seeing me at the door was an invitation for a housemaster to snoop around inside.

After Sanborn's celery and cake orientation Jim and I spent the whole night talking. We talked most of the next night as well. By then I could tell that he was glad we were going to be roomies. He'd heard about how I liked to drink and flaunt the rules and do a minimum of work, but he still liked me. He saw something in me that I couldn't see myself. Really, the only shame in rooming with me was the fact that the whole school knew about my visits to Dr. Bellini.

I wasn't the only Andover boy who had to see a psychiatrist, but I was about the only one who'd admit it. I told everyone that I had to go if I wanted to stay in school, it was the only way my father would let me. I never said anything about my mother paying my tuition. It was humiliating to think that my mother had to give up her leisure time on my account, especially when I was lying to her about all the schoolwork I was doing. As soon as school was under way whenever I got a decent grade on some inconsequential test I'd send it down to Dudbury to give her something to crow about. The only thing that pissed my father off more than the way my letters were slanted was the fact that mom had become a working woman because of me. Because of my craziness.

Still, from the first Dr. Bellini had refused to write that I was a dangerous maniac the way my father had wanted. I'd seen some of my father's letters when Bellini had to leave the office. My file was already full before my first month as a senior. I didn't dare read them from start to finish because they were long and I was afraid of getting caught, but I'd seen enough to know that my father was exaggerating my faults when he wasn't lying outright. Since he was no longer paying anything for my support I couldn't see what right he had to flood the mails with all these lies about me, but naturally the Dean and Dr. Bellini thought my father had a "responsibility" for me. Responsibility was one of my father's favorite words, even though there was agony on his face whenever he said it.

I called it a lie when he said: "I mentioned to Gordon how hard his mother would be working on his behalf and his reply was, 'So what?'" He was referring to that incident last summer after my mother had decided to support me at school by going to work. Maybe I did say, "So what?" about something along the line, but my father had been yelling at me for an hour before I said it. Also, wasn't it the same as a lie when he forgot to mention that he jumped on me when I said, "So what?," knelt on my chest and started pounding my face in?

The way I saw the incident it was sporting of me not to fight back after a beating which was going to leave me deformed for life. I could have smashed my father's face worse than he did mine if I had wanted. There was something about pounding your own father, though . . . especially when you could see he was out of his mind with frustration.

I thought the incident was forgotten (even though I was sure I'd never forget it). Then I saw that my father was trying to use it to get the school to step up their surveillance of me, if not their punishments. That was the point of all his letters, all that responsibility of his which was about as subtle as barbed wire. He figured that if I were more or less permanently on posting, which was a severe disciplinary restriction, and made it through the year without a breakdown, I might get into a decent college.

I'd already been on posting more than anybody still in school. I'd even been on double posting, which was so complicated I'm not going to explain it. To be posted meant that for two weeks you couldn't go anywhere but to commons, chapel, class and sports. You couldn't stop for an ice cream. You went around campus like a zombie ticking off your appointments. Back at the dorm at night, during the time that my father thought I'd be studying for lack of anything better to do, I would thumb through dirty magazines looking for answers to my predicament. It sounds crazy, but dirty books are what you look at before you tackle something like the *Il-iad*. If you can't respond to a naked woman, how are you going to get into a massacre?

Maybe I'd be able to tell Bellini the truth about my atti-tude someday. For now all he wanted to hear was how I felt about my father. Actually, I always felt the same about him: I loved him the way a son loves his father, and I hated his guts for picking on me. Sometimes.

"I don't care how it comes out, my love for him will never change. I know he means well. That makes a big dif-ference when you have to sit through one of his five-hour lectures."

"I'm going to level with you. I'm bewildered. You seem like a sensitive guy and your insights are worth listening to. I'm impressed with your sensitivity to your father's predica-ment. I think this man is going through some anguish. But if all it would take to please him is to start handing in your as-signments, why don't you make things easier for him? Try to find an answer for me, will you? I enjoyed our session to-day . . ."

Time to leave. I'd be coming to life.

The words might have been different, but Bellini's mes-sage was always the same: "Hit the books, why don't you?" I liked the doctor, but I'm not sure I respected him. He might have been too naive. You'd expect a religious man to be someone you could bullshit, but a psychiatrist? He should have realized that hitting the books for a solid week or even a month wasn't going to get my father off my back, and I wasn't going to turn into a grind. It was too bleak to think of studying hard more than a day or two.

Bellini's office was in the infirmary, which was as far from the Main Quad and the classrooms as you could get without going off campus. Near it was the cottage where I had lived as a lower. There were memories all over the place.

Gill had been the star athlete of Pemberton Cottage and went around with seniors. He could have refused to speak to the rest of the guys in our class and everyone would have understood. Gill wasn't that type, though. He was always glad to give you his opinion, and he returned the records he borrowed. In commons he almost overdid being a nice guy, sitting at the first table he found with an empty place.

Once early in the spring term I had his roommate's attack stick and Gill was showing me how to play lacrosse. From running around on the lawns near the dorm it was natural for me to think of trying the woods, "like the Indians." Suddenly Gill was off around our cottage and down Faculty Road, cradling the ball and whooping.

In the woods we were playing a dangerous game. The point was to remain within passing distance, but to make it a surprise when you passed. The game was dangerous because it was hard to keep track of the man with the ball as he flashed in and out of the dense brush. Still, we weren't trying to hurt each other. If one of us couldn't pick up the ball the other would holler, "Hey!" (That was all there was time for.)

By the time we quit our legs glistened red where they had been cut by the high grass and all over our bodies there were scrapes from the brush.

After my session with Dr. Bellini that Tuesday I decided to cut my French class and went down the winding road that led to the faculty homes. I left the road where Gill and I had done and went through the woods.

I had known that nothing would be the same. It was autumn and the woods were bare. The grass in the clearings was dead. There wasn't any mud and the hard ground was leaving a fine dust on my loafers. The dead leaves and branches loose at my feet made a sound like a bonfire as I made my way. My ankles literally burned where I'd skinned them trying to escape the claws that sprang from nowhere to seize my feet.

The trees were still thick with leaves changing color and the shrubs were still green but I wasn't afraid of getting lost. All my life I'd had the feeling I'd find something familiar in

forests if I kept pushing on: a road, a house, a fence or perhaps a steeple in the distance above the trees. I loved letting
my thoughts get lost, knowing my body would be safe. The
feeling of relief would be so strong in the woods that my
sense of pain would desert me and only much later would I
notice the scribbles on my arm—hardening and turning
black in the dusk as I walked home.

I went back the way I'd come and it was just my luck as
I was passing the infirmary to run into Dr. Bellini. He was
leaving by the main entrance on foot and might have been
headed for the commons to have lunch with the faculty.
Even though it was chance that I ran into him it had been
dumb of me not to take the long way around. What were a
few minutes one way or the other when I'd already cut a
class?

I pretended I hadn't recognized the doctor so that I'd be
able to say, "I didn't know it was you until you were so far
ahead . . . " If Bellini had seen me, though, he'd be sure to
wonder what I was still doing down by the infirmary. If
there had been a few academic buildings on the West Campus there would have been boys coming and going and I
could have blended in. But now we were passing through
the West Quad and there wasn't a soul around. Somehow
you knew all the dorms were empty. They were giant brick
buildings covered with ivy so green that you didn't miss
trees in the vast space they enclosed. I was trying to keep my
loafers quiet, but the buildings were commenting.

I'd lived on the West Quad my upper year, and in spite
of the screams, the usual sound was a hum while the boys
played catch in the near darkness or there was an informal
practice. When it was getting hard to see, high above to the
east a gray slate roof glowed orange.

I'd loved playing catch out in the middle of the West
Quad while summer warmth was coming. I liked any sports
that weren't organized. The way Gill and I had played lacrosse was an example of what could happen if guys our age
would use some imagination. Why should students go on

playing what they were told to play as they were told by teachers told by teachers told, with all the weight of the past pressing down? The civilized parts of the field house were stuffed with trophies and the walls were hung with pictures of championship teams with everyone smiling. All smiles— the ones who died in the war doing what they were told, the family men who'd learned their lessons and had gone to head up corporations and give everybody an ulcer, including themselves.

Maybe all the old P.A. men were smiling to please their coaches, and their coaches were only proud of all the smiling. I'd played team sports enough to realize that winning was small satisfaction next to having the coach on your side. By doing what you were told you could have the coach's admiration in a losing cause.

My dawdling was increasing the distance between Bellini and me and I began to relax. Dr. Bellini was an all-right guy. I hadn't been prepared to like him when I went to my first appointment last year, but that was because I was scared. Most of the time the doctor seemed to enjoy listening to my bullshit—puffing on his pipe, blinking, leaning back in his chair, sitting up suddenly, leaning back again. He never looked sleepy, and I found this remarkable. He was the only much older guy I'd ever known who could listen to me for more than five minutes without wanting to get in some advice, or at least a few stories about how much tougher things were in the old days, or how much better, or how cheap everything used to be considering nothing ever wore out.

The doctor was headed for the commons all right and it was time for me to put a building between us by taking a new path, but just as I began to sneak away he stopped and turned to me. He was smiling. He waved.

He must have known all along. I had to go up to him.

"Were you following me, Gordon?"

"No! I mean, I thought it might be you, but I didn't think you'd want to talk. Having lunch with us today?"

"Yes, I'm a guest of the Dean. That's a tough crowd. Academic people intimidate me. As a student I was a late bloomer. Maybe it'll be that way for you."

"Well, I hope you have a good time. I'll be seeing you next week, I guess."

"Gordon, look, I know your visits are required. I'm sorry you're being coerced into coming, but there's nothing either of us can do about that. Let's try to get somewhere next time. See if you can make a few strides in the coming week. How about it?"

"I'll try. Thank you, doctor."

"Next week, then."

"OK. Bye."

He hadn't suspected a thing. The smile was genuine. How could anyone get to be a doctor and be that stupid? I'd been having a heart attack for nothing.

Jesus, though, it was a breath of fresh air to come across someone who didn't know the rules so well, or didn't care.

THREE

I met her at the hardware store while I was looking for an extension cord. She had a package already and quick I had to think of something to say without asking what she had bought. I hated nosy people and didn't want her to think I was one. I hated small talk, too, in all its forms, but what could I do?

"Would you let me talk to you? I'm not trying to pick you up. I just wanted some information."

"What is it?" She blushed. I loved girls who could still blush.

"Oh, I wondered if you lived in town, or went to school here. Abbot, maybe."

"No, I went to high school. Graduated."

"Last year?" She nodded, pondering. "You don't know what a relief that is. The girls from Abbot are all hags. Hey, could I buy you an ice cream soda at Callahan's?" This was my big line whether it sounded like it or not.

She accepted, but she might have been disappointed. I hoped she didn't expect me to try to get her into a bar. She was an older woman, but not the type to sit around in the dark in order to drink during the day, and it was already too cold to sit around outside anywhere.

Seeing the way this girl had blushed and the poised way she could act I was glad that I had some of the same feelings about women as Barton. I liked being a gentleman, when I was getting to know a woman, especially—at a dance, for example. But no matter how pure they seemed I wasn't going to stop trying to get my finger wet.

The town streets were full of guys from P.A., but Callahan's was nearby so I didn't have to run the gauntlet. She was tall and knew how to saunter so that you couldn't have her walking at your side without being aware of every move she made. If we'd been on the streets of Boston or New York, going up and down new streets would have been a perfect way to spend a day.

In Callahan's there were a lot of teenaged girls—the kind who wore men's shirts—and there was no quiet place to talk. We got as far away as we could from the idiots. She seemed to sense that I didn't belong on their level any more than she did. I guessed she would only like rock and roll to dance to, and I found out later I was right.

While we drank our sodas she told me that she'd been to Europe and liked European men. That rankled because I had to find a way to stick up for American guys my age. The last thing I wanted to do was stick up for America when she'd been to places like France and Switzerland.

"I've never been out of the country. Well, once when my dad took us to California we went to Tijuana. I was about 11, I think. I bought firecrackers and had my picture taken on a donkey painted to look like a zebra." She wrinkled her nose. "I know, it was awful. I shouldn't have told you. What, have your parents got a lot of money? Are you *society?*" I tried to look so suave that she'd think I was too good for society, even though I belonged.

"No. My mother's dead. I'm an only child. My father likes to travel and he takes me along. I wouldn't say we're poor, though. He's an architect. What about you? You look like upper crust."

"No way. My father's a Shakespearean actor who's been reduced to making army training films. We still live in Dudbury, Connecticut though, which is famous for its coun-

clubs full of middleaged women with tans who never get fat."

She subtracted bubbles from her soda while she digested my description. "Maybe I've heard of it. We moved here from Minnesota three years ago. I don't know too much about the East Coast."

"Hey, that's great. Minnesota! That must be a fantastic place, all cold and deserted. I guess you moved here when your mother died."

"In some ways you're very perceptive, Gordon." We'd told each other our names on the way to Callahan's. "Janet McBride" didn't do that much for me, but "Jan" was nice.

"My English teacher thinks I'm perceptive. He's been known to write that on my papers when I bother to hand them in. I'd better warn you, I'm not much of a student."

She gave me a pained look and I was sure I was sunk. "I don't see how that could be. I'd say you were polished and well-spoken for a Phillips boy."

"Maybe I shouldn't tell you so much after just meeting you, but I've been in a lot of trouble over the past couple of years. I'm kind of a rebel. I do a minimum of schoolwork. I read, though. I know about Europe even though I've never been. Don't get the idea I'm out of it. I play varsity soccer and I pitched on the JV baseball team last year. I had a two-hitter against Methuen and tripled in two runs. I even sang in the school octet. It's like the Whiffenpoofs. Solos, until I got probation last year and had to quit."

I might have been laying it on too thick. She was sucking on her soda and wouldn't look up. She was smiling when she did! "You sound interesting. I don't know if it's such a good idea not to do your schoolwork, though. Unless you're tremendously smart. Don't you want to get into a good college? I thought that was what prep school was all about."

"Maybe I'll join the army first. I don't know if I'm ready for college if it's going to be anything like Andover. How about you? Are you a freshman somewhere?"

"No. I took time off to travel. I might apply."

"You'd better hurry! The guys in my dorm are already waiting to hear. I'm not. With my record I could never get into an Ivy League school and there's no way I could stand to go to UConn or some dopey state school with a bunch of guys from Dudbury High, or guys just like them. That's what's got my dad so pissed off. He likes to picture me at Harvard, it appeals to the snob in him, but Yale would be just as good. He knows the baseball coach."

"The baseball coach? That's a strange person to know."

"Ethan Allen? Nothing strange about him. He was a great major-leaguer, Dizzy Dean's former roommate, the best college coach ever. He's an authority on the game. He's written books."

"But why the baseball coach? Was your father a player?"

"Oh, he played a little softball for CBS. He wasn't too hot, I'd say. He just wants my brother and me to be good enough for the majors. He's the strange one. He's what they call a baseball nut. I wish somebody would shoot the son of a bitch."

"Your own father?"

"Yeah. The cat's out of the bag. We're locked in a death-struggle."

"Do you think your language might be a little strong?"

Her eyes slid to the side to indicate the rest of the people in Callahan's.

I gave her a pained look and something funny happened. She started to smile. No blushes, now. She looked just like that faculty wife who had given me a hard-on in the downstairs hall. She looked older than her age and more sure of herself.

"My language isn't so hot, either—not around the house." She kept watching me and smiling. "I like you, Gordon. I think it would be fun to know you better."

I was grinning back. I felt like jumping up and doing a turn like one of those weirdos from *An American in Paris*. I was in love, all right. The real thing. The other times I'd just been horny.

Before we said goodbye we were speaking French. I had a good accent, but she did, too, and she knew a lot more words than I. (No one over there spoke like Corneille unless he was dying.) Jan was *au courant*—very. Speaking French she looked older and more self-assured the way she had when she'd given me that sexy smile. It amazed me to see how a foreign language could change her personality. I'd be giving all my study hours to French from now on.

God what tits.

I kept thinking of her body as I walked back to the dorm. Or floated back. What an ass she had. She must have known I'd be watching as she walked away. Had she been wiggling her ass on purpose? It probably moved that way by nature, but she might have been able to slow it down.

Would I get my hands on her ass? Would I get my hands on her tits? My mouth? Oh, God, I could hardly wait to get back to the dorm to jack off. But Barton might be around. Hating him I kicked a stone. Sure, they were *our* rooms, but I owed it to Jan to jack off in bed while I thought of her. No way was I going to think of her while I was in the john and there were sneering guys outside telling me not to get any on the seat. She was turning me into a romantic.

God, what tits! The other guys were going to die when they saw her. She had the biggest tits I'd ever seen on a girl her age—who didn't weigh two hundred pounds, that is. In spite of her huge tits she must've weighed about one-twenty-five. All the meat on her was in the right places. When she said she wanted to know me and smiled like that I thought my hard-on was going to tip the table. If there'd been a little wet gum under there it might have done the trick.

Jan, Jan, Jan . . . She'd slipped out of her loden coat and through her blouse I could see the pattern on her bra and the dark places that were flesh.

I was a good French kisser. All the girls had said so. That would be the time to make the grab. God! If I could only get my hand under her bra. Forget anything more. That would be enough. I could wait for the rest. The rest! Her ass. Then that place between her legs, all wet and smelly and hot like spit or blood.

I may have faltered before, but I'd do it to Jan . . . during her period! Even if the blood were hot, still coming out hot, and I wouldn't care if it felt like eating an animal alive. With a smile like that she was on fire, no doubt of it. But how could I possibly be the reason? Could she want to hold *me*—my skin, my thing?

Maybe I had hot thoughts, but my body belonged to those lockers at the gym full of mouldy jockstraps. I always walked around with goosebumps when I had my clothes off. Blue lips. What did I have that she could want? No, I'd have to snow her. I'd have to hypnotize her somehow before I could get my hands under her clothes. I knew damned well that if I were in her shoes I'd rather let someone put a frog in my bra.

Maybe I was stupid to put myself down so much. I'd seen a woman once who looked like the Virgin Mary let a guy put his hand right up her dress and play with her . . . during his lunch break! That's right, a guy named Pinella, a big, hairy Italian. We used to work together at a greenhouse. It was a summer job in a town near Dudbury. The rest of us had our parents bring us and pick us up, but Pinella had a car. So did his girlfriend. She stepped out of her Chevy at noon like the answer to his horny prayers and brought him a sandwich and gave him his second wind.

What kind of sluts were they, anyhow, these girls who went to church and looked like nuns in nightshirts and would let a guy like Pinella put his hairy hand between their legs? I'm not trying to make anyone sick, but it's the truth that his fingernails were permanently black and there were thinner black lines that showed his fingerprints. Naturally, I looked at his hands all the time—with envy! Pinella was an idiot, but his life made a lot more sense than mine. All I could do with my hands was work and eat.

If I didn't stop cutting myself down I'd be playing with myself for keeps. There was a mystery about the way women let men degrade them, and you had to respect it. Maybe a girl like Jan would like her man to be rough and dirty, and somehow I shouldn't respect her less for that. I didn't care if she was a nympho who liked to do it in the mud, I'd never lose respect for her, not after the way she'd shown me how honest she could be.

It wasn't just her looks, great as they were, that drew me to Jan. She had character. She could admit when she was being phony. She was the first girl I'd ever known who could do that. Girls *never* wanted you to know what they were really thinking, I knew that much.

I was snowed when I asked Jan to come to my soccer game next week and she said "yes" right away. Then she asked if she could bring her father.

"Your father may not go for me," I'd replied. "Maybe he should stay home."

"Oh, I know he'll like you! He's wild about sports, Gordon. He'll be hurt if I won't let him come."

"Then I guess he'll have to. Are we going to get rid of him, though? Will we have the chance to be alone?"

She gave me that quick, haughty look which told me I'd caught her off guard. Then the sexy smile again. "You'd like us to be alone . . . ?" That didn't sound right to her. She'd gone too far. "Right after your soccer game?"

"I might try to kiss you. Come on, far from the prying eyes, OK? It's not only your father we'd have to shake. I've got a lot of friends who'll ride me about your looks. Very uncouth. Could we get together in town after the game, or at your place or something?"

She showed her character again. "I'm not ashamed to be seen with you, and I hope you feel the same about me. If your friends are immature, that's their problem. I know I can handle anything they might say. Anyway, they won't say much if my father is along. I don't want to sneak around when I see you."

She was already counting on meeting me more than once! She must have noticed how happy she'd just made me because I got another sexy smile.

"My dad is a sensitive guy. He'll leave us alone. He doesn't care what I do with men."

She must have noticed how hard it was for me to take my eyes off her. I'd never been so excited just looking at a girl and hearing her say things. Up to now pictures of naked women had been sexier than girls in the flesh with their buttons and clasps and their fearful nudity.

Barton was gone so I took a chance on jacking off in broad daylight—under the covers. It wasn't so unusual for me to be catching a few winks in the afternoon. Sometimes I didn't get out of a bullsession till four in the morning.

Now I wished I had Barton's room. The door could be locked from within. The room was wasted on Barton because I don't think he ever jacked off. He must have known how. I don't know, it was a sensitive subject with him. As big as he was and as mean at sports, no one wanted to ride him too much, including me, but the way he got red when the rest of us started talking about masturbation was a giveaway that he had some problem about it. Only Thomson, the Southern guy upstairs, had the guts to tease him.

Barton must have been downtown. He hadn't told me where he was going, but that was the only logical place on a Wednesday afternoon. (We only had classes in the morning on Wednesdays, which made Friday look feasible.)

I pulled it without really trying to come for all of ten minutes, listening for Barton and feeling safer all the time. Finally I got down to business by undressing Jan. It would have helped to know what her nipples looked like, but I decided to make them big with lots of pinkish brown around (and that's just how they turned out to be).

It was the damnedest thing. As soon as I thought of her

vulva I'd start to lose it. Not my chip—my hard-on! Nothing like this had ever happened to me. So far this term I'd been thinking of Sheila Burke every time and I'd be off in a couple of minutes. Sheila and I had never gone all the way—she was too scared for that—but I'd had my finger in her continually and I couldn't wait for high gear to drive one-handed on the parkways. When she let me look at it up close I could tell that she was embarrassed so I kept saying how beautiful it was. Actually, it had a well-chewed look and wasn't as cute as the one that had almost made a man of me the summer before. Playing with Sheila's in the dark had been easier to take. But I kept on telling her how pretty it was and making it juicy with a gentle finger. Suddenly I got the idea that she should join the campaign and I told her to play with it herself a while, since she knew better than I what to do. Sure enough, she flicked at it and glided over it, but she didn't slide the skin around as much as I did. (Odd, but she wanted me to keep doing it my way when I was touching her. I guess she figured a flick from me would hurt.) The noise she made aroused me more than anything.

Sheila Burke had been by far the sexiest girl I'd ever known. It was probably my fault if she got carried away at times because of my skill in persuading her that the dirtiest things I could think of were beautiful. Still, whenever I'd try to put my cock in, her eyes would get big and she'd scream if she had to. Then she'd be putting on her clothes, completely cold and not even wanting to kiss me goodnight. Naturally, I liked to see all the perverted things she would do—it was better than nothing—so I didn't try to force myself on her. Anyway, it was the slightly perverted nature of all this that must have made her such a good person to think of while I was jacking off.

I must have been a very scummy person because in spite of my feelings for Jan, I found myself thinking of Sheila Burke, and sure enough, the thing was hard again. How could you explain something like that? Sheila Burke meant nothing to me any more. In fact, if I weren't horny the thought of her vulva or whatever would have made me sick. On top of that, I was pissed off at her. She'd turned into a nympho after we broke up and was letting every guy in town fuck her.

I may have been partly responsible. I cheated on her with quite a few other girls, including the one I first went all the way with the summer before last, and she'd found out about two of the other girls, and maybe more. In the back of my mind I worried that she'd turned into a nympho to get even with me. There was nothing wrong with my ego, though, and it was hard for me to see how a girl would want to ruin herself just to get revenge on a no-good guy like me. *Her* ego wasn't getting the job done, that was for sure.

I was very close to coming while I was watching Sheila expose herself, but I forced myself to see Jan's face smiling down at me over Sheila's tits, and there it went again. The stupid thing was still swollen, but now it was like a swollen ankle, and hurt like hell.

I started over with Sheila, half in agony now. I think my cock was trying to spare itself further mistreatment because in no time its head was up and the tingle had started that would take me over the top. This time I waited till the last moment before I started looking at Jan and I had her open her mouth wide and show me her glistening teeth and say "Yes! Yes!" the way Sheila used to when I touched her. Success at last.

If you could call it that. The next part is nauseating even to me, but I want to tell what things were really like at school, and I wasn't alone in my dirty habits, believe me.

I'd had sense enough to throw back the covers when I came so there wouldn't be any evidence for Barton or a nosy laundryman, but once again I'd been so preoccupied with my human sacrifice that I hadn't remembered to bring a Kleenex. To tell the truth, I don't think I ever remembered. I hadn't bought any Kleenex in ages. I was such a grub that I'd cast around for some dirty clothes to clean up the icy puddle on my belly—maybe an old sock, or the shirt I'd taken off before I got into bed. For some reason I thought I was above suspicion with laundry that was all stuck together. The first time thinking of Jan I employed one of my new stratagems: pulling out the bottom sheet and using the edge to dry off.

I thought I was doing a great job of covering up, and I guess I was. Still, I hated the whole business of jacking off from start to finish. It was unnatural as hell, even though everyone did it (except Barton).

I longed to have my cock inside a vagina where it belonged, and I wanted my sperm to be absorbed by the body of the woman I was with, my so-called beloved. (If it was Jan, there'd be no need to make a face when I called her "my beloved.") If my sperm was going to give the woman a baby, so be it. I was willing to ruin my entire life for a few moments of natural behavior. I would become a family man and a laborer or something *gladly* if a woman would let me come inside her just *once!* Come to think of it, though, if I had to be a laborer for the rest of my life my wife would have to let me come inside her every night. No wonder the poor had so many children.

I always felt hangdog after I'd jacked off. Then I thought of a way to brighten things up. I'd promised to write Jan and she'd promised to write back as soon as my letter came so that maybe I'd have an answer before my Wednesday game.

I had to be very careful about the impression I was making so I cut the letter short, hoping to get it done before Barton got back and started asking a million questions.

(Letter-writing was Barton's main romantic achievement. He thought a letter with "Love" at the end and nothing dirty in it had the same chance as an ejaculation to tie up a woman's thoughts. I had more faith in sperm at one in a million, but I hadn't even figured out a way to get Jan's father out of the picture, so it was too soon to think of getting her pregnant.)

Dear Jan,

I've been thinking of you ever since we met and talked. I hope you'll believe me when I tell you that I've never flattered anyone in my life, not even a girl. But you're enough reason to make an exception. I like everything about you: your hair, your eyes, your skin, even your mind—and especially your temple where the hair is fine and I can see throbbing sometimes. But I'm sure you've been told many times about your beauty, even though you couldn't have been so beautiful for very long. There, that's off my chest.

I'm still worried about what the other guys are going to be like because frankly, they've never seen anyone like you around here. But maybe they do know about you if you went to football games with your dad. I was clear across the campus playing soccer so I was doubly screwed: I never got to see any football (or you) and I've had to play for small crowds. What a difference if we were in Europe! However, I know I wouldn't be good enough for a European team. Our right inside is from Latin America and you should see him. (As you may know, a lot of the best European players are from Latin America, too.)

Maybe you think it's funny that I'm asking you to come and see me on a Wed. afternoon. I wonder if I explained that I have an away game (Deerfield) coming up this Saturday. Sunday I've got to go to chapel (I'm all out of cuts) and that ruins the day right there, but to top it off, my choir's got a concert in the afternoon and I've got a solo. (I take choir for credit, so I can't cut that either. Not so bright of me. It's like having a class on the weekend.) If you get this letter in time you might want to come and hear me. Don't! The whole thing is pathetic. They've got the Abbot girls doing it with us. I never give them a glance, horny as I am from this goddamned place.

Anyway, Wednesday's my first free time and I'm dying to see you after the game.

Best regards,

I typed a draft of the letter on my portable and went over it a dozen times before I came up with the final version. Still I wasn't sure that the style was right. I'd had to risk sounding naive in order to muffle a tendency of mine to use big words. I wanted Jan to think of me as a sincere admirer, but not someone who was trying to impress her. I figured a girl as pretty as Jan was sick of people trying to get her attention by some extraordinary feat or turn of phrase.

I'd been sincere telling her about myself at Callahan's. I had known I was taking a chance telling her how I hated my father, how I'd never been abroad, what the school thought of me, and that there wasn't going to be an Ivy-League college in my future.

Somehow I had known that I had to confess to Jan and be the person I was. I wasn't afraid that she'd see through me if I put on an act, but I sensed that she valued sincerity, and thought she had found that quality in me. I wasn't going to lie to her until I had to.

It would have been great to tell anyone how I really felt, but to be able to tell Jan was such a miracle that it made me want to thank someone. For once I felt smallminded for *not* believing in God.

FOUR

When I got back from Deerfield on Saturday I went to the school post office to check my box. I'd been writing a girl from Dana Hall whose family had so much money they'd never have accepted me in spite of Dudbury and my family name. I hadn't had a letter from her in three weeks so I figured someone had found my name in the black book that is kept on people from old families who don't own yachts.

At the start of the term I'd been writing long letters to a girl from North Carolina who'd been visiting a friend in Dudbury over the summer. She'd only let me French her, but she was good at it and had a dark beauty. Also, I'd loved her accent. She'd stopped writing, too, and hadn't bothered to send me a Dear John letter. She must have found somebody who could get up and sit down, walk around a little, waft something.

Unlike so many of my friends I'd never received a Dear John letter. I made it a policy never to write a girl unless I was answering her letter, and all I did was answer. I didn't try to push our love any further. If I didn't hear from her, she didn't hear from me, and the relationship would fade away without a lot of insults and bad news. In any case it was my experience that relationships were hard to sustain through the mails. The more letters you wrote, the further you strayed from reality. It could be a letdown to see your

correspondent in the flesh with the poetic images in your letters coming back to haunt you.

Lately I'd been visiting my mailbox about twice a week
to pick up my father's shit and a few whimpers from my
mom. More often than not I'd look their mail over right
there in the post office and throw it away. Late Saturday I
went down in case there might be word from Jan. There
shouldn't have been. I mailed my letter to her on Wednesday night and if she answered right away I wouldn't have
word from her till Monday. To my surprise there was a letter
on good stationery right next to two of my father's business
envelopes. It was hers.

I tore open my father's letters and gave each one about
ten seconds. I wouldn't have read them if the ink had been
smeared with tears. There'd have to have been blood on
every page. I was tempted to open Jan's letter, but too excited. I'd go back to the dorm. There'd be privacy now because Barton always went to the Saturday night movie right
after chow.

Dear Gordon:

*I'm not wasting any time writing this letter because you
said you wanted to write me one before we see each other on
Wednesday. If there's a change in where you'd like to meet
me, I hope you'll clear that up when you write. I can find
your playing field don't worry cuz I've gone to games with
my father over where you are.*

*Really, I don't think anything has happened around
here since I met you that you'd care to hear about. I do want
to tell you more about myself cuz there's a lot you don't
know, and it's unusual for me to accept a date so fast. I'm
not worried about what I'm getting into, though. I liked you
right away and I told you the truth about your being the first
guy on the hill I've dated, but I should have said this year
because I went out with Alan Benson once or twice, but he's*

graduated now. Anyway it wasn't serious and my reputation isn't that bad. Just kidding! But Alan explained to me about your rules and I understand we'll have to be careful about some things, and that's all right with me. Kind of exciting, you know?

I'm doing some baking and I want to get this in a mail-box. My father is crazy about my cakes and my cooking and you will be, too. I'd like to have you for dinner sometime. We'll see. Take care of yourself and get ready for the big game you don't care about. (Isn't that what you said?) I'm looking forward to seeing you then right after on Wednesday.

Sincerely,

Jan

A letter like Jan's might have seemed tame to some people . . . Types who lived where there was lots of neon. My senses had never been dulled by too much of anything (except too much school). The nuances in Jan's letter bowled me over.

In the first place, she'd written it on her own without waiting to get mine. There was a world of significance in that. The next most impressive thing was her willingness to make a clean breast of her dates with Alan Benson. Alan Benson! I could hardly believe my eyes. He'd been one of the co-captains of the football team and started at attack in lacrosse when I was a lower. Here was a guy who was still remembered on campus for things he'd done two years ago. He was a legend, practically a god, and Jan had been his girl. Well, his date, at least.

After a few dozen readings of her letter I had a change of heart. There was something fishy about the "once or twice" she'd gone out with Benson. Obviously she was trying to play down the importance of the time they'd spent together, but she'd have known if it was once or twice or even four times, and "once or twice" was therefore nothing but a way of glossing over what had really happened. But what was that? Why did she stop seeing him?

I could get an answer to some of these questions on the spot. Thomson had played on the varsity football team as a lower, and he'd been good enough to have a few friends among the seniors. Thomson was likely to be in his room because a) he'd received a huge package of food from his mother yesterday and b) he never went to the Saturday night movies.

I've given an idea of Thomson's character, and I had plenty of reasons to dislike him, but here I was about to go up and mooch his goodies and pump him about Alan Benson and Jan. Mixed feelings explained the inconsistency. I had respect for him as an athlete, I respected his toughness. He was well-equipped to survive here, and I couldn't see where he was going to have any troubles in life when his schooldays were behind him. His family was wealthy, he was a top student, he was as big and strong as anyone in school and he had blond good looks. Maybe it was because he had so much that he wasn't likable. Anyway, even though he and Barton were at odds, I looked up to Thomson in a way. I guess I should have been looking down. But he took me for someone like him and enjoyed my company.

"Look who's back wi' slobbah on his mouf!"

No denying I wanted more of his pralines. Thomson was from a swamp in Mississippi and he had the strongest Southern accent I'd ever heard. About his pralines, for example, he might have said, "Mama makes 'em huhsel' lahke nub'dy in dis wuhld." I've got to compromise on Thomson's dialect. It would be a tremendous pain to render his words phonetically, and the better job I did, the harder it would be for a reader to understand him.

"Well, if you're offering."

"I figure you all will pay me back at that little party we got comin'." The booze party I was planning. He was trying to make me shudder by talking loud about it. "You gonna have some bourbon for me, ain't you?" (Beubon.)

"As long as you keep shelling out." I took a fistful of his pralines. "Look, Thomson, I've got trouble. First of all, did you ever hear the name Janet McBride?" So far I'd only told Barton about her.

"Never heard of the lady."

"All right, read this. Maybe it'll refresh your memory."

"Alan Benson. Now what she wanna get tangled up with him for?"

I snatched the letter. "That's just what I'd like to know. Didn't you hear about her? Benson went out with her back when we were lowers. He must have said something . . . "

"What she look like?"

"Then you saw him with a girl? You tell me."

"Looky here, Gawdon. I saw him with a girl or two. He had all the pussy at Abbot aft' 'im. Wait, now. There was one girl saw him regular, a townie with big tits." Tiyuts, Jesus. You could tell he was thinking of both.

"That's her. What color hair did she have?"

He was strumming his lower lip. "Yeah, going out with the fellas I saw her sometimes. I don't remember that girl at the games. Once't I had my helmet on I was like to forget all the yelling and the poontang. She was a purty thing. Dark hair, brown hair, I don't know. No blonde. Blue eyes, I think, but I'm a-guessin'. Is that your'n?"

"I'm sure of it. Well, can you tell me anything? Did he ever talk about her?"

"I know she'll give you some sugar. Anyone on the team could tell you that."

The bastard was having the time of his life.

"You're trying to make me believe that Benson was enough of a prick to tell everyone on the team about her?"

"I don't remember him telling no one, but that was the word. She was a townie and everyone on the team was raring to go, but A.B. had a hold on her. You got a hell of a woman there, Gawdon. I'd take sloppy seconds anytime.

You gotta expect they's gonna be broken in some, older wimmin'."

"What do you mean, older? She was one year younger than Benson."

"No suh. That I do know. She had to be a senior at the hah school here in town, or else in college already."

"You're kidding. How could you know a thing like that? You'd almost forgotten her."

"Tell ya what, everybody on the team was lookin' for her come our upper year and Benson gone. She must have graduated. No one ever saw her again and over the years I kinda forgot about her. But if she back in town and you got something cookin', Gawdon, you one lucky fella. You get her pissed off at ya, let me know. She give you a disease and you don't want her, pass her on to me."

"Knock it off. You know how I feel about her."

"I feel the same way mysel'!"

There was a commotion in the hall. The movie was out. I knew enough from this bastard.

Ah, a mistake. I'd snatched Jan's letter back from Thomson but the envelope was still on his desk and I caught him studying the return address. He had on the slight smile which along with his cold eyes was what made him look so mean at times.

He handed me the envelope. Better not to mention what we both knew. I could warn Jan about Thomson. I could tell her to watch out for him. I didn't think he'd try to make a move as long as I was still interested, but I'd ruin his chances in advance, even if I had to fill her head with lies about him.

Barton was sitting downstairs and Kingsley had followed him in. Kingsley was the flit next door and he was just waiting to be shit on, but then Channing and Hobbs dropped by. Barton only wanted to tell me about the movie, but the others had come to iron out our plans for Thursday night. That's when I was getting a shipment of booze from Ed Nye.

Nye's father was a liquor distributor in town who didn't drink. The Nyes had a cellar full of booze that came to them in the course of business and it saved them ever having to buy someone a present. Ed was a day student, and though I didn't know him as well as I did my friends in the dorms, he was a reasonable guy. For ten bucks he'd let me have a case of booze, enough to last a term, or almost enough—this was our second shipment and the Thanksgiving recess was still more than a month away. With Channing and Hobbs in the dorm, and Thomson, and that bruiser Teasdale, it was hard to keep any booze on hand. The party on Thursday coming would be our biggest yet—eight guys.

Barton drifted away when the planning started in earnest. Oh, Jim did his share of drinking in the dorm—which would have surprised his coaches and teachers—but he was sore at me for making him take the shipment through his window. Barton's window was on a blind side of Sanborn's house where the cellar door was at 45 degrees. With careful footwork to get me to a ledge above the doors I could hold the shipment high enough for Barton to take it reaching down. Knowing P.A. it was a wonder there wasn't any barbed wire to worry about. However, Sanborn was a trusting housemaster. You had to make a hell of a racket to get his attention. He might have been half in the bag himself most nights.

Barton was sore because he thought it would be safer to take the stuff in through the front door—right under Sanborn's nose—in laundry bags.

Never in the history of our school had an Andover man been seen after dark with a laundry bag, but Barton was a great one for clean clothes and thought he could get away with it. When the chips were down, though, he wanted *me* to sneak the stuff in. The fight over his laundry bag idea was the biggest we'd had so far this year.

I was well-known to be someone you never saw with a

laundry bag. The faculty probably knew about me by this time. The kids who had plenty of money all term used a laundry service from town, Rutter's, whose trucks were crawling over our campus so much of the time that we never noticed them any more, any more than we would the flies when there was a turd on the lawn, or let's say dung beetles, because of all the trundling.

As a lower I realized that Rutter's could make some shitty shirts of mine look decent thanks to their heavy use of starch. As soon as I was sure I wasn't going to grow any taller I went to a thrift store and bought all the shirts my size (that weren't messed up with colors). Just once at the start of each term I let Rutter's restore my crummy shirts to the kind of purity that was only fit to be cutting into the neck of an angry priest or the forehead of a nun. I could get three days out of a shirt if I stayed out of food fights, and then it went on the pile in my closet that was huge by the end of term and so famous that guys visiting from other dorms would some-times knock on our door wanting a look.

Other kids with the same money I had to live on for a term would have had to cut back on snacks to pay Rut-ter's—to keep from lugging a laundry bag and keep starch in their clothes. I never had to cut back and probably saved enough to pay for our booze.

Anyway, I'd won the battle over the laundry bags and had every guy in the dorm on my side. Laundry was a matter for common sense and Barton was too much of a romantic to have any. I hated to admit it, but he was scared, too, and everyone had seen it. I felt sorry for Barton and hated to see him miserable, but he was getting to be embarrassing with his dumb ideas based on nothing but fear and survival in-stinct.

Channing went into Barton's room and came out with him right away. Channing would be a diplomat someday, I knew it. Someone who'd speak the language wherever he went, with mistresses and mansions where he could stay for nothing. My wildest dreams would be business as usual for

Channing. But if he turned into a Bowery bum somehow, which was what my father was always predicting would happen to me, I was going to be a lot more cynical than I was now. Maybe someone scared who played by the rules like Barton.

Concerning our booze party there wasn't that much to get straight tonight. Kingsley wasn't invited to the party, but I was paying him to be a lookout. The party would take place in Channing's and Hobbs's common room, which was right above Kingsley's (and Barton's). All Kingsley had to do was leave his door open so he could see Sanborn coming up the stairs and rap on the ceiling with my hockey stick. It would be up to Thomson and Teasdale to intimidate the non-drinkers so that no one would use the stairs. Half the dorm would be at the party, so movement in the halls would be easy to detect.

Channing and Hobbs were great guys. High honors students who lifted weights during study hours, ordered pizzas by cab all the way from town and in other ways were hospitable to people who would drop in and help them fritter away their evenings. At one time or another everyone in the dorm had passed a few hours in their common room and it was the logical place for a drinking bout. A lot more logical than my room, which had been the scene of the first small party. Things had happened then which had worried Channing and Hobbs and they wanted to know what my ideas were if Sanborn made it all the way to their door. I explained that this Thursday coming there'd be an extra floor between us and Sanborn. We'd have the Kingsley warning system. We'd make sure that none of the light drinkers had too much. The big guys who could hold it would be in charge of the bottles. This was important because at our first party a kid named Goulet had puked on my rug. (The whole school called him "gullet" from then on.) Then someone had dropped him when they were carrying him upstairs.

Sanborn found me scrubbing the rug.

"What was that racket?" he wanted to know.

"Barton and I were having a fight."

"It sounded as if it came from the hall!"

"It started in the hall, but he finished me in here." Plausible enough. Our boxing team was no joke. I knew things would go better for us if I were the loser.

"What are you doing cleaning that rug?"

"He hit me in the stomach and made me puke."

"For the love of Pete. What's the matter with you boys? Where's Barton? Is he all right?"

"He's pretty banged up. He's in his room, though, see for yourself."

Sanborn took a peek and there was Barton all crumpled up and groaning, a great act for someone who was unconscious. The next day he couldn't remember anything that happened after midnight.

"Well, I want this kind of thing to stop. Maybe you and Barton should come to see me tomorrow sometime after athletics."

"We'd be glad to, sir."

It was early in the term and Sanborn didn't know yet what he was in for from me or he'd have been a lot madder. When he was clattering down the stairs to his apartment all the doors in the dorm moved a quarter of an inch and were completely shut. At the moment none of us were connected up but you could still feel a collective relief. Boozy breath being let out without a sound.

Why didn't Sanborn smell alcohol? He'd had quite a few himself by one at night. That's why his face had been so red and his eyes had looked smaller behind his glasses. The mystery was why he bothered to investigate noises in the dorm when he'd had a few drinks.

If all the new precautions weren't enough for Channing and Hobbs I'd come up with a system for collecting glasses and bottles and stashing them here and there under sofas and beds and chairs. As a final touch the guys at the party would bring their notebooks and spread them out on the floor so that Sanborn—if he ever did get a look inside—would see us all studying together. I could tell this idea was big with Barton. "Yes, Jim, you'll be able to study for real if you want."

"Nothing wrong with your plans. They're pretty cute. I still say you're taking a lot for granted. If there's a slip-up out back there won't be a drop in the house."

"No more shit about the delivery!" Yeah, but if it didn't come off there wouldn't be a Bancroft or a Barton in the house, either, because you got expelled automatically for drinking in the dorms, it didn't matter who you were. Of course Channing and Hobbs didn't sweat how we were going to take the shipment since Barton and I would get all the blame if something went wrong. Up on the second floor Channing and Hobbs could stomp around all they wanted and nobody but Kingsley or Barton would be annoyed. I had Sanborn's dining room under me and a mistake might show up in his soup.

When we'd been over everything about twenty times my guests finally got the idea it was time to leave. As soon as they were gone I fished a Coke out of the canvas bag which hung from my window and unlocked my filing cabinet to finish off a bottle of rum I still had. Barton never moved from his chair until I handed him his glass. Barton had curly black hair and his skin could be as pale as death sometimes.

"I feel like I really need one tonight," he said. "You know, Gordie, sometimes I think it's all getting out of control. Everything we worked so hard to achieve—oh, I don't mean you. But most of us. How would we take it to be thrown out in the middle of the fall term—our senior year? How would I take it is what I'm really wondering. I think you'd handle it better because you don't have any prospects."

"Sure I do. They're just all negative. I expect the worst and you know how that goes. A few good things happen from time to time and I'm really grateful."

"Yeah. You might be right, but don't forget you don't have anything at stake. Think how you'd feel if you'd been grinding away the way I have since I came to this place. I want to see my work pay off. Yet I chose you for a room-mate, and I'm letting myself get involved with all the illegal stuff you do. Don't worry, I knew what kinds of things would be going on. We may not have been in the same dorm last year, but I heard about your exploits, even things you've never told me to this day. I must be trying to destroy myself for some reason. Maybe I'm the one that should be seeing that guy you go to, Bellini . . . "

"Nah, there's nothing he could do for you. You've just got a hankering for fun in you and once in a while you give in to it. When you're out of school you're going to be a real hellraiser, Jim—that's what I think. As for me, I want the chance to drink and screw around until it isn't fun anymore. Until nothing would be so boring as another bar, another car, another woman. 'Oh, look at those tits,' 'What an ass,' and so on. You can't tell me that it won't get boring eventually. When I'm finally fed up with all the pleasures that no one wants me to have, I might try to figure out what those peo-ple at our concerts are up to. The ones who get the polite ap-plause. I think there's a place for that stuff, Barton, but not when taking someone's coat can give you a hard-on."

"I know. A lot of hypocrisy comes from pretending our baser urges don't exist. It'd be different if we were the only ones pretending, but for the school to pretend that we're hungry for culture is kind of a joke."

"It's good to hear you say so, man. It means a lot to know that someone can understand, especially when you're someone who's able to live by their code. I see your side, too. I know it makes more sense to work hard and accept what they've got in mind for us. I really am screwed up. I know I could study and toe the line if I tried harder, but way down deep I'm afraid I don't care . . .

"There's something maniacal about everyone doing what they're supposed to. And there's no doubt that this school is turning out some cutthroat bastards. Maybe that's what we need in this world. Not people who play by the rules—don't try to tell me that's what we're learning to do. No one thinks the rules are good enough to play by. We just learn to manipulate them until we're old enough to make our own."

"I don't know, Gordie. You get me depressed when you talk like that. You should see your face. Go ahead and have another drink or something. The world isn't all that bad a place. Hey, even the guys here at P.A. have it a lot better than most people our age. How'd you like to be a farmer from the age of eight, or selling vegetables from a cart?"

"It's really Jan that's got me down. God, I'm in a lousy mood."

"Why don't you get it off your chest? I'm not being nosy. What's new with her?"

"A letter came. I've got it on me. See for yourself."

He took a lot longer to whistle and say "Alan Benson" than Thomson had, which goes to show what a fast reader Thomson was. That must have been the biggest reason I didn't trust him. In spite of his drawl his thoughts were moving ahead like lightning and you could tell his mind was working even faster when his mouth was shut.

"She must be quite a girl if Alan Benson would take her out. That's great, Gordie."

"I was happy for a while. Then I went up to see if Thomson knew her."

"I know what's coming. He told you a lot of dirt about her. Don't believe him. He may have played football with Alan, but Alan wouldn't tell Thomson anything about his girlfriend."

"Well, Thomson says he did, and he's pretty convincing. What's more, he claims she's really two years older than I am. Nineteen or twenty. He says she graduated high school two years ago and left the town. He knows because a lot of guys on the football team tried to find out what had happened to her as soon as Benson wasn't around. I tell you, if Thomson is right, that means she lied to me, Jim. And here I've been telling you how honest she is. That's a pretty big lie for someone her age. I could see an old bag shaving a few years off her age. Past thirty women are getting desperate if they haven't got a man interested. But why would *she* lie? Wouldn't she realize I'd see a big advantage in her being two years older? Free to live her life any way she wants? Everyone knows a girl of twenty will put out. That's the difference between high school and college."

"Not so fast. I still say Thomson's lying about something. He probably doesn't know a thing about this girl and he's making all this up to mess you around. After all, in the letter she said she went out with him 'once or twice.' Benson probably went out with a lot of girls once or twice, especially the ones over at Abbot. How would Thomson know which one she is . . . this Janet McBride? Why would Benson run around saying, 'Hey, fellas, I'm taking out Janet McBride.' What would that mean to anybody?"

"I don't know, but something tells me Thomson is right. I think Janet McBride is a whore. I'm thinking of one of the first things she said: 'I spent some time in Europe. I liked the men.' It all adds up. She told me she'd been three years in this town, but no one's seen her for the last two because she's been humping her way across the Alps. That explains her sexy smile. No girl who hasn't been around a lot could look me right in the eye and smile like that."

"I thought you said she blushed a lot, she was the type who could blush . . . "

"It's true, but what if guilt makes her do it and not innocence? Maybe she gets ashamed of herself at times for the way she's been passing herself off as such an innocent young thing, the way she's roping me in."

"What are you going to do?" He sounded dejected.

"I'm going to give her every chance to prove her innocence. But if it's true, and she's been whoring around, I'm going to try to love her just the same."

"That's great, Gordie!"

I knew my man.

FIVE

The next day, late Sunday afternoon, Barton was true to form again. He couldn't believe I could be in love with Jan and still want to go to the Abbot Mixer.

"Ever hear of morbid curiosity?"

"I've heard of it but thank God I haven't got any."

"Some Abbot girl might be just the ticket for you, Jim. Never know when a new face will turn up."

"All you ever say is what sluts they are. I know you, Bancroft. If I go with you you'll try to get some laughs at my expense. Say, introduce me to the biggest slut they've got."

"The Abbot girls aren't sluts, Jim, they just talk dirty. I went to all the dances last year and the best I could do was cop a feel in some rhododendron bushes. Not even inside her clothes . . . "

"Well, if that's what you do this time, I don't think much of this great love of yours for Janet."

"But how do I know Jan will still go for me a week from now, or a month? Take my word, if we were out in California and not stuck in this hole I'd have Clark Gable for competition."

Every year they held the Abbot mixer early in the term so that Andover guys and Abbot girls would get the hots for each other. Relationships would begin only to be nipped in the bud by schoolwork and busy schedules. There was no way to get to each other except through the mail or in broad daylight, patronizing the local soda fountains on weekends. Intimacy in surroundings like that was so degrading that necking in a back alley could seem like a classy thing to do.

Intimacy breeds frankness and enables people to acknowledge their shortcomings and laugh at themselves. Proms, cotillions, and well-supervised affairs like the Abbot Mixer represented the least intimate possible way for the sexes to get together. Nobody told the truth. Everyone was wearing a smile, but it was just nerves—nothing was funny until you thought about it later. As we lurched around the room pretending to study the decor or the other dancers our eyes were glassy. Best friends didn't know each other and if you called out the name of someone staring at you he'd be startled, get hot cheeks and look away. Probably a lot of us were thinking dirty thoughts and that explained the leaps in the air when we suddenly heard our names.

Those among us who knew how to talk to girls (I was one) were more intellectual than our counterparts at Abbot. Or so it seemed. Abbot girls weren't stupid. They knew all they had to do to enslave us was dance close enough to let us feel their tits against us, feel our thighs brush. Why take chances with their intellects?

I have to admit that Abbot girls in general had more poise than we did. This was so because they'd been brought up to believe that crudeness was the worst trait in a girl. Their trainers prized wit and courtesy. Wit could be elegant as well as stinging. Courtesy could be cruel. These rich girls had mastered cruelty and elegance before they went away to school, but in the Abbot dorms there was no way to suppress crudeness. Still, it surfaced in disguise. An Abbot girl could drawl the dirtiest words with a gleam in her eyes and make them sound right for an afternoon tea. Our guys were still saying them by accident and looking around to see who had heard. When I say poised I'm thinking of the women who made chitchat and nibbled on delicacies while lions were devouring the early Christians.

I'd been to a lot of formal dances over the summer and I'd become an expert at arousing the girls I danced with—in spite of all the crinoline and courtesy—with my right thigh. I could get away with this because I didn't crowd in on a girl's upper body while we were dancing. I leaned back to hear what she had to say and to let the world admire her. But my right hand on her lower back was a vise, and whenever the music was right for dancing close I put my right knee as far as I could between her legs.

With my rhythmically plunging bony knee and her jelly thighs, dancing with me was like having sex on a grand scale and when the music died I'd take my partner off her feet, lean back still further, then let her slide back slowly onto the floor, so that for a tense or squirmy moment her crotch would lodge against my knee. I'm sure the chaperones took this gesture to mean, "Wasn't that fun?"

The girl herself might not have realized how serious I was. I was doing research when I went to dances. I knew by their responses which girls my age could go for me. Sure, I'd end up with the girl I brought, but when I telephoned one of the others she'd know I wouldn't be content merely to kiss at the movies. One of the girls I'd screwed last summer had confessed that she'd gotten wet pants as soon as she recognized my voice over the phone. Oh, I knew my way around a dance floor.

The mixer was informal. The way some girls and guys got together you'd think they'd known each other all their lives. Newcomers to both schools were spinning out of the social orbit, skirting the dance floor or drifting through space in search of someone they knew well enough to cling to. I was bold at dances and stood on a chair to see if any of the Abbot girls I knew had improved. I spotted Eleanor Adams and decided to cut her out of the herd.

Ellie was a redhead I'd met at the Mixer when I was a lower. She was my grade at Abbot but a little older. We were eye to eye back then, but over the last two years I was looking further down to find her eyes each time we met. She was a quiet, sensitive girl, very ashamed of her acne, and in the beginning we'd enjoyed being untouchable together. We'd both changed for the better. She was finally dressed to show off her sensational tits and she'd always had a big, springy ass. There was no denying I was tall, dark and handsome no matter what could be said about my mental health. Furthermore, I'd never had a problem with zits and I was smelling of something called Knize 10 which always reminded me of the varnish they put on yachts.

"Oh, my gahhhd. Gordon Bancroft. When are you going to stop growing?"

"That's all over now. What about you?" I looked right at her tits and made my eyes big.

Her color came up but she was saved by the music and said, "Let's dance."

Her tits were so mountainous that her zits were hardly noticeable. Oh, she still had an archipelago across her cheeks that made her forehead look like a snowy plateau. As soon as I'd learned acne wasn't contagious I began to like rubbing cheeks with the zitty girls, they were sexy to me. Something was brewing in them that they couldn't help or hide. It was a suspicion of mine that redheads were zittier than blondes and brunettes, and everyone knew that redheaded women liked sex. That was more than a suspicion—I had proof.

Ellie knew all about my right knee and I don't think she cared what I did with it as long as she had her clothes on. In spite of the way she was displaying her body, however, I got the feeling she wasn't aroused. Her face got so tight when I started probing you'd have thought I was the dentist.

"Maybe you won't want to see more of me this term," I said at one point.

She dropped her arms and stopped cold in the midst of all the obedient zombies. "What makes you say a thing like that?"

"The way you are when I hold you, dancing. Did you get raped this summer or something?"

The Abbot girl took over and she smiled. "None of your business. But if I had been I wouldn't encourage you by saying so." We were dancing again. Now I stopped.

"I can't help it, I think you've turned into a prude. Or else you're in love with somebody."

"Would it be so unusual for me to have a boyfriend at home?"

"Hell, no. I can't believe how you look now. But your personality isn't what I remember. You know how we used to talk . . . "

"In my experience people who talk a lot about sex aren't getting any." This was more like it, but her condescending tone was wrong.

"Well, let's go outside and get some, then."

"Nobody's leaving yet. Christ, Bancroft, we've only been here half an hour and the sky is still red."

In spite of this vague promise her inner thighs were wary as we danced on. Something was wrong. When someone cut in I set off like an electron. I had a lot of reactions and it was dark out by the time I got back to Ellie.

"Let's blow this popstand. We'll say you're sick and I'm walking you back to your campus. That worked last year."

"Not with me."

"Sorry, you're right, it was someone else, but that's a good one. They can't refuse and they'll even let us back in if I say you're feeling better."

"It's too obvious. No one else is leaving."

"The hell! I saw two couples go slinking off!"

"Yeah, while the rest of us were exchanging glances. Too bad trying to get some privacy has to be such a public gesture. Anyway, one of the girls is a prep, doesn't know any better, and you know the other one."

"By reputation, I read you. But there are places on the way to your campus where we could fool around. We could even go all the way . . . "

"You slay me, Bancroft. As long as I've known you I've never had a letter."

"I wrote you one!"

"Maybe so, right after we met, but you were all business."

"What do you mean?"

"Making alliances, trying to make friends. I was doing the same thing. When you're out of it it's hard to be sincere."

"I know. It's like being poor people who overdress when they're invited to watch the rich get married. I can't believe how flowery my letters were then. When I read them over they just don't sound like me."

"Did you get that many back?" What? "To read . . . "

"No, I have the drafts. I always roughed out my letters a couple of times. I didn't want some girl to get the idea I was a real person. As a fantasy I could keep her interest. If she wanted me for a lover, I'd have been sunk. I may have been puny but I was smart."

"I don't remember you being puny."

The music stopped and we sat the next one out.

"I had my first affair last summer," she told me presently. Clever way to say she wasn't a virgin.

"Hey, that's great! Is it over now?"

"I don't know. I look forward to seeing him again. It's not impossible."

"Want to tell me about him?" I hated to be a friend to girls who were in love with someone else, but I was hoping to ruin it for her, get her to admit that the guy didn't care enough about her, that she was miserable alone . . . Whereas I really did care and always had and I . . . was here.

"I'd rather not. Too much to tell, and it was crazy. What about you? I noticed the change right away: you're in love."

"How'd you know?"

"It's the way you're buzzing around and making a hit with all the girls. If you wanted to fall for one they'd play hard to get. But someone must be in love with you. You're acting like a married man. The challenge is to see if one of us has what it takes to make you stray."

"You're going too far. I'm in love, OK, but I'm not sure yet what she feels for me. She's beautiful, too, but you're full of shit if you think I'm acting like a married man."

"Maybe so, but look how much you've told me. Now I know where I stand."

"So you're involved with a married man . . . "

"I'm not either!"

"All right, I believe you, but you've been involved. I hope that doesn't mean that we can't make out later. Look, I've never kissed this girl. We haven't even had our first date."

She looked sophisticated as she sized me up in spite of her zittiness. "Have you just got a crush on someone? That isn't like you, Bancroft . . . "

"No, it's more. I can't explain. It's . . . Look, the main thing is, let's get out of here. Before long they'll be loading you on a bus. If we leave now I can walk you back and we'll get there when the bus does."

"I'll get there."

"Sure. We'll say goodbye a few blocks away. I won't let anyone see us. Hell, we both know how the bus goes."

We left with two other couples and we all took off in different directions to do our mixing. What all of us wanted to mix at the Abbot Mixer was juice. Only the juice of our mouths, true, but I never lost hope . . .

There was no moon and where the streetlights were weak I found some shrubbery with inky gaps and steered her in. So much caution doesn't make sense in retrospect. The townies didn't know us, and necking was tame compared to what they could do in their cars. Our masters were looking the other way tonight, as they would during the Winter Ball and the Spring Prom. In fact, dark places were dangerous now. What if we bumped into another couple from the Mixer? What if we got something going and another couple bumped into us?

We Frenched a while and I remembered how good she was. I didn't like it when girls let their tongues expire and threw their mouths open for an autopsy. Better if they jousted with me, or like Eleanor, pushed inside my mouth with a firm, exploring organ.

Groans made our mouths buzz. On the sidewalk syncopated footsteps grew more pronounced and passed. Couples too engrossed to notice us. Or perhaps our mouths were muting each other, the sound was only loud within. Now the rest of the world was closing around—cool, waxy fingers, clawed. Our mouths never came apart. Imagination danced away with our thoughts. Our bed of leaves could have been mud . . .

God, a girdle—I'd forgot.

"Gordon, I don't want to."

"Come on, it's no big deal to put that thing back on."

"That's not the point. I can't."

"Your period?"

"No. More serious."

"A disease!"

"You idiot, no! I couldn't respect myself if we made love. I swore I'd be faithful to Carl."

"*Carl.* Did you put it in writing?"

"I swore to myself."

I could have ribbed her but I knew I'd have to stay with her sincere tone.

"Hey, call me Carl. It's what you need. I'll call you Jan. Think of him. I'll think of mine. It might work. You feel so good, you probably feel better than she would. Maybe we could be some help to each other. What are friends for?"

"I don't think so. I don't think I want to be a surrogate in sex."

It was time to face reality. This compost heap we were on was even more ridiculous than her reasoning.

"You'll still walk me back?" she asked as we scrambled out of the bushes.

"Of course! Not just because it's the polite thing to do, though. Maybe you'll weaken and let me kiss you again."

"Better if you don't. I'm sorry. I'm attracted to you, but love is something more than an attraction."

"I'll say. Love is saying to hell with everyone else and diving into the bushes."

"I won't say it isn't. Maybe love should be a bit like that, but what if there aren't any bushes? You know there wouldn't be if we were seeing each other. Or only a few times in the year. I'll wait for Thanksgiving recess to see Carl. Christmas, Easter. Summer at last. He's in college and he lives away from home." With that news I gave up on her completely. "What about this new girlfriend of yours? How soon can you see her?"

"Next Wednesday after my game."

"Wednesday! She comes up for your games?"

"All my home games, I hope. She lives right here in town."

"She's a *townie?* Bancroft, how could you? You're *disgusting!*"

"That's what everyone keeps telling me. Lucky for me I don't take myself that seriously."

"How could you make love to me behind your girlfriend's back?"

"I told you, she's not my girlfriend. At the moment she's nothing but a noble ideal. I thought for sure you and I could get something going as soon as she found out how disgusting I was. Anyway, what about you? How do you think Carl would like it if he found out where your tongue has been tonight?"

"You make it sound worse than it was. Anyway, it's not the same. I'm a mature woman and I'm forced to be alone for months at a time. If Carl found out I'd kissed some boys, I'm sure he'd understand."

"He might understand if he's up to the hilt in college coeds."

"Stop! It's bad enough that you're a degenerate, but you don't have to talk like one."

"All I heard from you last year was 'fuck' and 'shit.'"

"I'm not the same person."

"I get it. This Carl is a divinity student."

"No. He wants to be an electrical engineer. And he's not religious. I just think it's childish to use dirty words to shock people. Attention-getting . . . "

"Somebody had better get your attention, quick, and get through to you. What a waste of a beautiful body if you're going to be faithful to some guy you can't even see. Might as well be a nun."

"Gordon, what about this beautiful girl? Why the sudden interest in me?"

I took her arm and stopped us. At the bottom of the hill we were on and a half-block to the left on a main road was the entrance to her school. "I think I'll tell you even though we may never be friends again. I'm so crazy about this girl I can't sleep at night. It's more than simple horniness. Or maybe it isn't. I'm so guilty about the other women in my head that I can't even jack off properly."

She winced, but she was waiting for more. So was I, expecting more of a response before I could go on. "You're in love, then," she said. "But why were you kissing me so lovingly? Were you really thinking of her?"

"No. I don't know what was going on. Probably I wasn't going to see you again till the winter term, but tonight I wanted to make love to you. I know I'm nuts."

Another pause. "I admire your honesty. Maybe you'll feel better if I tell you I wanted you to. Make love to me. Thanks for not saying 'fuck.'"

A bus passed on the main road below. There'd be another one soon.

"I've got to run. I'm close enough. Go back, now. Sorry to disappoint you, Gordon. Maybe we'll see each other later in the term. Or not. Our paths don't cross. I can't act or sing.

At the Winter Ball! Even if your girl comes, I want some dances with you. I'd love to meet her . . . " She was off.

I started back to my dorm feeling like a loser leaving a playing field. Even if she'd tricked me, Ellie Adams had to be a much better person than I'd ever thought. Oh, no doubt she'd tricked me. She was kissing me with such fervor that I forgot to unhook her bra. Now maybe I'd never get to know what her tits were like, the rest of her . . . Where did she get so much character, though? Why hadn't I seen it before? She admitted being excited, but wild as she was she was able to stay loyal to her stupid Carl. It probably wasn't healthy to respect her so much, or any of the others. I'd give myself a complex and never be able to do anything dirty to them again.

Suddenly I saw Jan's face before me, speaking French. Her teasing smile, the glint in her eye. The day before I'd had trouble remembering exactly what she looked like, but here she was, entire. Not a vision, but a demon, coaxing. I felt a surge of confidence, a joyous warmth. The soft, rising French phrases. Her eyes. Her repeated smiles taking hold like tendrils. She wanted to possess me, she'd been trying to entice.

All the long way home I saw her before me. I ignored the bushes by the side of the road and had completely forgotten the girl that I'd been kissing a while ago. I was possessed, Jan was possessing me and sustaining my delight.

Two days later in Bellini's office I was babbling about them both. I'd already made up my mind not to see Ellie again, or think of her, but I couldn't escape the memory of what we'd done. How easy it had been to hold her and kiss her, how good it had felt, how thoughts of Jan had never intruded. Hard thought pointed to the fact that I had been afraid all along that Jan was too good for me, or that I wasn't good enough for her, while Ellie with her acne might think she was lucky to have my love. But there was more to it.

Last year as an upper I'd given up on god for all time, and I'd never had any use for the supernatural except in movies, but now I was convinced there was something demonic about Jan. People had visions of the Virgin Mary, but I'd never heard of a vision that followed you around and crossed the street with you on green. Jan was no angel, though. Where was she when I was kissing Ellie? My philandering had her approval. She just stepped in when I was alone to make sure that sex was all I thought about.

The doctor was smiling, but I wasn't making sense to him or he didn't care. If I'd been to bed with one of these girls he might have tuned in. There wasn't a psychiatrist alive who wouldn't want to hear details about them, especially if I described them first. Visions of Jan weren't interesting to him as long as I wasn't hearing voices. Oh, there was a sound-track. I remembered the sound of her words and the shape of her lips as they were formed. She was repeating her end of the conversation at Callahan's.

"I'd like to hear more about her, Gordon. She sounds interesting. I hope she'll be a healthy influence. However, since you're still letting your work slide, I think for now it might be better if you put this girl out of mind. I'd like to see if we can't uncover some of the thinking behind your self-defeating behavior. But first let me ask you: have you done anything to get on the right track over the past week?"

"Nah. Well. Maybe. Not much."

"Why don't you tell me more about your dad? As I recall, you were painting a somewhat idealized picture last week. Tell me what you don't like about him. You may find it exhilarating to get rid of your negative feelings. Don't hold back."

Ever since meeting Jan I hadn't thought much about my father and it was hard to get him in my sights. Then I thought of him in his bathrobe and I was rolling.

With sex on my mind so much it wasn't suprising that my first bitch had to do with the way my father had made me squirm when I was learning about it. Before the junior high stepped in with their movie about zygotes my father had already sat me down at the breakfast table in front of my mother to tell me in detail what it took to satisfy her, how she had to use her own hand to help, sometimes. Now I had Bellini on the edge of his seat. I'd shown him a picture of my mother, who had a figure that wouldn't quit. Bellini must have been a leg man.

"It made me want to puke, you know? Maybe he did it to make her feel like a freak. Deep down he's pissed off at her for taking my side." I went on to relate how as an 8-year-old my father had told me to say "fuck you" to my mother during one of their fights. There might have been some confusion in it for me because my mother had washed my mouth out with soap for saying it the year before.

"Some hush-hush kind of Nazi thing is going on, I'm pretty sure. I've heard the sound of slaps on rare occasions. Tom and I have always been too scared to set up some kind of diversion, but I remember wondering how they'd like it if the fire department showed up during one of their fights.

"I don't know how Tom felt, but dad was always more of an irritant to me than a pain. He pressed me to go out with the prettiest girls in my class, and whenever I had attractive dates he'd have to nuzzle them and kiss them on the cheek . . .

"It sounds as if I'm going out of my way to find fault with my old man, and that's because it's not easy to dig up dirt on him. Sure, if you're going to look at somebody's entire life in a few minutes it's easy for the bad things to stand out. But wait. In one area he hasn't got a saving grace. Baseball."

I related how my father's tragic flaw first came to light when he'd hit fly balls to my brother and me and some neighborhood kids and paid us when we caught them. I asked Dr. Bellini to reflect: assuming my dad knew something about insurance, wasn't his behavior suicidal when, with full knowledge that six-, seven- and eight-year-olds were ball-shy, he could see fit to bounce flies off the heads of the neighbor kids?

"I thought your father was a Shakespearian actor . . . "

"Between jobs he was always threatening to go into insurance. He took some test and came out first in the state."

"First in what, exactly?"

"First in ability to sell insurance. My father thought that was what they told everybody who took the test. You know, to fire them up. I tend to think my father really did come out first and was afraid to live up to his ability. There's no doubt he can read minds. If he'd had more time to practice hitting he could have been another Ted Williams. He always knows exactly what a pitcher is going to throw. Ted Williams is his idol, you know. He knew Williams in San Diego when Ted was using a homemade batting tee and shagging his own balls. If you get the idea that there's nothing stopping my brother and I from taking advantage of the god-given opportunity to grow up to be as good as Ted Williams, you've got my father in a nutshell.

"For pure craziness, though, get this. He didn't confide it at the time, but last year he told me he was glad that I had so many girlfriends. Why? I had long legs when I was twelve and when I was sitting on the bench with my friends in the Little League he thought the way I crossed them was effeminate. He was afraid I was going to turn out homosexual. Me!

"Once I almost got even with him. He was putting up the Christmas tree lights on the front lawn. We've got a huge spruce growing there and each year he gets the extension ladder and goes up into the tree to put the lights around. OK, I heard him telling my brother to be sure not to switch on the lights while he was up there. They worked on a switch right inside our front door that also put the porch light on. It was a switch easy to flip by mistake, but he'd have known I did it on purpose if he lived.

"I now realize that his chances of getting blasted weren't very great, but at the time I'd been convinced by my

father's fears. I stared at the switch the whole time he was
up on his ladder. I wonder what I would have done if it was
a much taller tree and he was sure to die. Anyway, winter-
time had arrived and I was having my revenge . . .

"He didn't stop pestering me then. I could be practicing
my French horn more. But he looked kind of lost in his
heavy clothing. Sometimes he'd take a bunch of us to a
bowling alley, but his heart wasn't in it. Needless to say, I
became an expert at things like bowling and ice hockey. At
the dinnertable my brother might say, 'Hey, dad, Gordon
scored three goals today at Tillie's Pond.' Dad would muster
a phony smile and say, 'Well, well,' but you could tell it
made him sick to think I could waste my time getting good
at hockey when he had to flog me to get me to pitch to him.

"I know I was giving him a hard time, but I thought I
was justified. Other fathers stood behind their kids, but I was
always wrong till proven right. If I came home with a black
eye I must have done something to deserve it. If I gave one
to a neighbor kid he'd 'tan my hide.' Ah, but when rock and
roll came along he was really up a tree.

"For a couple of years I played that music all the time.
Like a hypocrite I was practicing my French horn and playing in orchestras. Yet I was walking around with a head full
of doobie-doos and dang de dang-dangs and so on, driving
my father out of his mind.

"Picture one of his winters. No baseball to give him
something to do. Having a log on the fire, trying to read, and
from my room in the corner of the house comes this beep,
beep, beep, beep bum dahdle-ee-dah . . . Sounds that mean
nothing to him imported from the slums of New York."

"You took up this music to persecute him?"

"Nah. I don't know why I liked it. I'm ashamed of myself now."

"Under the circumstances I think you've got a balanced
opinion of the man. It's heartening that you recognize his
good qualities and his love for you, as you told me last time.
I'm sorry to see you in so much hot water. However, Dr. Ea-

ton writes that your studies are 'going ahead aimlessly,' your 'reasoning is tangential,' your 'interest is sporadic.'"

"What's that?" Bellini had been reading from a paper in my file.

"I'm afraid it's a copy of a letter which has been sent to your parents. I declined comment except to say that we were making progress. That's what I told the Dean, but my rather guarded good opinion was left out of the report."

"I guess there's no way you'd let me read it?" He'd already put the report back on the stack. "Nah, I don't think I want to, anyway."

"Your teachers and your choirmaster and your house-master are merely reporting what's going on."

"Yeah. I suppose the choirmaster had something to say about me lying on the floor."

"Lying on the floor? No, I don't think that's caught up with you. But he thinks you've been singing flat on purpose."

"No point in denying it. There's been some clowning."

"This is all the time I can give you today. Try to make it to your French class instead of wandering around the West Campus, OK?"

Oh-oh. Still, he wasn't trying to look all-wise. "Maybe next time you can help with my girlfriend?"

"I'd like to hear more about her. Please, you're going to be late to your class."

Bellini was sure anxious to get rid of me. I was ashamed of all that I'd said about my father, all the badmouthing, and it was good to be outside.

Minutes later I was bounding up the steps of Samuel Phillips Hall on my toes to give my calf muscles a workout when I had a premonition that drained my strength. I flopped onto the stone steps where the other men sat who were early to class. Everyone was doing some last minute memorizing with closed eyes or had an equation written on his forehead.

I was a mile away. I was back in the infirmary listening

to Dr. Bellini . . . reading from a paper that had been sent to my parents. Who would surely respond. What would they do differently? Wouldn't they just fire off a new round of warnings to tell me all over again what an ungrateful son I was?

There was something unusual about this report, and it was just dawning on me what. I'd been taken off probation. I wasn't on posting at the moment. There was no reason for a report from all these people. My fate was being decided in some new way that the school didn't think students should know about.

I felt like one of those guys in a spy movie who has just found out he's being used. I thought I knew all the rules, I thought I knew when I was safe, but the way I'd been seeing the school had set me up.

There weren't any special reports about students who made high honors and kept their noses clean. For that kind of guy the school was everything it represented itself to be. But for the problem boys there was a lot of consultation going on, and if a teacher took a different tack with me it might have been because of something he had heard about me at some war council, and not because of anything I'd said or done in class or in my dorm.

Andover might kick me out, and soon. Pressure was building behind the scenes. There was no such thing as a third probation. Until I came along there had been no such thing as a second. Perhaps that was the reason for all the whispering. If they could pin something on me that would be good enough to warrant a third probation they'd have an excuse to give me the boot.

Why was I so scared of being expelled? Andover was all that kept me close to Jan. If I had the time and the money I might find a room, a job. But even if one of the Andover guys would lend me money, what would her father think of someone who'd been kicked out of school? He must have known what a great school this was if he went to all those games.

I wasn't so worried about her father. I wasn't worried

about her past. I knew that what I felt about her had to be protected. If I were a failure my feelings would change. I'd never feel good enough for Jan. Sooner or later—even if she were a saint—she'd be ashamed of me. The social pressure on people our age would be too great. Jan would be made to see how much she'd be throwing away to stay involved with a guy like me.

I'd have to start studying. I'd have to change minds and enlist supporters. I'd burn so much midnight oil that Barton was going to think I had an icon.

It was a good resolve, but I was off to a lousy start. Trudging up to French class I realized I hadn't even looked at my assignment and had nothing to hand in.

What was worse: as soon as I saw the look on Mardelet's face I knew he was going to call on me.

SIX

In all the time I'd been a part of the sports program at Andover I'd never played a game of any kind before a grandstand. That said a lot about my athletic interests, if not my ability.

Actually, I wasn't a half-bad athlete, and I could have been a standout if I'd gotten bigger sooner. With two years more experience pushing people around even the coaches would have been afraid of me.

Instead, playing soccer and hockey as a puny lower, my heart wasn't in it and my mind was a blank. I went into a daze when the coach put me in and after I'd been smashed around long enough by the bigger guys he'd yank me out. Having done his duty he wouldn't look at me again for the rest of the game.

Too bad I didn't exist from the start.

As an upper I'd put on a lot of muscle, but I didn't have any skill. That was when I started playing fullback on an intramural soccer team. Fullback was the only place to put me because I wasn't quick enough to scramble ahead with the forwards, but I was tough enough to lay them out by the dozen when they were coming at me.

In the degraded soccer I played my upper year I was always being pitted against fellow Andover guys, so it was considered bad form to put somebody in the hospital. That didn't stop me. The chance to put one of our snotty Andover bastards in the hospital was for me an incentive to play the game. I never wanted to be taken out and seldom was. (On the bench I was the type who's always asking to get back in.)

At fullback I got the reputation of an assassin or a psychopath. Sure enough, this prompted a visit from the varsity soccer coach. He watched one game and tapped me to play fullback on next year's varsity team. It was a miracle to most people, but I'd expected some attention as soon as word got around.

My methods were simple. I needed no coaching. In soccer a tackle was defined by coach Smythe (my first coach) as any point in play when two players dispute possession of the ball. (He made it sound like a minuet.)

As far as I was concerned the best way for this to happen was for both guys to try to kick the ball in opposite directions at the same time. One of the players was likely to go down with a sore leg.

Since forwards and halfbacks were always smaller than fullbacks, they were the ones who went down. With my right foot in contact with the ball (without contact the move was illegal) I'd run right into my opponent, or over him, and if I stepped on his face in the process, so much the better.

Because a steel cup and shinguards were our only protection, I could kick the algebra out of our boy geniuses. It was great sport. By comparison the contact in football was impersonal. You might as well hit your head against a wall.

The varsity coach broke me of some of my bad habits and used me a lot in games but I knew I didn't have the talent to go very far in soccer (which didn't bother me because pro soccer was a European game). Still, I was intimidating and fairly helpful and I could kick the ball downfield pretty much where my teammates wanted me to put it. Before they put me on the varsity one of my worst faults was kicking the ball the length of the field every time there was a free kick. Our forwards were in a frenzy as they watched the ball sailing over their heads into enemy control. Whenever there was a free kick coach Smythe would start screaming, "Don't root the ball, Bancroft!" But unless I wasn't right on target I'd root the ball a tremendous root, and screw everybody.

The day Jan came to see me we were playing some tough high-school punks from a town about an hour away— which on second thought I'm not going to name. There was a lot of town spirit in ___, and school spirit, too.

Because there weren't any bleachers there were small mobs of people standing by the field and I had trouble making her out until she waved. Dad had to be the big guy standing beside her.

Mr. McBride was a guy my size with black hair and ruddy skin and he looked young to be her father. I didn't resent him right away as I thought I would—and that was strange, I didn't know him yet. The way he stood beside her seemed just right. Best of all I didn't feel I'd be judged from the sidelines the way I would have been had my own father been standing there with my mother or one of my girl-friends.

When my father shook his head or clucked his tongue the women went right along. I'd seen them in action when my brother was playing. (My father had been almost as tough with my brother as with me.) Around my father women thought they were becoming sports experts. It was pathetic.

There was a difference having a father on the sidelines now that I was playing soccer instead of baseball. I didn't have to worry so much about skill to wow my fans. I had to get good and angry was all. I knew I'd make a big hit with all the fathers who were watching as long as I ran over a few of the fancy Dans who were trying to score on us. I'd have been making a big hit with Dan's father if he was anything like mine.

As soon as the game started I forgot all about Jan. The only time I thought of her was when I found myself showing off, or when Rogers, the other fullback, thought I was. This kind of thing happened a lot when I was heated up. I'd get out of position and take a tackle away from him. Often this worked out for the best. Rogers would be right there to clear the ball downfield. Still, Rogers might have felt I was making him look bad, as if I thought he couldn't make the play himself. One of the reasons Rogers was so touchy was that I had improved all season and was getting more playing time than he. Coach Knapp was always taking him out for a rest.

God, I played my heart out that day. I must have been aware of Jan. Maybe I was forcing myself not to think of her, but the adrenalin was flowing. Was it ever. I felt like the Grand Canyon rapids were going through me. I don't know about the Grand Canyon, but I felt twice my normal size.

We kicked the shit out of ___. They didn't score a single goal on us. I was tempted to say on *me*, because I was the main reason they didn't. There were only a few scattered shots on our goal which were soft enough for Hopkins to handle without diving. Rogers stopped being pissed off and did his best to help. In fact he did most of the kicking downfield, but I did nearly all the banging. The way I saw it, no one would think I was a showboat if Rogers looked as if he knew what he was doing.

To show what coldblooded bastards we were, after winning a game the Andover players usually ran off the field to the gym without looking back or getting together for a victory dance the way some of the stupid high schools did. Today, however, ___ had been so badly smotched that we gathered around the bench for a minute to tell each other how great we were. The coach had never been so gung ho and his face lit up when he saw me. He gave me a big hug, something unheard of at my school. I was so dumbfounded I pushed him off me. For one thing I thought he was an idiot not to see that I'd been hogging all the work at fullback and probably giving Rogers a complex that he wouldn't be able to shake for the rest of the season. If Rogers didn't start the next game Coach Knapp would go down in my book as a bad coach. (Rogers did start, though.)

When I came to Jan and her dad I was so covered with

sweat that it was embarrassing. The wind was getting under
my shorts and my scrotum was squeezing like a fist. Whenever a game was over my jockstrap would feel gritty and
itch me and my wet skin would suddenly get cold as hell. I
felt like running off the field, if only for my health, but here
I'd have to walk with these two and be composed and warm
and even modest as it turned out.

"That was some game you played, son. Got a bang out
of watching your team on defense. Those other fellows
couldn't do a thing."

Jan was beaming, her face full of color. The skin was
tight around her eyes and her cheeks were firm because her
expression was getting away from her. I forgot my suspi-
cions, discounted Thomson. Still, I was glad he was at the
other end of the campus in a football game. Far as it was, we
could hear the roar of the crowd at times, screechy music,
bass drums. Of course I hadn't heard a thing or thought of
the football game while we'd been playing.

She introduced her father as Frank McBride (for Francis) and he gave me a handshake that was supposed to mean
he liked me, or at least that he had admired the way I'd
played. He had a pipe going and up close I could see the
gray in his hair, but he still looked young to be the father of
someone built like Jan. It was his red complexion and his
dark beard. You could tell his beard would have been all
black if he let it grow. He'd given himself a close shave and
his face was smooth and maybe even soft. I know that's
what made him look young. The only lines were from smiling. He looked like a movie-star, but I'd expected that after
seeing Jan.

He did a nice thing as we moved off the field. He'd
been walking between us, but he moved to his daughter's
other side so I could be next to her. I had a rotten thought at
that moment which showed what a suspicious person I was.
If he was so anxious for me to get something going with his
daughter, could it be because her reputation was ruined and
no one else was interested? I was ashamed of myself when I

84

began to take in the dignity of her appearance. At first I'd been scared to look her up and down in front of her old man so I'd been looking sideways like crazy, mostly at her face. Then walking along I began to relax, and while her dad was talking sports I gobbled up her fine points.

She was wearing a maroon turtleneck under a cream-colored cardigan—the kind only women had, with a collar and so thick that it was really a coat. She had on a plaid skirt and knee socks that matched the maroon and a gold brooch on her sweater. The sweater had a belt instead of buttons, and she had it closed at the bottom. Now and then she'd pull it closer and retie the belt, but as soon as she took her hand away her tits were pushing through again. She had the kind of body that must have been a nuisance to dress in the kinds of clothes nice girls her age were supposed to wear. She dressed well, though. Class all the way. It was impossible even to think of the word "whore" when you were looking at her unless you were someone like Thomson or someone who hated women.

There was a town road between the West Campus and the East Campus and I had to cross it to get to the gym. Since the McBrides were parked up by the road I thought it would be better if they waited for me by their car, so I had them point it out. A snazzy Buick. They seemed taken aback that I wanted to go buzzing off so soon, but I told them that there were nothing but sweaty bodies over by the gym at this hour, and that I could run to the gym, shower, change and run back a lot faster if they weren't along. I realized I was being rude, but I was freezing my balls off and our stroll had become an endurance test.

I ran off and didn't look back until they were about to lose sight of me. Jan and her dad were loitering beside their car. He was talking. She was looking up. Her face looked red, but I remembered how up close the cold had powdered it pink and blue. What a dope I had been not to have taken her hand. I was sure she'd have let me in spite of the dirt on mine. I'd been too dazzled to make a move.

She would be inside the Buick getting warm now. But maybe it was all in my mind that it was cold. I was dripping wet from head to toe. It was probably mild as hell for October.

I ran hard for the tunnel under the gym and I didn't slow up much when I made it. My cleats were screeching. Down into the stink. The smell of one thing only—sweat in cloth, some of it a month old. You didn't smell the mildew until you got next to an open locker.

In front of mine I unwrapped my legs and threw the tape and my soggy shinguards onto the fermenting heap at the bottom. Jockstrap, shorts, shirt—they made it onto the heap as well. Laundry day was long overdue. Maybe it would never come.

I ran down the aisle to the showers, not bothering to stop and talk, though I heard guys calling my name. I used the school soap again without losing any hair. Just my luck that today they had one of the trainers dusting us for jock rash. A long line. I butted in babbling about an emergency and Andy gave me a squirt of dust to the left and right of my balls before the guys in the line could raise a shout.

In dry clothes I began to feel sure of myself. I'd shaved and my short hair was nearly dry. The McBrides had invited me to their house and the way I was looking and feeling now I'd be right at home on a carpet. The first carpet since I left home—that told you something about the way we lived. To cover the mildew I stole some Old Spice from the guy next to me, who was in the shower. I was all ready now, but I thought better of running back for fear of working up another sweat. It wasn't cold out at all. It was hard to be subjective, though. I was on fire with thoughts of Jan, wondering if I could sit next to her in the car. I figured they'd have to let me in spite of my size. Wouldn't it annoy them more to have a big stranger breathing down their necks?

Jan moved over and made room for me as if there had never been any doubt where I belonged.

So she could sit back and get comfortable she put a hand on my thigh to push off. It was only there for a moment, but her fingers stood out like jewels on velvet. Her nails were a strong pink, unpainted, and her knuckles were reddish, probably from cold. Veins showed through on the back of her hand and there were a few faint freckles. The shape of her hand was beautiful. Long, tapering fingers and oval nails. No rings, but there was nothing like a nun about her hands. They would have been perfect to hold a delicate glass of red wine, or to run through her hair. They were much too beautiful for scrubbing.

We were moving. I sat back myself and my knees rode higher. Mr. McBride carried the conversation since I was holding my breath the whole time, or just about. I was dizzy, and that must have been the reason. My heart was pounding, but that wasn't as bothersome as my light head, because my heart was telling me that in spite of how strange I felt, I was still alive.

"This is where they'll be building the new junior high."

That sounded like a lot of fun. "Hey, that's right. Jan told me you're an architect." Deep breath.

"Oh, I've got nothing to do with this. No doubt when they're done I'll be glad I'm able to say that. These days I'm doing restoration. My projects are small, but never boring."

"They are sometimes. That's why he likes to travel. He means that his work doesn't tie him up the way it used to."

"I've never been off campus except to go to town. Never knew what these neighborhoods were like. All the schools and children come as a surprise." Why don't I let a fart and get it over with, I was thinking. They were too puzzled to think of a way to change the subject. "I mean . . . there are people who *want* to live here? Who don't have to?"

"Gee, dad, I think he's insulting us." She must have known I didn't mean it that way. If she'd have looked me in the eye she'd had seen my irritation. Instead she did an amazing thing. Taking my hand she squeezed it hard a few times, and then she began to slide her thumb against my own, slow, slow. My cock stirred ominously.

"Hey, this street reminds me of my home town." I had to say something to take my attention from Jan and keep from getting a hard-on right under her father's nose. But the street did remind me of Brookside Road, winding and rising with the trees joined overhead at times and the cleared land mostly on one side with the big houses.

"Where do you come from, Gordon? Jan didn't tell me."

"Dudbury. Little town in Connecticut." It was happening. I could already see the bulge.

"Oh, sure. I know some people there . . . " Well, this might be one way to get it to go down, depending on who the people were, and how well they knew me. Dudbury thought as highly of me as of someone who had poisoned the water supply and was about to get out of prison for good behavior.

The suspense was killing me.

"Go ahead, tell me who you know. The people in Dudbury aren't all jerks."

"I went to school with a guy called Wilson Church."

"The architect, sure. You must have studied together. He's got a kid my brother's age. I don't know him too well, but I've seen him at the country club. The kid, I mean. I don't know Wilson Church at all, but I might have caddied for him a couple of times."

She stopped rubbing my finger, but it was much too late. I was hard as stone. Naturally, I had my right arm crossed over my lap to cover up, but it was going to be hell getting out of the car. Even the thought of so much embarrassment didn't send it down.

"You caddied at the country club where you belonged?" Jan asked. I was sorry it had to be her.

"That's right. My father still hates me for it. There were four country clubs in our town, so he didn't understand why I couldn't ply my trade at one of the others. But the kids at the other clubs were tough, and at my own, where at least a few people knew who I was, I got to go out. It was dog eat dog for caddies when I was growing up."

Her father laughed. Jan was squeezing and rubbing again. I couldn't take much more before I shot my wad. I thought of concentration camps, of scrawny old women pissing into buckets, of all the things that used to work when I was called to the board in algebra class (back in Dudbury. Anyone who got a hard-on during a math class at Andover was going to be having some strange sex later in life.).

"I'll bet you went to dances at your club when you were older, though."

Maybe she wasn't too bright. There was a cliche about women as beautiful as Jan.

"Sure, I went to all the proms and cotillions at the different clubs. Only in the summer, of course. To tell you the truth, I'm out of touch with the people in my town. Like it or not, school is my world. I have to get a summer job to work with older guys who are out of school. My old friends in Dudbury . . . Well, when I write home there's no one I ask my folks to say hello to before 'Love, Gordon.' It's just jealousy."

"Does your mother call you 'Gordon?'"

She saw my astounded look. How could she be two years older than I was and talk like such a dimwit? At the thought that she might be a touch retarded the blood in my dick finally started to get back into circulation. As if she could sense my waning interest I felt a finger stroking the center of my palm. With her father sitting there, that was a whorish thing to do. I was hard again in a flash. If she were a whore her intelligence didn't make any difference. I'd still take her out—socially—as long as I could tell her what to say.

We made it to their driveway before there was a dark spot on my pants, and even though the driveway was half a mile long, I was so relieved to see the house that my hard-on faded. When I took my arm away my pants weren't even taut.

Hard-ons throve on danger, that was one thing I'd learned about them. When I wasn't supposed to get one I was sure to. Once last summer, when I'd been lying naked with a girl, there was a period of half an hour when I couldn't buy a hard-on. Only when she told me how glad she was that I wasn't forcing her to screw, how scared she was to have a baby, did the thing go up again.

Perverse is putting it mildly to describe a thing like mine. I wasn't alone, though—I had that satisfaction. The three whorish girls I'd been with last summer had told me plenty about the other guys. It was some comfort that I had to push so hard to get them to talk because the one thing I could kill a girl for would be telling my friends what I was like during the act.

Her driveway was asphalt and there was a big field between the town road and her home. Some small evergreens were sticking up here and there, but nothing else was growing in her field but grass, and it wasn't mowed often. I figured Mr. McBride had let the grass in the field get long because it would soon be under snow. There was a small lawn and a flagstone walk to the front door. There had been a flower garden between the lawn and the field. Only the roses were holding up.

The house was basically a saltbox. A back wing gave it a rambling look. Dark red, white trim, white shutters. There was nothing plain about the place, but I'd been expecting sliding glass doors or a skylight and maybe a fountain. An abstract jumble wouldn't have surprised me. A rolled dice feeling.

There was a double garage with a Healy 3000 inside.

"Hey, Jan, don't tell me this is yours!" I checked her dad's face, afraid I'd blundered again.

"Sure is," he said. "She's had it quite a while and it still looks new. You're good to your baby, eh, sugar?"

Jan got out before her father put the Buick away. This

was the first second I'd been alone with her, but it was the wrong time to bring up her age. Thomson had been right, though—she had to be twenty to own a car like that for "quite a while." If she'd bought it new I could figure out her age if I knew what year her car was, but Austin-Healys didn't change style every year like American cars. She'd probably worked to pay it off. Unless they were a lot richer than she'd told me. No matter what story was true, I was up against a lie of hers.

I took a chance on her old man to see what I could find out.

"You're sure great for a dad, I'd say, to let your daughter have a car like that."

"Oh, Jannie needs it," he said over his shoulder, taking us to the front door. (I think we could have gone in through the garage but it was tight with two cars in there and all the junk.) "Maybe she didn't tell you, but she's the lady of the house. She does all the shopping."

"Yeah, she told me about your wife's passing. Sorry." I tried to sound sincere, but I was still probing.

"Well, that's not quite true." Aha! He left it there while we went inside.

"Dad knows about the dumb things I told you," Jan began when we were in the door.

Her dad switched on the living-room lights. "We'll be comfortable in here. Let's wait to talk till we can sit down, shall we? Gordon, I'll get you a cocktail or something but I don't want you to be in trouble when you go back."

"My housemaster can't smell booze in the evening. Drinks himself."

He asked me what it would be and I told him, sherry. Ever since I'd found out that students at Oxford were served sherry by their tutors it was my standing order at the home of a parent.

Jan had her "usual" (!): a glass of red vermouth with a lemon-rind. I knew this was a taste acquired in Europe. My parents and their friends never drank the sweet one straight, only in Manhattans. Our bottle was in back beside the dusty bottles I stole from.

"Jan's mother and I are divorced," her dad began when he had settled into what was obviously his favorite chair. "She's mentally ill and spends most of her time in a home. She visited us quite often when we were living in Minnesota. I still see her there when I go back at Christmas time. I've got some wonderful friends in Minneapolis as well. Can you see why Jan told you what she did?"

"It's just so much easier," Jan put in. "I think of her as being dead. As far as her ever being my mother again, she might as well be."

Instead of being touched by her plight or her mother's my first thought was to wonder if the reason that Jan had sounded lamebrained back in the car had something to do with her mother's genes. In spite of my visits to Dr. Bellini I wasn't all that tolerant of people with mental problems. In fact, I'd sooner have had a leper in my room.

"Well, then, I guess the way this place looks is all your doing." A dumb remark like that was needed to ease the tension.

"It's a mess at the moment." She jumped up and busied herself putting papers away. "I've no excuse. I knew you were coming. Or I thought you were because I planned to ask you. I'm glad we've cleared the air about my mother."

"I wasn't being sarcastic, you know. It's like a palace here compared to the rooms we've got at school. Wait, not a palace, either—so homey. It's a miracle that you could make a place so homey without a mother, Jan."

I was being sincere about the house. It was one of those places with a lot of shelves where dishes were turned on their sides. There were knick-knacks on all the tables that had a story behind them. Jan and her father could tell it quick: "We got that in Morocco . . . " At least it wasn't a dead place like a doctor's waiting room with nothing but furniture and ashtrays and magazines.

Jan told me she'd show me the rest of the house some

other time, that she was behind in her cleaning. She and her father went on in this vein for a while, telling me about their daily lives, all the friends that came, the bridge games—Jan was good, and I didn't even know how to play, so she was no lamebrain. No matter how much we all tried to be interesting the ghost of Jan's mother wouldn't go away. Or else it was the lie that Jan had told which was still hanging over our heads. Even after the lie had been exposed, she'd as much as wished her mother dead.

Finally her dad got up and came to me with his hand out.

"Gordon, I'm glad to have met you. I enjoyed watching you play today, and having you here, and I hope we'll see more of you. I'm going to leave you two alone, now—I've got work to do. Honey, I might go over to Ruth's later, but I'll be back before midnight. Gordon, help yourself to anything you want to drink . . . " I could tell he didn't like the sound of what he was saying. Andover men were all minors.

"I'll be discreet, Mr. McBride. I know what I can get away with. My parents let me drink at home, and I think it's civilized, but I try not to bend the school's rules more than I have to."

Telling big lies was easy for me. It felt so good to believe in them, if only for a moment. Sure I was a hypocrite to expect honesty from Jan, but there were mitigating factors. I only lied out of necessity, and I couldn't see any reason for Jan's lies—yet.

"Good. Look, honey, if Gordon doesn't have to be back by ten, why don't you kids go out for a while? Plenty of time for a movie. Or stay here by yourselves . . . As you like . . . "

He left the room with a hand waving behind which signified "I don't know what you want" and "I don't want to be in the way" at the same time.

SEVEN

Jan got me another sherry and sat beside me.

"I wanted to ask you about something else you told me, Jan, but I was afraid it might be another lie, and maybe one you didn't tell your father about."

She waited, holding her drink steady, watching me squarely.

"You're older than I thought, aren't you?"

The sexy smile again. I was learning that she used it whenever I found her out.

"Yes. I lied. Thanks for not bringing it up. Don't think it would have come as a surprise if you had, though. I knew what I was letting myself in for when I mentioned Alan Benson in the letter. I had a feeling you'd try to find out about me. That would be natural. Alan was a big man on campus, right? Anyway, if you didn't know already you'd have guessed when I brought you here. I don't live like a high-school girl. I'll be twenty-one in January."

"Oh. I'll be eighteen in February. But you're only two grades ahead of me?"

"I don't know. I only had a year of college. How do you want to figure it?"

Maybe I'd caught her out again with this one . . . . Unless her being a senior in Benson's time was just a rumor that Thomson had picked up . . . Or an attempt on his part to seem knowledgeable about her. Whatever the case, she was a lot more mysterious than I could ever have imagined a townie being.

"Why did you try to fool me?"

"I wanted you to think of me as the type of person you'd normally go out with."

"Then why did you snow me with all the stories of Europe?"

"Is it important, Gordon? If it's so important maybe we shouldn't try to see each other."

Her words hurt, but I knew the tactic, I'd known girls who were quick to put our relationship on the line. She was bluffing and I told her so. "You like me a lot, and I feel the same about you. Let's not be stupid about it."

She bit her lip without losing her smile. "All right. I liked you right away and I must have thought you'd lose respect for me if you found out I'd dropped out of college."

"What's college? Everyone thinks Andover guys are geniuses, that's the trouble. Maybe there are some, but I'm not one of them. For one thing I barely passed math. I was an honors student in everything else at one time, but I don't want to live my life between the covers of a book. I can tell from the way you talk you're smart as hell."

"Come on. What did I say that was so smart?"

"About Benson. How you had figured my reactions."

"There was nothing smart about that. That was my woman's intuition. Or call it cunning."

"So you didn't make good enough grades to stay in college?"

"I was a B student at Bradford."

Bradford was right up the line from us. It had a good reputation, but Andover guys thought any college but the Harvard kind was shitty.

"I might have done better," she was saying, "if we hadn't been so new in town. It was hard to forget my old friends and make new ones. I helled around a lot, too. I suppose that's the real reason I wasn't an A student. Oh, I could have coasted through, but I was bored, the school was too

95

small, the men around here were all too dumb. I put in a few months my second year, then I quit and went to work and saved all my money so I could travel. Dad helped, too. I'd had some French in school so France was my goal."

"What do you mean when you say you 'helled around a lot?'" The horrible truth was that this girl might have been someone like *me*. "You mean there were other guys besides Benson?"

"I guess you're assuming I went to bed with Alan. You must have heard that about me. Golly, the boys up there have long memories, don't they?" She was toying with me and she knew it. "Gordon, I'm going to tell you this point blank so you won't have to do any more research into my past. I lived with a man in France."

My first thought was: "So it's true. She's a whore." But looking at her as she sat there smiling, drinking, trying to guess what I was thinking, I was able to see the stupidity of the word "whore," at least the way it was used by the guys at school. She was older than the girls who had interested me till now. What should I think, that she'd "been around" or that she'd "traveled?" Did she have to be a whore just because she was getting laid in France? Why couldn't she have been like a lot of girls in love who wanted to live with a guy first to see if they thought a marriage to him would work out? That's what I would do if I ever wanted to get married. Why was I such a hypocrite? I was the one who was supposed to hate Andover for turning out a bunch of vicious bastards, but maybe I wasn't turning out any better. Here I was with a heart of stone judging a girl whose mother was in the nuthouse, a saintly girl who was trying to keep her father from going crazy by taking care of him like a wife . . . The most beautiful girl I'd ever seen . . . And you normally didn't expect hard work from such girls . . .

"Well, Gordon, do you think you'll survive the blow?"

"What blow? I was just thinking what a great person you are to take care of your father the way you do."

"My father? I don't do anything . . . Oh, he makes a big

deal out of the little things I do around the house. We've always gotten along well. We're good buddies."

"You've been through a lot together, I can tell. Say, what about a ride in that car of yours, Jan? We don't have to go to a movie. That's a little dangerous for me because I'm not supposed to be off campus after eight."

"We don't have to leave to be alone, you know. My father will make noise coming down the stairs. Intentionally." At last I was seeing a smile that didn't tease. I knew she wanted me to kiss her now. She had the guts to make the first move, but she wanted to see how I'd handle myself. She was in for a surprise.

I'd learned a lot about how to snow a girl over the summer, and I had absolute confidence in myself, even with a girl as beautiful as Jan, who was older and more experienced than I was.

The most important thing I'd learned was to be completely serious even if a girl was laughing in my face. Even if something ridiculous happened—a belch, say (not so ridiculous considering how much beer I drank on summer evenings)—I never let it break me up. I might smile, but I wanted the girl to see a distant look in my eye. I didn't want a glimmer of doubt to exist that what I was doing had to be done, was the only possible response to her beauty.

While my expression was as steady as could be I tried for a light touch with my hands. Playing with a few strands of hair next to her ear, or the ear itself. Touching her cheek gently. By the time our lips were together she must have thought she was the most beautiful creature on earth. At least I had her believing I thought she was.

I might kiss her hard, now, but I wouldn't try to trap her with my arms. For a while I would let her feel my fingers stroking, teasing. If she pulled away at any point she never got the chance to see me slobbering and panting. All she saw was my distant look, my patient smile.

Time to catch her breath and take a look around to be sure she was where she thought she was, with the person she thought I was . . . all alone at the beach, or at the side of some deserted road in the front seat of my parents' car with a breeze at the window and a sad chirping in the night. Then she had to go on with the game to find out how much I really wanted her, or maybe just to see what would happen.

What usually happened was that she wanted me to be serious with my hands as well as my eyes. When she was convinced that I was serious as hell—relentless—there was still a good chance that she'd pull away again. But by that time she'd be contending with the fact that she was beginning to be serious herself. She had to admit that she didn't want me to stop, even though she knew it was wrong for me to go on. But we had to go on because nothing had happened. So on we went, until the only thing she was sure about was how she felt and she didn't know what was happening or even care. But I cared to the end. I wanted to do everything right, and seriously, down to the last detail of the mopping up.

It seems almost cruel the way I describe it, but it wasn't when you consider what a guy had to go through to convince his girl that the thing they both wanted was possible. I'd much rather have jumped on her the moment we got in the car and torn her clothes off, but that was the summer before last, and I'd learned my lesson.

I edged closer to Jan so I could get my arms all the way around her and there was that sexy smile again. I didn't bat an eye. Slowly I brought my hand up. Instead of putting it behind her head or even on her shoulder, I stroked her cheek. This move was meant to cause an orgy of confused thoughts. Did I feel sorry for her? Was I hypnotized? Why did I think I had so much time? Was I just toying with her?

The sexy smile vanished. Her face showed something more like panic. Her eyes were wide. Maybe this was the first time in her life that a guy didn't press her against him and get the feeling of her breasts against his chest—that much at least—before she pushed him away and the dream was over.

I turned my attention to her ear and watched my fingers take up the lobe as if it weighed something. Then I had an inspiration. I took my hand down and sighed, then turned away to look for my drink.

"Gordon, what's wrong? Why were you looking at me that way?"

I took a sip and put the glass down before I turned back.

"Wrong? There's nothing wrong I know about. There's certainly nothing wrong with you." Dead serious. "Is there?"

"How can you just let me sit here? I want you to hold me."

"I want to hold you, too. First I thought I'd like to look at you. Your dad was around so much today that I didn't get a chance to drink you in." Not inspired, but I was under control.

"I want you closer, that's all." She let herself back against the sofa and raised an arm to invite me. There was no way I could diddle around any more after a move like that.

As soon as I put an arm around her she had both of hers around me. I think my last calm thought had to do with how sweet her breath was, how sweet her lips were from that slop she was drinking. Then all hell broke loose. She was chewing my neck and moaning and touching me everywhere and when I was slow to start feeling her up she took my left hand and pressed it hard against her breast.

I had sense enough to squeeze a little, but I was confused. What did she want me to do, fuck her right here in the living room with her father upstairs doing his homework? Hadn't her father said he was going to see somebody in a while and wouldn't he have to pass right by us on his way out? What was going on?

I must have stammered an objection and got through to her because all of a sudden we were looking at each other, panting and slobbering, and she was speaking to herself in French, saying the equivalent of "bullshit," I suppose, but I didn't know the words. Then she took my hand and said, "I know it's not your fault."

I'd stopped seeing stars by now. "No, it's not my fault that I've got half a brain. My god, he's probably already heard you. You're incredible, Jan. I never made out with a girl like you before."

"I'd almost forgot that's what they call it. 'Making out.'"

"We don't have to stop. Couldn't we do a little necking without tearing each other to pieces?"

"There's more privacy in my car, if that's what you want."

"We'll go for a ride, then."

While I was drinking up I thought of the kind of car she had and what it would be like to get a gearshift up my ass or maybe an emergency brake.

"Didn't your father say he was going out? Why don't we wait for him to leave and we'll have the house to ourselves?"

She considered a moment and shook her head. "I don't want to make love to you tonight."

"Who said anything about making love? You must think I have a hell of an ego. It's only our first date. I thought we'd be more comfortable here than in the car, that's all."

"Gordon, you're making it difficult for me . . . " I think I was. "If you stayed here with me and we went up to bed together, I'd want to make love. The reason I don't want it to happen is that I'm afraid of what you'll think of me. You brought it up: 'our first date . . . ' The code they go by at your school or in your home town might make it hard for you to respect a girl who would go to bed with you on the first date."

"I'll tell you the truth. I'd have respected them a lot more if they had."

"So you've been 'all the way,' as they say?"

"I'm no virgin! What made you think that of me?"

"I don't think it. How am I to know? But let me ask you this: what do you think of the girls you slept with *now?* Or maybe I should ask you first, did you ever sleep with a steady girlfriend, someone you cared about, again and again?"

"No, to be honest. The most was twice with the same girl. Two different nights."

"Before you dropped her."

Her quiet tone increased my shame. I didn't think she'd written me off as the world's biggest rat, but I would have to be careful about what I said next.

"I didn't drop anyone, Jan. Let's face it, I wasn't interested in those girls except to get in their pants."

"I'm sure they didn't see it that way, did they?"

"Well, they weren't prostitutes. No. I guess not."

She had me in a corner. I was a rat, all right. Still, the kindness in her voice led me to think that I might have her love if I was honest and stopped looking for a way out.

"The fact is, I seduced them. I was getting pretty good at it before it was time to go back to school."

There. I was at her mercy.

She got up slowly and went to get more of her crud. I heard the ice in the alcove.

"Want some more sherry?"

"OK." I wanted to get dead drunk was what. Most of all I wanted her to like me enough to let me take her in my arms again, but I was beginning to think I'd lost her. The tremendous energy she'd shown earlier was starting to have meaning. It was dawning on me that the girls I'd fooled around with all summer were just that—girls—in spite of all the fancy equipment.

Coming back with the drinks she was faintly unsteady in a way that made her look tired, not drunk.

I told her my thoughts. I compared her to the girls I'd been with before.

"It's plain I don't know anything about women," I concluded. "I thought I had the whole thing figured out. It's this crazy life I lead. You can imagine how much the guys talk about sex in the dorms. All we ever talk about is *seducing* women. No one ever talks about love—except my room-mate, Barton, maybe. And to show you how much he knows, when I told him about French-kissing a girl he said, 'I suppose you'd use her toothbrush.'"

She laughed and her face stayed alive.

"All of us talk all the time. Talk, talk, but really none of us has been around women as much as some dipshit in the 10th grade of high school. Probably we're scared of women, that's what. That's why we depend so much on technique. It's supposed to be like learning to drive. As soon as you've had your fun with a model and it's as good as everyone said it was, you're taking another one for a test-drive."

"I guess the image is good, but what you're saying makes me kind of sick."

"Well, it makes me sick, too. Especially after what just happened with us. You've got a power I don't know how to deal with. While I was kissing you I went to pieces and forgot everything I ever learned."

She put down her drink, came close and put a hand on my thigh. Inches . . .

"That's the way it's supposed to be. Just go to pieces."

"But what am I supposed to do with my mind? I'm not used to being unable to think. It's like being so drunk you can't remember where you did your drinking."

"Say love words. That'll keep your mind busy."

"Now? I can't. I'll have to kiss you first."

"Kiss me, Gordon."

This time she was holding back—for my sake, maybe. She let me take the lead and I fell back on the things I'd learned. I didn't know what else to do. This time she really was like a whore because her heart wasn't in it. I could do whatever I wanted and she merely made it easy for me: reaching up behind to unfasten her bra, opening her legs so that I could slip my hand all the way to the top and still have room to wiggle my finger.

There was an unbelievable amount of juice in her. Her flesh was so soft that her panties were like a warm, wet sponge. No doubt she'd manufactured all the juice when we'd been at it before. It might as well have been Vaseline, the way she was acting now.

When I took my hand away for a moment to wipe it on my pants she said, "Don't you like me?" Her voice was cool, but she wasn't teasing.

"Are you kidding? You're beautiful." I wanted to tell her how I really felt, but we heard her father coming downstairs, whistling. We stayed huddled together, a couple of culprits, too sleepy to care if we got caught.

"All right, honey, I'm going out. You two look comfortable. Watch the time, though, will you, Jan? The booze can play tricks. We'll feel terrible if Gordon gets in trouble."

I was about to holler out some reassuring word when the door closed with a click and a thud.

She squeezed my arm. "He's right, you know. We might get sleepy and let the time go by too fast."

"I wanted to tell you . . . before he came . . . I liked you better the way you were before. Wild. Maybe you think you were too wild for me. No way!"

She gently kissed around my eyes. I took the opportunity to get my palm under her heavy breasts. I marveled at how springy they were.

She was encouraging me. *"Vas-y. Suces-moi. Tu m'excites . . . "*

I eased her back and opened her blouse. Lifted her bra off and settled it above her breasts. They were swollen, the nipples reaching out. I grazed her nipples with strokes of my hand until they roughened. I didn't suck them. That was too obvious. Rather I licked them lightly as if I had a razor right at the tip of my tongue. I could feel her tension mount and bit her gently when it was high, starting from scratch with her other breast.

Suddenly she was kissing my forehead, my eyes, and I

thought, "Here we go again . . . " But no, she pulled away. Now she was smiling and expertly opening my shirt.

To bring her lips to me I got as much as I could of her breasts in my hands and gave a slight tug.

Down she came. I found I could tug at her breasts in the most delicate way and move her entire body from side to side or up or down.

Wherever her head was she took up my skin in a kiss while her tongue slid quickly back and forth within her lips.

"J'aime ta peau," she was saying when she moved away. *"J'aime l'odeur de ta sueur."*

When I thought about it later the naturalness of Jan's French was more surprising than the fact that she liked my skin and the sweaty smell of it. There was nothing theatrical about her words, they were passionate. I was responding to the passion in her voice and her meaning reassured me.

My cock was up again, and not just to see which way the wind was blowing. Earlier there had been too many messages in the air—nothing about Jan's behavior that I could count on—and my cock had been flying up and fading away like a performing porpoise. One minute I'd be sure of her excitement, the next I'd be afraid that I was boring her.

None of my old doubts could change the way I felt now. All I wanted was to wield.

Even though she wasn't pressed against me she must have sensed my condition. Somehow she got my meat out without any blood. I felt her nose scudding down to my stomach. All I could see was her thick, dark hair.

I'd heard about blowjobs. That was all the guys talked about. I'd only had one, and it was a bigger fiasco than my first attempt to screw. The skin of my prick had got caught in her braces . . .

Terror is mainly what I remember about the experience, and not because I was afraid of a torn-up sex organ. I had this near-blowjob before I knew Channing or any of the other guys who could talk about sex, so I only had my omniscient father's word to go on.

He'd told me about blowjobs, of course, using words like "intromission," but as usual he hadn't told me what it was like, so I'd been expecting this girl to blow on me. I wouldn't have been surprised to see her cheeks bulge out like Dizzy Gillespie's. Look what nature did to toads.

When this poor girl started sucking me it felt like she was trying to get me to come in her mouth, and this was seriously perverted for a girl who was a grade behind me in school. Getting snagged on her braces was probably the best thing for both of us. Well, for her it was a reprieve straight from God. No way could I have kept it quiet if she really knew how to give blowjobs, but now that I'd been caught in her braces I'd never breathe a word.

Anyway, Jan got sidetracked by my navel and was doing something with her tongue that made the roof of my mouth tingle. When I felt her hand come around my cock, which must have been so big by now I wouldn't have recognized it, I started to relax.

All the girls gave handjobs. That wasn't such a big deal, even on a first date, if the girl was already someone you wanted to spend the rest of your life with. True, you tended never to see some of those girls again, but when you were starting to find out about their bodies it was amazing how promising some of them were. Which was why Barton's attitude about sex might ruin his life. He'd be prone to think that the way he felt about a girl before sex was the feeling he could trust. It didn't take much experience to know that the only test of true love was how you felt about her after.

All of a sudden she had me scared all over again. She seemed to be kissing her way down. If she wasn't careful she was going to get a big payload of goo right in her face.

"Gordon, why are you stopping me? Let go! I want to!"

I started massaging her temples as if that was the reason I'd put my hands in her hair, but she shook me off.

"What are you afraid of?"

"Well . . . If you knew how close I am . . . "

"Is there something wrong with that? I take pride in being able to excite you."

"Maybe I've never been with anyone who had so much experience." I was starting to lose my erection, which was just fine. "I'm sorry I'm so . . . "

I didn't get to finish this. She still had her hand there and had felt the chance in me. Now she was bringing me back like an experienced nurse tapping up a vein. Then I felt her mouth trying to cover all of me, and slowly, the lewdest thing any woman had every done. Then her mouth was gone. I knew it, something had gagged her! Forget the little mess I was capable of making, I'd be lucky if she didn't spill her stomach contents all over me.

"I just wanted to give you a preview," she said then, smiling up at me from under her spilled hair. "Maybe next time it'll seem right to you."

"A girl already did that, Jan. I'm not as naive as you think."

"Then why can't I?"

"Because it's only our first date, unless you count the soda at Callahan's."

She may have been hurt, but she was still smiling when she got her head back into the conversation.

"You're afraid you'll lose respect for me?"

"No. I'm afraid something stupid will happen and screw up our chances. When a girl gives you everything right away it kind of screws up the logic behind dating. Don't think I don't want to do it with you . . . everything. But maybe I would like to know you better, so it's really you I want and not just relief or something."

"Maybe you're right," she said, walking a hand over my chest and ending the congestion there. I had about six organs that could be clenched like a fist, which might have been an anomaly. Every time it happened I'd tell myself to ask the guys in our next bullsession, but after countless bullsessions I hadn't remembered once.

"Going so fast might have been something you learned in France."

"Thanks for suggesting that. I have an excuse. There just isn't anything wrong or bad about sex the way the French see it. If you adapt to the life there it's hard to go back. Still, I know everything will be all right with us. We'll give each other time."

I never loved anyone so much in my life, and wanted to start over and do everything. She may have been onto me. We'd kiss for a while and then she'd stop and give me sly looks that were sexier than anything she'd done with her hands. Finally she had me begging for something to happen. Not in words, but she must have known. Still, she made me place her hand. She knew what I wanted and I was gone in a flash.

She brought me about ten kitchen napkins, but she didn't stand around and watch me mopping up, which showed how sensitive she was to my feelings, or maybe she was afraid I'd say something stupid about the mess and make her ashamed of being such a skillful lover.

When Jan reappeared she had her thick sweater around her and a woolen scarf. Could this be right? I hadn't done anything to satisfy *her*. Even Barton might think that was naive.

"Were you trying to tell me something? You were laughing."

"Oh, Barton. My roommate. He's so sensitive. I was wondering what he'd think."

"When you tell him about me?"

"Tell him? I wasn't going to tell him anything. He puts women on a pedestal. He thinks it's immoral to do anything with one unless you're married. No, I just couldn't help wondering what he'd think if he knew how messy sex can be even when it's the most beautiful experience you can have in life."

"Go wash up and I'll get you some cologne if you like."

She motioned me to the downstairs hall while she climbed the stairs.

It never occurred to me to wash my hands any more. To wash my hands I had to find my soap and my towel, go down our ratty hall to the washbasin and put up with the smell of recent shit. Most of us were content with our shower after sports to keep us clean for the rest of the day. Oh, Channing and Hobbs had a lavatory and didn't even have to leave their rooms to piss. Unheard of. That's why they had a more civilized veneer than the rest of us. They could have shaved three times a day if they wanted.

Before we got in her car Jan asked if I was hungry and I admitted I was, but told her I didn't want to go back inside and see her working in the kitchen. She wouldn't tonight, she said, but she'd like to cook for me real soon. Instead we'd go to a place where there was take-out food. I could tell her what I wanted and lay low in the car while she ordered it and picked it up. (You could find a member of our faculty at any joint in town.)

Everything went off without a hitch and right in the parking lot, feeling like a thief, I polished off some fried chicken, French fries and sliced tomatoes. Jan said she wasn't hungry, but she had a milkshake. There were extra napkins and she had let me bring the sherry along since the bottle was low. It was the best meal I'd had all term.

On the road again we didn't talk much. She was more subdued than I was. I wouldn't say depressed, but dreamy.

I'd driven a Healy before but I let her drive. I had a hand at the back of her neck and I was stroking her leg with the other.

I could smell the ocean air before long. I was always amazed to look at a map and see how close I was to the Atlantic. Only the guys who went out for crew knew anything about it.

She pulled over when we reached the last high land and we saw the lights along the shore and under low clouds a sprinkling of lights out on the water—boats or buoys or channel markers. Some were twinkling, some glowed. You could see the horizon and the sky lay in a mist over the black water.

I swigged at the sherry. The bottle was a long time dying. We talked softly and kissed.

We talked about things we might like to do together someday, ignoring the last frantic hours, content to know each other as well as we did. She was as much a mystery to me as the black ocean, but I couldn't imagine spending time with another woman or even thinking of one. I wanted more than pleasure from Jan, I wanted her to be more than a joy to me. There was work ahead. I'd have to sacrifice for her. She was my calling.

Barton had a lot to tell me when I got back, a lot to ask.

"Where have you been, Gordie?"

"Who's been looking for me, Sanborn?"

"No. Gill was by. He wanted to see you. I offered him some rum. He knew where the key was."

"Sure—Gill's always welcome. How's his leg?"

Gill had broken his leg in a motorcycle accident at home over the long weekend. He was out for the rest of the football season and his leg wouldn't heal in time for hockey. Too bad, because I thought I might make the varsity this year and hockey would have been our first chance to play together for Andover.

"He wasn't complaining. He looked like death, though. He hasn't shaved in days. I guess they're going easy on him. He's got a right to be depressed."

"I'll say. Sports is all he likes about this place. Gill's no ringer, though—he's bright. He doesn't care what he has to learn, that's all. He just wants the grade."

"I heard you played a great game today, Gordie."

"Yeah, we tromped 'em."

"Did you go off somewhere to celebrate? With your girl, I mean." Barton had known I was meeting Jan after.

"You might say so. To her house."

"With her folks around? You look kind of bombed. I can smell it. Did everything go OK?"

I told him, "Fine," but I wasn't so sure. It was a relief to be back in my dingy room after all that had happened with Jan. To have Barton sitting there in his pyjamas thinking his familiar thoughts and being concerned about me. I was where I belonged and yet the things around me had only a sentimental meaning. I was already beginning to miss Barton and the desk I'd avoided. Yes, because sometimes I would sit there late at night with Barton asleep and the study lamp warm on my arms, writing my lying letters home or to some girl, looking through the books full of things I was supposed to learn, and dreaming. I'd miss my desk, and the window that showed me the street at night under its blue light, the hood of a parked car gleaming up out of the murk like the head of a seal. The street was grainy as an old film—rolling off into a darkness filled with people using their minds and married people touching and children sleeping.

Sitting at the school was all I was doing these days. Just soaking up the atmosphere. I knew this life would be over soon and I'd be caring about different things in a place I couldn't imagine yet, a place that would have edges just as sharp as the ones in my room. I'd forget what it felt like to be a student—if I ever knew. When I was kissing Jan a while ago I had known that my future life had come for me. It was like dying: some were taken before their time.

I was ready.

EIGHT

Overnight my attitude about P.A. had changed. My interest in Jan had awakened a host of others. I didn't have enough time to turn around a record of failure that started five terms ago, but I was eager to show my critics what I had in me.

If I wanted to go to college next year I might have to settle for a state school, but damn the prestige. I didn't care what my father thought. He was beyond hope, he'd heard too many solemn vows. Whether I vowed to become an astronaut or to clean up my room he had no comment. His wasn't a "wait and see" attitude, either. He'd waited too long and he'd never seen anything.

I intended to let Bellini and Sanborn know that I'd finally decided to give the school a chance, and was ready to apply myself and see how much I could learn before the year was out. I was willing to let them take the credit for the change in me if that was what they wanted.

I wasn't thinking ahead. I was absorbed by my present situation. It was like being a new student. I wasn't afraid of my teachers any more because I was too caught up in proving myself.

Still, I didn't have the force of character to call the party off. In spite of all the changes Jan had wrought in my thinking, I couldn't go against my image of what a good man should be. It was too ingrained. Backing out of the party would cost me my prestige, and I had worked hard for it.

Waiting for Nye to show up I was reading an idiotic French novel as part of an assignment. Barton didn't know what to make of me. I could sense him taking a peek now and then, but I kept my attention on Anatole France. Yes, Barton's door was open. I'd told him I wouldn't do anything to bother him tonight, and now he believed me.

At 8 o'clock I jumped out of Barton's window and got lost in the shadows behind the dorm.

There wasn't a car on the road for long minutes. My dorm and a few others were old houses on the fringe of the campus that the school had gobbled up somehow. The townspeople were next door. There appeared to be a lot of single-family dwellings on the road leading from the campus into civilization, yet there were hardly any comings and goings. No one ever went out for a beer. I had the feeling that all the decent citizens in the neighborhood were old Andover alumni who were still thinking in terms of study hours and lights out. Or night workers that did their catting around during the day while I was in class. The town was as mysterious to me as our school was to townspeople.

Nye showed up at quarter after and his old Ford was only the third car that had gone by. I was stiff from the cold when I went to meet him because I'd been so lost in thought that it hadn't occurred to me to do calisthenics.

The transaction was swift and soundless. There I was on the street with a case of booze. I scuttled into the bushes to check out the haul. Sure enough, nine bottles of hard stuff: gin, rum, bourbon, scotch.

No one but a student here could appreciate how incongruous a full bottle of liquor looked on Phillips Academy soil. The only time in my life that mere possession had been so exciting was when another 11-year-old had boxes of explosives in his attic that his parents didn't know about. Enough to blow the roof off his house. For months my pockets bulged with smuggled fireworks.

Carrying contraband put me in high spirits every time. Yet the few times I'd had a big wad of money in my pocket I'd felt fearful and melancholy. Maybe I would always be down with the dregs turning money into contraband and never up with the bigshots turning contraband into money.

I got up on the cellar doors like a cat-burglar. High and away I tendered the prize with the nails of my other hand digging into the shingles behind me. Barton was reaching down with the expression of someone defusing a bomb.

When I scrambled down from the ledge I was so full of energy that I bounded like a kangaroo through a dark part of the street. My sneakers didn't make a sound on the lumpy asphalt.

The minute I was inside Barton was after me to store our supplies in my filing cabinet and put dirty clothes in the empty box. He didn't like the name Hiram Walker and wanted our new laundry box in the closet. He was right, though, it was dangerous to leave anything lying around because when Sanborn knocked on your door, you had to open right away. If you didn't he thought nothing of tearing your room apart to find what you needed time to hide.

The bottom part of my filing cabinet had a door that could be locked. The entire haul wouldn't fit in my little locker so I put two bottles in with my empty file folders. Am. History, Biology, French . . . what a joke. At the start of the term I was always a fiend for organization. I'd figure, this time I'm going to study, but then the assignments would get handed out and I knew I'd never have any trophies for my filing cabinet.

The remaining bottle—rum—I cracked open and mixed with some coke that was cooling outside my window.

"Why you wanna start so soon, Gordie?" The old refrain. "The other guys are gonna be watching to see how much you can drink. You don't want to let Thomson drink you under the table . . . "

"Do you realize you said that before the last party? Hey, man, do you think I care what they think about my capacity?

At the end of the school year I'm never going to see any of these guys again."

"Afraid so, where you'll be going. But you do still care what they think or you wouldn't be throwing this party at all." He knew he'd found my weak spot. "Why are we running all the risk?"

"What about Channing and Hobbs?"

"OK, most of the risk. We supply the stuff. We've always got some. Your friends know they can stop by our rooms and have a drink. What if someone had it in for us?"

"If anyone ratted he'd have half the senior class against him. He'd probably die on a playing field."

"I hope you're right. Listen, Gordie, are you serious about turning over a new leaf?"

"Dead serious."

"I never saw you work so hard. Tonight your chair didn't even squeak."

"I knew you were watching. I guess it's kind of surprising. I was sure I'd lost the 'study habit,' if I ever had it."

"Look, the hell with the college you have to go to your Freshman year. If you work hard the rest of this year and the next, I'll bet they'll let you transfer to Harvard, and I'll get you into Adams House."

"God, Barton! One year at state wouldn't be too big a price to pay for everything I've done wrong around here!" I jumped up and grazed the edge of my desk, nearly spilling my drink. "My father hasn't even thought of that! That asshole, he's always holding the state college over my head like a salt mine. Jesus, they even have girls at state college. That wouldn't be such a bad place to spend a year. Don't worry, I'd study."

"Maybe you could get your girlfriend to go there with you. Then you wouldn't be distracted by the campus queens."

"Barton, I love you sometimes! Have a drink, you deserve it."

"I can see tonight is going to be shot as far as studying

is concerned. I'm OK, though. I had a light load. How you gonna make up so much work, Gordie? That is, if your teachers will let you."

"I'll go around to the teachers and ask them if they'll accept my work late and give me a grade. Sure, they'll tell me I can't get a grade, but when they realize how hard I'm trying to make amends, maybe they'll just say, 'Forget about the papers you owe me. Just do all the work from here on.' I hope so. Otherwise I'm going to be working every weekend from here on out."

"I say, leave 'em free no matter what. You can't risk losing Jan or there goes your reason for working."

"She'll understand. Being such a good person she'll be glad that she was the one responsible for the change in me. She would never be selfish where my future is at stake, that much I can guarantee. God, how I love her."

"I think you're finally mature enough to see things my way."

I gave him a withering look. "Mature enough? You've never even had a girl's bra off, Barton. What are you gonna do when it's your wedding night and you find out that your blushing bride wants you to treat her like an animal?"

"Knock it off. The future Mrs. Barton will be human in every respect, I can tell you that much."

"If you can get sick seeing a frog on the dissecting table, what's going to happen when you find out what a woman's thing is like? If you don't get some experience you're going to come face to face with the real thing and it'll make you sick for life. You'll turn queer or something."

"I guess you know I'm not afraid of you, Bancroft. I can take you in a fight."

This was surely true, unless I wanted to murder him for some reason.

"I'm telling you these things because I care about you. You're like a brother to me. How can you be such a straight arrow?"

"I'm not a straight arrow. I'm just not a cad like you or Thomson."

"Cad? Come off it. Nobody says that. Really, Jim, sometimes it's embarrassing. Do you want me to show you some of the letters I got last year from Abbot? Thomson might be filthy but he's not perverted."

"The hell he isn't. I've heard the stuff that comes out of him. I'd rather find out what's at the bottom of a cesspool. He's evil. And Teasdale is a sadist."

"Come on, we don't even know if those cat stories are true."

"You can tell by looking at him. Say something gory and watch his eyes. He's a monster. As for Channing—I won't say anything about Hobbs because he's a follower with no mind of his own—Channing has a Don Juan complex. I'm sure you've read about that. He can never stay with one woman. As soon as he's conquered her he goes on to the next one. Types like that are supposed to secretly despise women and might even be homosexual. There's your homosexual."

"Channing? You're out of your mind. I don't care how many women he's had, he loves them all. He even eats it."

Barton changed the subject. Anyway, it was almost time to go upstairs.

The party was a big success at first. I felt proud to belong to such a superior crowd. Someone older and wiser might have thought my friends were a bunch of snotty bastards, silver-spoon cases, people who would be ruthless when they came to power and make life miserable for all the poor slobs affected by their decisions. Maybe they were, maybe they would. They represented the new ruling class, but they weren't quite ready to spill blood. They were getting the feel of all the different games, more worried about rules than ruling.

The guys had brought their notebooks so that instead of milling around and making noise that could be heard all over the building (eight guys was a big bullsession in our dorm) everyone was staying put unless he wanted to piss in the sink or lift weights (the sound of barbells was the ordinary thing in this room). As a further attempt to reduce the hubbub there was one bottle for each two guys—in theory, a pint apiece—and the guys were to sort themselves out according to what they wanted to drink and who they wanted to drink with. There were two extra bottles for the survivors.

Pissing off Thomson and Teasdale I went through a drill to make sure everyone knew what to do if Sanborn knocked at the door. Naturally, all the Coke and 7up could be left lying around—a realistic touch.

Finally the caps were off and everyone tried to get plastered as fast as he could.

Early on there was discussion of a remark a guy named Winthrop had made in a dorm over on the Main Quad. Winthrop was just another vicious bastard, but his remark would make him famous because it was sure to filter down to the lower classes and live on.

A guy named Brian Pinnock had lost both his parents in an auto accident. The school had given him leave to go home and join his living relatives, and he'd been excused from his classes for a week. He could have had the rest of the term off if he'd wanted is what I think. None of the masters would dare give him a lousy grade after he'd taken a shot like that.

Pinnock didn't leave right away for some reason. Probably he was in a daze. He was moping around his dorm the night after he got the bad news, and he wandered into the bullsession where Winthrop was holding forth.

Winthrop jumped up looking overjoyed, stuck out his hand and hollered, "Congratulations, Brian, we just got the word! When's the money coming in?"

Pinnock was stunned. He didn't know what Winthrop meant right away. Eventually he broke down and smiled. The point in being a "good man" was to be superior to emotions of pity or even sympathy, as Winthrop had been. If

Pinnock had punched out Winthrop he would have been ostracized. That was our code.

By three drinks or so the guys were showing the effect. The bad actors began to act badly. Teasdale wanted to play Frank Sinatra records on Channing's stereo and Channing wouldn't let him.

"If it's supposed to look like we're all in here studying there shouldn't be any music," Channing told him, speaking for all of us with half a brain.

"Fuck you and Bancroft and this stupid playacting. I oughta take this bottle back to my room."

"Do it and that's the last drop you'll ever get from me," I said.

"Don't worry, I wouldn't let that bottle out of my sight," said Farnham, who was sharing it with Teasdale. "Nor would I spend the rest of the night in Teasdale's room."

As soon as this ruckus had died down Thomson challenged anybody to wrestle him, looking straight at Channing, who was on the wrestling team. Thomson was always trying to pick a fight when he had a few drinks in him, but once he'd beaten up a few guys he turned into a jolly drunk and he'd still be yukking it up when the last drop was gone. He boasted he'd drunk corn with the men in his hometown. I believed him.

Soon Channing and Thomson were going at it on the mat. It was something to see because Thomson must have outweighed Channing by 50 pounds. Still, Channing was 170 or so and all muscle. In no time he had Thomson pinned. Thomson couldn't understand what had happened to him and wanted to go again. Channing pinned him this time, too, more quickly than before. Thomson muttered something about being able to throw Channing out the window with one hand if he wanted and Channing let the remark pass.

Now Teasdale had to get into the act because he was pissed at Channing for not letting him play records. In his shrewd, Nazi way Teasdale must have thought Channing would be worn out after his session with Thomson. Channing was soon twisting Teasdale's arm off and smearing his face into the mat. This was the high point of the party for everybody but Thomson, who identified with the big guy.

When the bottles were down the nasty stuff began.

"Well, Gawdon, you gonna tell us about that pussy you been into used to be Alan Benson's?"

Naturally I had nothing to say to Thomson. I kept drinking and thought of things I could hurt him with if he went too far.

"That's right, boys, ol' Gawdon got hisself some regular. Hear tell she's the hottest thing in town."

"Not from me you didn't you stupid hick."

"That was the word from the guys on the team. That woman know how to love. She make your eyes roll back in your head." When he was needling you Thomson would talk like a Negro. But now he was making a sound like a car revving up which was pure white boy, showing his teeth and making them chatter.

"A snapping pussy, I get it. Only a dumbshit like you would think that's something to snicker about. If you knew anything about sex you'd know that any woman can do that if she's got the brains."

"Don't admit anything!" Barton's whiny voice.

"Shut up, Barton. I noticed you didn't have anything to say when Thomson started shooting off his mouth."

"I'm with you, Gordie. I'm not afraid of him. I'll take him right now." Barton had a dangerous gleam in his eye.

"C'mon Bahton, you piss-ant. I'm not afraid of those boxin' moves of yours. I'll tear you' balls off, boy!"

Thomson's voice was loud as hell and Mamelakis told him to keep it down. Thomson wheeled round and looked astounded to see a foreign face so close to his own. I don't think he'd looked at Mamelakis all night. He had wanted to drink with him because the Greek was too self-controlled to drink much and Thomson could hog the bottle.

"Am I gonna have to kick your ass, too, Mahmaduke?"

"You're not going to kick anybody's ass."

It was Channing, cool as you please. I hoped he wasn't pushing his luck. Wrestling was a sport, after all, and it was different from an all-out fight.

"You've got about four people I know of pissed off at you right now and I don't think you'd like the odds if there's going to be a fight. Even if I have to take you myself, I can guarantee that you won't play any more football this year. I want to warn you that I know a lot more about fighting than a few wrestling holds, and if you try any dirty stuff I'll break both your arms."

Channing's voice was so calm and menacing at the same time that it gave *me* chills. Thomson got the message. He put on his good-old-boy face and claimed not to have been serious in anything he had said. The incident was past. Well, the part of the incident concerning Thomson was past. Barton would never stop reminding me that I'd discussed my girlfriend's "private parts" in front of half the dorm. I swore that I never would have done so if I hadn't been drunk. That was the only way to shut him up.

Around eleven we had a hell of a scare when there was a knock on the door. Hobbs had passed out on the sofa, but Channing helped me clean up and I got the door open after a reasonable time.

"What are you doing here, Kingsley? What's happening?"

"Sanborn and his wife are out. It seemed awfully quiet downstairs and I didn't see any light out of his livingroom window, so I went out and checked. The only light is the one he always leaves on, in the hall. And his car is gone. They must have gone out."

"What about his wife's car?"

"It's still here, but I'm sure she went with him. Maybe she's having it."

"That's still more than a month away. Good work, then. Well . . . when he comes home, don't come up here and tell us. He might be right behind you. Just listen and give us the signal."

"No problem. Say, do you mind if I have some of that?"

Channing let him drink out of his own glass and Kingsley managed not to gag himself.

I wondered aloud what we should do about Hobbs. Channing suggested we "let sleeping Hobbs lie," and Thomson thought he'd wake up before there was any danger. I finally prevailed. Thomson and Channing and I carried Hobbs into his room and threw him on the bed.

Sometime after midnight nearly everyone was dead drunk and no one gave a damn about Sanborn or the empty bottles or anything else. It was hell trying to keep the noise down and it seemed that Channing and I were the only ones who were trying to. Barton had gone the way of Hobbs, but he was too big to move at a time like this, drunk as we were. Thomson was laughing a lot and too loudly, Farnham was talking incessantly, Mamelakis was studying as if this were a night like any other and Teasdale had an ugly look on his face and would shout something like "bullshit" every few seconds in response to something Farnham had said. He was probably irritated with Farnham for keeping up with him drink for drink. Finally Teasdale had had enough and went disgustedly to his room.

Three knocks on the floor. Three more knocks, closer together. Then three more knocks, really frantic ones this time. Even though Channing was already helping me to clean up he had a word for Kingsley. "Jesus, what's he trying to tell us, it's a police force coming up?"

Thomson was on the floor, laughing. Bottles were rolling and clanking. Mamelakis and Farnham were frozen where they sat. I was dragging Barton into the room where Hobbs was when there were knocks on the door. I put a notebook over Barton's head. That didn't look right. More knocks, louder this time.

Inspiration! I pulled down a top window. Ran to get the barbell, noting at a glance that it was at 125 pounds. With all my might I threw the barbell out the window, a tremendous heave. The 25-pound plates just cleared the window frame.

The moment the bar was out—it lingered a long second in the light from inside—I let out a bloodcurdling scream. Hobbs woke up hollering and through the door I saw his feet swing round and come down on Barton as he sprang from his bed.

I ran to the door, still howling. It was Kingsley! I didn't have time to bash his head in, if Sanborn were home he'd have heard my scream. I ran down the stairs, past Sanborn's apartment without looking, around the house and into the garden where the barbell had fallen. I couldn't see it! It had vanished in thin air!

Footsteps. Someone was right on top of me. Channing.

I was tracing an arc from Channing's window to the garden when a beam of light found me. I was blinded when I looked.

"Bancroft? What fell into the garden? We heard a scream!"

"There's a barbell somewhere in your garden, sir."

"Who's that with you? Channing? Are you in on this?"

"It's right down here," said Channing, pointing his right foot. "The soil must have got soft today."

The beam of Sanborn's flashlight played about our feet.

"I don't see anything. Is everyone all right? What was that scream? What did you say fell, Bancroft?"

"A barbell, sir. It fell from Channing's window."

"Fell? *Fell* from there? I've never heard of such a thing."

"Well, I had to throw it out or break the glass. See, I lost control of the bar. That can happen sometimes. You lose your balance."

"I don't know about this. I guess anything is possible where you're concerned. What was that scream we heard? Was that you?"

"Yes, sir. Suppose you were out for a midnight stroll in

the garden? You can't blame me for screaming. That would have been murder."

"All right. Where do we go from here?"

Channing: "I'll help Bancroft dig up my barbells. I'm sorry if we disturbed your slumbers."

"All right, you two. Get the barbells back upstairs, but no more weightlifting tonight. The mania for fitness around here—it's getting out of hand. I think we're going to have to make a rule against weightlifting after such and such an hour. You'd think you boys would get tired of so many rules, but now you can see the need of them. I believe Mr. Kingsley has a room beneath you, Channing, isn't that so? I wonder how he likes to hear that barbell being dropped in the wee hours. Mr. Barton is below as well, but he wouldn't complain—his roommate is up there dropping it. Enough. I don't want you fellows standing around in the cold dressed like that. Get that thing upstairs and go to bed."

His window squeaked shut and the flashlight bobbed and died.

I felt completely sober now, the effect of so much fear and the night air. We reached deep into the soil at opposite ends of the entry marks. Dirt was impacted between the plates, but nothing was broken. Loosening the red collars we wiggled the plates and the dirt fell off.

The weight was light between us.

I crooked a finger at Kingsley on the way past his room. Of course he was still peeping out. He followed us upstairs.

Everything had been cleaned up. I guessed the small amounts of liquor left had ended up in Thomson's room. Hobbs was already back asleep. Barton was gone.

"All right, Kingsley, why did you give us the signal while Sanborn was asleep in bed?"

"I heard someone on the stairs. You told me to signal if I heard anyone on the stairs. When I looked it was only Teasdale, but you'd be surprised how much down can sound like up out there."

I just stared at him with the evidence of my stupidity gaining weight.

Channing patted Kingsley on the shoulder which was taken to mean there was nothing more to say and Kingsley could go back to his room and get some sleep.

"That was quite a move," Channing told me, closing his window. "Too bad Sanborn wasn't out for a midnight stroll in the garden."

NINE

The day after the party there was genuine brotherhood when we left for morning chapel thanks to our hangovers.

I was still feeling rugged when I went back to the dorm before lunch. There was a note from Sanborn under the door. Jesus, a sealed envelope. He didn't want Barton to be contaminated by the tone he took with me.

Bancroft: Please report for a conference at 2 PM sharp. I will write an excuse for your athletics. Important.

O.F. Sanborn

I didn't bother to look for nuances. All this note meant at the moment was "nap time."

My alarm got through to me at zero hour. There was an apple on Barton's window sill and I scraped the mold off an old piece of cheese from the bag outside. Practically a meal. At least I wouldn't be sitting there having stomach cramps in front of Sanborn.

He opened right away. Ushering was in his blood. He showed me the living room.

"Sit right here. Make yourself comfortable."

Fat chance. How could I be comfortable in a chair smack in the corner when the one he was pulling up for himself had a seat a foot higher? The way Sanborn positioned

125

himself you'd think he was trying to keep me from making a run for it. On top of that, he had a hard chair and mine was so soft it was impossible to sit up straight. He wanted me lolling there while he probed.

The wary once-over lasted a minute. "I guess you know why you're here." It was always the same opening.

"The barbells in the garden," I said wearily. "I can explain the whole thing."

"It's not the barbells. I don't want to discuss last night. The fact that you were lifting weights at one in the morning might have some bearing."

I was looking around the room. I guessed that Mrs. Sanborn was an antique collector. The place looked like the one your country relatives lived in thirty years ago. All that was missing was flypaper.

"I'm worried by some of what I hear, Bancroft. Your instructors are concerned about your work. It might go deeper than that. Are you aware of the letter to your parents?"

"Dr. Bellini told me," I yawned.

"Bancroft, this is serious!" His bushy eyebrows were going up and down. "You could be expelled from this school! Only the most radical change in your behavior . . . "

"Save your breath, sir. There's no need to give me pep talks any more."

Surprise had ripped through his mask, but then suspicion started sewing. "What do you mean?"

"Remember that last chat when you told me you liked my poetry?"

He was disappointed. "I did like your poem, Bancroft, but that was the start of the term. I don't care if you've got a pile of poems up to here." The flat of his hand was two feet off the floor. "You haven't been doing your work. All your teachers have written me. I got three letters this week alone, plus a copy of the report the Dean sent to your parents."

I knew damned well that Sanborn had said bad things about me on that report, Bellini had told me he was one of my detractors. I would need a good opening to snow him about the change in my attitude. It would have a better effect if he'd worked up to a frenzy first.

"This is the last time I'm going to talk to you, Gordon. You're at the end of your rope. It reflects badly on my qualifications as a housemaster that I've been powerless to prevent one of my boys from being expelled, especially when I've only been charged with fifteen of you. In my defense I'm afraid you've become a bad influence on the other boys here. Soon they'll be hearing from the colleges where they've applied, and all will have been accepted somewhere. There's a notorious tendency among senior boys to slack off over the last term of school. What incentive will they have to keep up with their work this spring when they can say, 'Look at Bancroft, here. He doesn't do any work, yet he's allowed to remain in school.'?"

Up and at him. "I'd be the best influence you could possibly have in this house."

His mouth fell open.

"I guarantee it. I'll be the only one studying night and day, all weekend, every chance I get. The only one who hasn't got time for a bullsession. I still intend to lift a few weights, you understand. When muscles get as developed as mine they go to fat in no time if you don't keep up."

"What are you telling me? Do I understand you correctly?"

"I hope so. I'm going to try to make up all the work I've let slide. I spoke to two of my instructors this morning. They're willing to give me special assignments that will count toward my grade. In other words, I could affect some of my low grades with extra work."

"This is excellent, very good. Why the sudden change in attitude?"

"Oh, I got to thinking about some of the things you were saying . . . "

The idiot, he was buying it.

"I know it might be too late to influence the colleges,

but at least I want to have a good record to look back on. I want to have the full benefit of my last days at Andover."

Sanborn always made a point of telling me that no amount of effort would get me into the college of my choice. I was to study my ass off "for myself."

"Bancroft, I hope this isn't a song and dance. If you're on the level this is some of the best news I've had all term. There's nothing so excruciating for a man in my position as to watch a young man like you throw his life away. A young man with so much to offer . . . "

On and on he went, telling me all the wonderful things that were going to happen now that I was going to hand in my homework—how there would be a stock market rally and dancing in Times Square.

At one point a couple of guys came crashing through the front door and I realized that there was only a thin wall between Sanborn's living room and the downstairs hall. When the two arrivals went upstairs the racket was unbearable. I'd hated those stairs all term and it was strange to think that Sanborn might have been just as annoyed. There were metal guards on the edge of each step that made a sound exactly like a cake tin. You had to wonder how he got his wife pregnant with the students traipsing in and out and the johnny-jump-ups that made the ceiling growl. You had to wonder how his wife had kept the baby this long.

Sanborn had rough, ruddy skin and behind his steel-rimmed spectacles his eyes were wide or narrow according to his enthusiasm. On this occasion he seemed enthusiastic about my future, but there were frequent doubts about my seriousness that brought on a squint, as well as second thoughts about all the bad reports he'd written about me. He was so worked up by the time he excused me that he beamed and shook my hand before closing the door.

I was demoralized as hell as I walked away from the dorm.

Gill had left word with Jim that he wanted me to come over. He was rooming alone his senior year and his room was incredible, even for Andover. A term's worth of Boston Globes completely covered the floor. They came to your knees. Dark cracks showed where his chairs were wintering. His rumpled bed was a raft iced in by yellowing events. The top of his desk stood above the mess, bare.

Gill was sitting behind the desk when I came in, but his right leg was sticking straight out, he was turned to the right in his chair. I'd simply knocked and entered. He didn't look surprised.

"I've had it with this place. I'm joining the Marines."

He looked like one already, a Marine who'd just spent a week in the jungle. He had a heavy growth of black beard that showed a scar.

"Why would the Marines want a guy with a broken leg?"

"Maybe you gotta break something and step back from what you've been doing to see how meaningless everything is."

"That might be true for me, but you've got a future."

"I'd rather be in a war. That would mean something. You gotta survive. All it is around here is a bunch of games that are meant to simulate life. It's a lot of training. I want the real thing."

I went to the highest mound and unearthed his armchair. "Mind? Jesus, Gill, if someone dropped a match in here you'd be gone in a cloud of smoke."

"You'd join the Marines, too, if it wasn't just a pose, all this rebellious shit you pull off. There are some people I want you to meet. Why I wanted to see you. C'mon, they're expecting my call."

Watching Gill wade through his rubbish, slamming a chair with his plaster leg, I saw real trouble ahead. I knew that if Gill wanted to give me a lesson in how to break the rules I would have to go along. Ever since I started getting in trouble for losing track of the time I'd been attacking the school's unnaturalness, rules that kept following us after we'd left the chapel, the refectory, the classroom . . . that followed us into the bathroom, ticked away on our desks while we studied at night, yanked us out of our sweet dreams, compulsory coitus interruptus.

What a hypocrite I'd been last night, coming up with so many rules for the sake of a good time, censoring everything my friends wanted to say or do. What was the point of outsmarting the school if we couldn't be spontaneous enough to laugh out loud or talk in a normal tone of voice? Gill here was the real rebel, pounding down the hall, banging down the stairs, wielding both crutches in one hand to force back the imaginary people blocking his way. Gill had once been more careful about the rules than I was, a lot more had been at stake. The cast on his leg had given him the absolute freedom of a mad bomber.

He used the phone by Benner House. The call took half a minute and I made sure I was too far to hear anything.

"Fifteen minutes," he said, swinging his cast out of the booth and motioning down the town street with both crutches. "I'm waiting outside, but go on in and have something if you want."

He was on his crutches now and moved the rubber tip of his right one a foot in the air toward the small group of wastrels clogging the entrance to the snack bar.

"I'll wait with you. Is this going to be worth it, Gill? Who are we waiting for?"

"You'll see. Big alumnus. You'll recognize the car."

From the corner where the kids with snacks in their hands could see us we were heading off campus. It was no sweat for Gill to swing his heavy body, he wasn't slowing me down, but his crutches were squeaking, a helpless high-pitched voice was telling me over and over that something was wrong, that I should do something.

"Your leg'll be all right for lacrosse this spring."

"Big deal. No college will give me a football scholarship."

"On the strength of last year?"

"Without knowing how I come out of this?"

"But you don't need a scholarship, Gill. Your folks are doing all right, aren't they?"

"My folks . . . Sure. My mother has the same shitty job as a salesclerk and my father is still pushing a wheelbarrow."

"Pushing a wheelbarrow!"

"It's not the end of the world. A lot of people have to work for a living."

"I thought he was an architect. Didn't you tell me that once?"

"Probably. Landscape architect is what he calls himself. He's just a glorified gardener."

"Now I get the picture. Your old man must have shelled out plenty to get you in here. How come you didn't get a scholarship?"

"I didn't qualify. With both of them working all these years, they're doing all right. But this place has cost them a bundle. All worth it if I get a football scholarship to a big-name college."

"They want to brag about you."

"My father, yeah."

"Wouldn't he have your ass if you joined the Marines?"

"He'd never speak to me again."

"What I want to know . . . Do you still love the guy?"

"Sure. He's worked all his life so that I could have a few things he never had. A good education—that's number one. No, I can't join the Marines yet. I'll have to settle for a school that isn't so famous and my father will have to swallow some of his pride."

I told Gill how I was going to start studying again and he didn't believe me. I told him what I'd been up to with my "townie girlfriend" (I didn't tell him her name) and he had to concede that no one could get so carried away with a story he was making up.

"That's why I've got to study, Gill. I can't risk getting thrown out. Keeping my girl is all I care about, and I'm afraid of losing her if there's a distance between us. What's worse, I'm afraid that I might look different to her if I'm not an Andover man anymore."

"Is this your way of telling me you want to chicken out on me today?"

"You haven't even told me what's supposed to happen! Sure I'll chicken out if I think you're taking a big risk just because you stopped giving a shit."

"This guy's a big friend of the school and his wife is a dish. Do I have to spell it out for you?"

"Yes! What are we supposed to do, fuck this woman while her husband is watching?"

I remembered Gill's grin from two years ago before he became such a cynic. There was so much gloom on his face all the time that a grin like this had the effect of a belly-laugh.

"C'mon," I went on, "I won't take the chance if you don't tell me something."

"Let's put it this way. This guy is filthy rich and he thinks nothing of helping needy students." I started to snicker and Gill caught me in the shin with his crutch and said, "He isn't queer."

"Hell, no. He got his balls shot off in the war and all he likes to do is watch."

"Up to you, Bancroft. You don't have to take his money and you don't have to do anything."

"Why would I want to come along, then?"

"To have a drink with me and get to know this guy. Maybe you could find a way to have a good time here that doesn't put your standing on the line. As it is, you haven't got a chance to finish out the year. I know all about the stunts you pulled last night with Channing and them."

"You must have heard from Barton."

"You might be surprised how many people are talking. That's our guy."

It was a dark-green Jaguar saloon I'd seen prowling the campus on weekends. The guy who drove it had been pointed out to me, and I'd seen him hanging around the playing fields looking exactly the way we'd want to look when we were rich alumni, though I'd never seen his wife.

Gill got in front and told me his name while I was climbing in the back. Paul van something put his hand back without turning in his seat so that it was upside-down. The warmth of his hand was startling. I'd grown used to the cool fall day it was while we were waiting.

All Paul wanted to talk about was football so I was content just to memorize the way. I heard the names of friends of Gill's who were playing for college teams now. What a thing to hold over him! But Gill acted pleased to hear any scrap of information about his old teammates.

Paul lived in a mansion in the same part of town as the McBrides, though he didn't have as much land. The road he was on was the last turn-off before Jan's place. The wife was expecting us, had the door open before we reached the stone entrance.

"Lynn" was immaculate and dressed young. If it weren't for an odd crack in her neck she could have passed for someone our age. I saw her neck when she bent to offer me pinkish canapes that were to accompany the glass of champagne I'd served myself. In bad light she'd have been in Jan's league—she was built the same and she was even as tall. There was something potentially evil about an imitation Jan and our host, Paul, didn't help by the way he seemed to eat it up when his wife was looking us over.

Gill kept yammering and acting like he didn't notice that she was feasting her eyes on him, with her mouth hanging open. While he was telling them about his leg she moved her chair closer, a diningroom chair she'd turned around. Following her lead her husband came closer, too, sliding to the end of the couch without taking his eyes off Gill, reminding me of a dog that's trying to get close to the food on a table by sliding his snout between two elbows.

By this time I was completely out of it in an armchair on the other side of the sofa with my champagne and my pink shit on toast and the crystal figurines they had and an antique grandfather's clock to talk to across. To see if Lynn was going to put a move on Gill I had to crane my neck, so crane I did. Back in the shadows where I was anything was possible.

Essentially Gill was telling them the same sob story he'd told me about how he was finished as a football player, and therefore might not get into an Ivy League school. Our hosts were a Yalie and a Smithie. They had to be childless because the house was old and there wasn't a nick anywhere in the wood or a missing speck of plaster—either that or they'd raised something in the basement.

The way they were perched over Gill it occurred to me that they might not be sex fiends, after all. Maybe they were crazy sports fans like my father who didn't have a boy to live their lives through (lucky unborn little tweedball).

"Hey, Bancroft, you going to pitch for the varsity this year?"

I'd been staring at a clock that wasn't ticking.

"If I last that long." The van somethings had come out of their huddle. Gill was slumped at the center of it.

"Don't worry about your visits here," said Paul, weakly hearty.

"We've been having boys for years," said Lynn, no fly in her peaches and cream in spite of the possible *double entendre*. "Paul knows all the rules, so none of you boys has ever been reported."

"I went to P.A.," said Paul. "All the privations never did make sense. Tobacco was tabu in my day along with the wine and the women. A little wine never hurt anybody, and the best way to get your mind off women is to have one once in a while." He waited the appropriate time for me to be scandalized. "Instead they legalize tobacco, in designated areas—a substance that does nothing but harm."

In the next minutes of chitchat Paul slid back to the middle of the sofa and addressed the empty room in front of him as if it contained an audience, and put his right arm and his left arm out to us as if he wanted to make sure we were still a part of it. He was trying to tell us something about the importance of belonging even if you've got a cast on.

"That's all I ever wanted since I came to the place," I burst out, "to belong, to have some kind of role to play. Since I got my growth late all I could do was be a buffoon, you know, take chances. People left me alone when they could see all I was doing was trying to hang myself."

Now I was making a hit. Paul was beaming and Lynn was shifting into my orbit with her chair.

"I never heard such a crock," said Gill, staring at the pink goo on the cracker he'd chosen. "The rest of us have been competing against each other and Bancroft wants to get out of having to hurt someone and be hurt by him because he can do a better job of hurting himself. What crap. He's the meanest guy on the soccer team, practically a legend, and the only reason he can't keep up in class is because of his townie girlfriend—he thinks he's in love. There's your problem boy."

Now I was basking in the admiration of Gill's two perverted friends.

"Anyway, that was the old Bancroft," Gill went on. "He's grinding now so he's sure to get through the year and be a real Andover man, after all. Maybe he can get into the same college that takes his townie."

Gill had always been a master at changing my feelings of admiration into pure hate.

"Maybe it's time something good happened to you, Bancroft, but after all the years I've been grinding quietly I'm going to resent it if your instructors let you snow them."

"What kind of friend are you, then? You just want me down at the bottom of the class where you can feel superior to me, is that it?"

"I'm going to find more champagne," said Paul, getting up.

"While he was gone Lynn went over to Gill and knelt by his chair and called him "John." "John, I think you're bitter, and you mustn't be."

The sound of the word "John" in her mouth was as intimate as the sound of a zipper laying his pants open. *Nobody* could call him John. Then to clinch it she put a hand on his good thigh and tried to find something to squeeze.

When her husband came back with the bottle she was sitting on the left arm of his chair with a hand on his right shoulder and one of her big tits against his ear. I looked up quick to see how Paul was taking this. All I could read on his face was something like pride or encouragement. Then Paul took a step back and the whole scene cleared. A couple of lushes, of course that was what they were!

Suddenly I remembered who it was Paul had been reminding me of: a guy at our country club who ran up tremendous tabs and then disappeared for a week or so from time to time. These were supposed to be his "benders" but I figured he checked into a hospital now and then to dry himself out before it was time to start on the Scotch again. For a guy who sucked it up like this friend of my father's, to go on a bender he'd have to drink half a bottle of Scotch at a swallow.

The sexy way Lynn was acting and Paul teetering back and forth with his fresh bottle were all part of the general relaxation of morals at this place, and I finally got into the right frame of mind to join in. I'd have given anything to be where Gill was now under the weight of that breast. I'd have let Lynn do anything she wanted to me, and toasted her husband while it was going on, listening to his stories of the good old days.

We didn't get much drunker, but I saw Paul slip Gill a twenty at one point, and his wife got in Gill's lap for a while, so it was easy to imagine a wild ending to the parties here. If I listened to the van somethings, who wanted me to come back "any time at all" I might get so drunk some night that I'd find myself in bed with Lynn, thinking about Jan, who was right around the corner, after all, and not seeing anything wrong. No wonder there were so many drunks in life in spite of the headaches that took all day to go away.

Paul dropped us off at Gill's dorm so that he wouldn't have far to go. I chose to get out with my friend. I wanted to ask him more things about Paul and Lynn, but I knew Gill well enough not to be surprised when he told me to find out for myself.

I walked to Benner House to give Jan a call, and before you know it my new friends with their breasts and champagne were far from my mind.

Thoughts of Gill and his father were depressing me so much that I took no delight in the fact that I would soon hear Jan's voice on the phone. I was staggered by the realization that Gill had lied to me my lower year. He'd been ashamed of his background.

It was unthinkable that a guy like Gill should be socially insecure. Sure I'd been flattered that he considered me a good enough friend to be entrusted with the truth, but Gill had sunk in my esteem. He'd become one of the rest of us.

That wasn't quite right. Rich Andover kids didn't have to lie, and the very rich kids were quite modest about their attributes: being sure of themselves in society, well-dressed, well-fed, well-read, well-traveled. Somehow boys from poor or average families became aware of subtle differences between themselves and the rich no matter how modest and unassuming the rich kids might be. A kid like Barton or Gill, who had grown up in the lower class (or lower middle class—the line between them was blurry to me) earned his prestige by fighting for it on the playing fields and racking his brains to keep up academically, or even to shine, but he could never rest on his laurels, the struggle had to go on, because if he ever stepped out of his starring role, or didn't make the starting lineup, he was just another kid from down the block. That was why Gill was so worried, that was the real reason. Now that he'd lost the chance to prove himself he was beginning to doubt what he had.

I couldn't have told Gill my feelings or told him the understanding I had of our predicament even if it would cheer him up to have an ally. A good man never talked openly

137

about social concerns. The best shunning was always quiet. If you had to give a reason, *you* would be the idiot.

I hung around in front of the snack bar for a while waiting for one of the two phone booths to empty. Some rich bastard was always calling collect to Hawaii and talking for half an hour. Even when I didn't need to use it I couldn't stomach the Andover type who would tie up a phone to ask how his horses were doing.

She answered right away. Good sign. I'd told her "sometime before dark," and she'd given me her early evening.

"That's the voice I've been waiting to hear."

"It's good to hear yours, too."

"I'm talking low because some stupid preps are standing around waiting for the phone, i.e., listening."

"That school . . . I'll be glad when you're out. We'll have this summer."

"I'll get a summer job up this way. And listen, I've been thinking . . . How'd you like to go to college with me next year? It doesn't matter that you can only get into a shitty school. I'm in the same boat. We could go together! Doesn't that sound fantastic?"

"Don't make me respond over the phone. We'll talk about it. About next summer, if you could get a job up this way it would be great."

"All I know is, I wish I could hold you now."

I had to whisper this, it was no joke about the guys outside.

"I've got good news for Saturday night. My father will be here in the afternoon, and we can bring you back after the game. Dad wants to talk to you some more, he really likes you. But in the evening he's taking his girlfriend to Boston—you remember, Ruth—and they're going to spend the night."

"He must tell you everything. God, it must be great to have a father like that."

"Why aren't you telling me how glad you are that you can stay with me?"

"The things I want to tell you are hard to say over the phone. I want to make love to you, Jan."

"Oh, I want it, too. All night."

"I don't know about all night. I might bring some books along."

"You *what?*"

"That's right. You've only got yourself to thank. You're turning me into an honors student. I'm going to work my butt off till the end of the term."

"That's great, Gordon, but do your studying before you come. Promise? You'll make me feel guilty if I keep you from your books."

"You wouldn't believe what it does to me just hearing your voice. I haven't got anything more to say, but I can't leave like this in front of all these guys. Do you get me? Say something."

"So long, Gordon."

"No . . ."

"I'll see you after your game tomorrow. We'll stand in the same place, just for luck."

"Aren't you going to let me tell you I love you before I hang up?"

"I'll stay on the line for that."

"I love you. Don't hang up, you bitch. Now you've got to tell me."

There was a long silence while the people at the telephone company played the Jew's harp.

"I think I love you, Gordon. I'll tell you when I'm sure."

She hung up.

Considering she didn't even have a picture of me . . .

TEN

We'd won again! This time Mt. Hermon got slaughtered, 3 to 0. The ride to Jan's was more like a triumphal procession because we knew each other now. There wasn't a word about Dudbury or architecture. We talked about the game and life at P.A.

It turned out that Mr. McBride had gone to Hotchkiss, a school I admired. I was surprised to hear that he had wanted to go to Andover but had been turned down. "Lucky for you," I told him. "I'd have given anything to go to Hotchkiss." I wasn't trying to make him feel important. At a small school like Hotchkiss I would have made varsity in everything.

I'd been by Hotchkiss twice with my father. He was always driving up to Sharon, Connecticut, which was right nearby, to look at houses. Buying a house in the country was an obsession with my dad even though he couldn't afford the land it was on. He talked a lot about converting a barn but my mother had trouble persuading him to pay a hauler to clean out the garage. I hated to tag along and listen to his lies to the real estate people. Maybe he just wanted to be treated like a king in a part of the state where nobody knew him. Anyway, Sharon was beautiful, and so was Lakeville, and Hotchkiss.

This time I chose the back seat. Jan turned and gave me a huffy look when I got in, but she purred when I put my hands on her cheeks from behind. When I rested them on the little bit of chest she had before her bosom she covered them with her own and began stroking.

When her father glanced over to see what was going on there was a smile around his pipe.

I was so happy I forgot the cold wet day it was, the icy mud I'd just been in, the smelly gym. The McBrides were like my new family. I didn't feel like Jan's husband yet. That would have set me against Mr. McBride. I didn't feel like a brother, either. I guess there was no word for what I was, but I knew I had a family now. Some people had finally adopted me.

Mr. McBride had another bottle of sherry for me. I hated to think he'd replaced the other on my account, but in the alcove where they made drinks I glimpsed enough bottles to keep a neighborhood bar in business. Mr. McBride simply might have pulled another bottle of sherry out of storage.

With the van somethings' as another place to go each week where someone would fix me what I liked to drink there was a chance I'd not cause any more trouble at school or elsewhere. I felt like a king with people like Paul and Mr. McBride to serve me, showing contempt for the law.

Jan was sitting next to me on the sofa and at one point had her arm around me and her head against my shoulder, making it difficult for me to hold up my end of the discussion. Her father's manner suggested that what he had to say to me was more important than anything his daughter was doing. His being so tolerant didn't impress me as much as it had in the car. In fact, I was having bad thoughts. Could it be that he was used to the way she behaved when her admirers were around? How many had been around, sipping a drink and having a chat with him while Jan was draped around them?

When Mr. McBride got around to his plans for the night he surprised me with frank words and that was when Jan stopped hanging onto me, so maybe she was surprised, too.

"Gordon, what's your feeling about a man and a woman living together when they're not married?"

Deserted by Jan, I was suddenly on the carpet.

"Yeah . . . Wow! It's all right, you know? I think people should find out everything they can before they get into something as binding as a marriage."

"I wasn't thinking of a probationary arrangement."

My heart sank at the sound of that big word. He must have gone to a lot of trouble to fit it in.

"What about two people who might want to live together out of wedlock for an indefinite time?"

What torture. What to answer? I thought Mr. McBride might have a liberal side. I didn't think he was the type to trick me into having the wrong opinion. But I was afraid of admitting too much feeling for Jan and then having to get a job to support her. Marriage was too ridiculous. I couldn't see myself returning from some trench and singing out, "I'm home, dear!" That would have to wait for about ten years, when all my other schemes had failed. Jesus, I didn't even know what I wanted to be yet. Maybe I wouldn't have minded being Jan's husband if I didn't have to be anything else, but I didn't see where I was going to get the million dollars to make that arrangement possible.

"I have to be honest, sir. I don't see anything wrong with it. If two people love each other there shouldn't be a lot of laws in the way. On the other hand, it wouldn't do a kid much good to be born a bastard, especially if he wound up at a place like P.A. where social status means an awful lot. It's hard enough to hold your head up in a crowd like that without having parents that were too lazy to get married when they had you."

Mr. McBride sat back in his chair, puffed on his pipe, got red in the face. When he took the pipe away he was beaming. I couldn't have been happier if one of my old math teachers had beamed at me.

"I agree with you, Gordon. Well, almost. I don't think being illegitimate matters so much. As long as the child doesn't know about it, I can't see where it does any harm. I'll go further—I don't think most kids would be stigmatized by illegitimacy even with full knowledge of it. They'd be getting their ideas about marriage from their parents. I do think marriage serves a purpose in protecting children, however. The law protects children when marriages break up, and some mothers—and fathers, too—would be in a hellish bind without any support from their exes."

"You can explain things better than my English teacher, Frank." It was Frank instead of sir because he'd asked me to call him that back in the car. It still didn't sound right. "Marriage is kinda phony, though. If all it's good for is protecting children, then why is there so much mushy stuff written about it? If you're not willing to marry a girl that's supposed to mean you don't care for her enough to, you know, have her love in any way. But marriage might change the way people feel about each other. Married guys have told me they liked their wives a lot better the way they were before marriage. They went out of their way to be nice to them then."

"I see their point, but not because of my ex. Jan's mother was a special case."

"I don't agree with either of you. Without marriage I don't think you can have a *home*. And without children you can't have a home. A woman wants a home more than anything, and the way I see it the husband and the children and all their feelings are part of the home. It's the home that keeps your feelings from changing. To have a home you've got to take responsibility for your wife and children. The man I marry will want that responsibility. There's no reason it should be a chain around his neck."

"Wait a minute, Jan," I blurted. "I'm not against marriage. Who doesn't want a home?"

She ignored me. "I've done a little traveling now, and I've had my share of affairs . . . "

My smile had suddenly become an effort. She made it worse by looking right at me, cool as you please.

143

"I think I know something about the kind of freedom men want. I can understand why they feel that way. When they get tired of someone they don't want to get stuck. And people get tired of each other fast. They meet, they fall in love, they say they care. It lasts a week or a month or even longer, but sooner or later when the sparks are gone, they start resenting each other. There might be a thousand reasons why it happens that way, and I don't pretend to know half of them—I just know that it happens."

I caught the resentment deep in her and had to be careful not to sound as if I knew better. "Well, what are people supposed to do, though, get married and hate each other the rest of their lives?"

Her father was watching me with clear, quiet eyes and I thought for a moment I might have fallen into a trap. Maybe the two of them were in cahoots, trying to draw me out! I kept my eyes on my hands and Jan went on.

"I think it must be the hardest thing for a girl . . . to think she's found the man she loves . . . only to find out all her feelings have been an illusion based on love words that were just words . . . and acts of kindness that were thought out in advance . . .

"I don't think it hurts that much to part. What hurts is to see the process repeated. Maybe the whole thing could be avoided . . . I guess I'm addressing you men, though. Women are more naive about marriage. Never make love to a girl you wouldn't want to marry." Obviously she was addressing me. "Never fall in love with her, or say you love her, unless you want her to marry you."

The collar of my shirt was scraping like a rope.

Her father broke in gently. "I'm sorry, Jan, I know how you feel. You've been hurt a few times. What you say is wise, and true. But maybe it's only true for you, honey, or for people in your situation. What Ruth and I have together . . ."

"That's not the same thing at all," she flung at him. "Who cares what you and Ruth do?"

I looked to see what her angry face was like, but she was already grinning. They'd been over this ground before . . . Then it dawned on me.

"Here I thought all along you were afraid about my intentions toward your daughter," I blurted. They both looked at me deadpan. "Whether I wanted to live with her or would marry her, I mean. Well, I'm right, aren't I? Weren't you just wondering how I'd feel if you and this Ruth woman wanted to live together?"

"Could you seriously think of living with Jan?"

He was about to crack up and so was Jan, unfortunately.

"Don't worry, I'm not going to say anything about how long you've known each other."

He gave Jan such a quick look that it was practically a wink.

"What I'd like to know is where Andover fits in your plans."

"Oh, I was thinking of what might be on the horizon. Who knows how long it'll be before I'm in a position to support her? Who knows if we'll still be in love by then?" I looked at Jan helplessly. "I sound like a dope, I know. It's too soon to be telling your father how I feel. You don't even believe me yet yourself." No help there. I turned back to her dad. "I'm sure I'm in love with Jan. She's already told me she's not sure about me, though, so there's still hope for you if you don't think I'm right for her."

"From what I know of you, Gordon, I think you'd be wonderful for Jan."

It wasn't always such a big relief to realize that the earth hadn't swallowed me.

"Still, I'm not sure if I know what you were talking about a moment ago. This future when you and Jan are going to live together, this time on the horizon—it's not so distant, is it, really? Weren't you planning to set up house as soon as I leave tonight for Boston?"

Incredible. No sooner had I breathed a sigh of relief than he had my heart pounding again. I'd have been dizzy

from it all if I'd tried to bullshit Mr. McBride the way I did
my father, or Sanborn, or even Bellini.

"No. I mean, yes, we were planning to spend the night
together, but no, I didn't think of it as living together. I can't
offer Jan anything but a one-night stand."

Jan's face told me my little joke wasn't going over.

"Saturday night is the only time I can risk spending the
night because Sunday morning we don't get a cut for skip-
ping breakfast and we can stay in bed until the Sunday service. I don't have to tell you how it is if you went to
Hotchkiss. The rules might not be intentionally cruel. The
authorities don't think a guy my age could fall in love. If
they're trying to make things hard for me it's because
they're afraid my love wouldn't do a woman any good. Parents feel the same. All the ones I've known. I think they
might be wrong, but it's dangerous to go against them. I
don't want to get thrown out of school or have my parents
stop sending me because that will make it harder to offer my
loved one some kind of life. I might be able to offer Jan a
good life if we lived together while we went to school, living on part-time jobs. I'm talking about what it might be like
if we went to the same college next year. I know my folks
would help us out, and if we got married, maybe even you
might want to . . . I'm going too fast, though. For now, if we
can be together once in a while I'll be grateful."

"You can spend the night here whenever you want, as
long as Jan would like you to. I think you're a fine young
man, and I'm glad to know you." He tossed off the rest of
his drink and bit some ice. "I've got to get going. I'm glad
we had our talk. I agree with most of what you said, but it
might have been unfair of me to bring up that question when
I did. Jan will be on her own before long and I think Ruth
and I will live together. Jan and I have been a good team.
It's going to hurt like hell when I have to lose her, but I
know I will someday and I'll be glad I have someone else
when it happens."

I was speechless. I could have had tears in my eyes, but

146

I had tremendous self-control when it came to crying. Even if the tears came out at times, I was able to keep a straight face, so that they looked like the kind caused by beauty.

As soon as her father pulled out of the driveway Jan and I were all over each other. Like the first time, she was in a frenzy, but it was better now because we were standing.

It was our first chance to fit to each other. I was six-three these days so it didn't matter about Jan being tall for a girl. I think she was five-eight. It was a good thing she was a little taller than average because if she were a short girl with such a big ass and tits she'd have been nothing but a blob in winter clothing. Anyway, when I buried my head in her neck and reached around behind, her ass came right into my hands.

When I dug my fingers into the bottom edge of her panties and pulled I got enough of a hold to lift her right off the ground. When she lost contact with the earth she really went out of her mind. Her body was jackknifing and rubbing me rhythmically. This was so much better than any dry-humping I'd heard about that it deserved another name.

She got tired of this before it became a big effort.

"We'll go upstairs," she said hoarsely, but she made no move. Rather she put her hands on my shoulders and held me at arm's-length. "Let's make up for all the days we had to wait." Her eyes were cloudy and I thought of a third eyelid, a nictitating membrane, the biology lab . . .

The flecks in her eyes crystallized. "If we saw each other every day you wouldn't think I was sexy."

"No . . ."

She smiled. "It's all right. I don't feel like I'm seducing you after the way you held me just now."

I let her pull me along but I was uncomfortable about the way she wanted our sex to be. It was as if she wanted us to bound up the stairs and start bouncing the bed in one continuous motion. I wanted to fool around more. Sure, I'd wanted the real thing as much as she did while she was writhing in my arms, but I wasn't sure I'd feel the same way after a trip through a part of the house I'd never seen.

"C'mon, we'll use my father's bed. It's big and hard. Perfect for making love."

I followed her into the master bedroom, but now my doubts were serious. For one thing, how did she know how good her father's bed was for making love unless she'd been doing it there with other guys? Could Alan Benson have dropped her because of the competition?

The closet door was open and there was a rack inside full of Frank's big shoes. I wanted to be in a room full of bras and panties. Lacy things that were hard to make out under a dress. I wanted all her frilly things to be crisp and white in the light. There'd be a plain white sheet. Her hair would be the only dark thing and her skin would be as pink as her cheeks were the day she first met me after the game.

She'd stripped off her clothes and turned back the covers, but I was still standing there with my shirt half off. I'd never seen such beauty in the flesh.

"What's the matter?" she had asked over her shoulder.

"I don't know about this deal. I don't think I can go through with it. Not on your father's bed."

"Don't be silly. He's not going to know. Even if he found out, he wouldn't mind."

"Yeah. It's fantastic to be so welcome. Still . . . couldn't we go to your room? This is our first time. I'd like it to be in your private place. In here I feel like we're sneaking some fun . . ."

"All right. I know what you mean." I gave her a hand getting up. "But take off your clothes. Don't let me be the only naked one."

I didn't get the chance to object, she was undressing me. When we were both naked I made a bundle of our clothes. I wanted to hold them in front of me, but she'd have caught on. I wasn't hard and I was ashamed of the wrinkles. She seemed to have simmered down, though. I asked to see the other rooms upstairs, and she showed me. Walking

148

through the house with my free arm around her I got used to being naked.

Her father had a big studio with a messy desk. Things on his drafting table were laid out neatly. I kissed her in his studio until I saw the hypocrisy and pulled away before she did. She hadn't been responding the way she did downstairs.

When we got to her room my heart was pounding. There were the frills. The top drawer of her bureau was open and that was where she kept her underwear. She got in bed right away and asked me if I wanted the light out.

"No. I like the light. You're so beautiful. I love to be able to see you."

"That's sweet," she said, but I could tell that whatever passion she had felt for me was gone.

I got in beside her and our feet were cold.

"Jan . . . It was like this before, remember? You're excited one minute and you lose interest the next. Or that's what it feels like. You're tolerating me, you even let me touch you, but you don't want me."

"That's not so. I still want you to touch me. You're right, there's a change, but I like being with you just as much the way we are now."

"Can you explain what it is, though? What makes you change like that?"

"I get too excited. Don't take it the wrong way. Then a moment comes . . . I don't know, something breaks the flow and I'm watching us. I like that just as much, though. And it gives me something to remember."

"If we'd made love when you wanted back there . . . then the flow wouldn't have been broken, right?"

She looked at me with the deadest eyes. "Sex is best when it's wild at first. Call it 'animal' if you like. I can't like a man who's too respectful. At first! I mean, the first time. There's nothing worse than a lover who doesn't know when to take it easy . . . "

I didn't want to hear any more. There was something about her tone of voice, her lack of expression, her whisper.

This was the second year I'd been an atheist and I thought it was just as stupid to believe in devils as it was to believe in gods. But the demonic—even cheap horror movies—created a murky excitement in me, and that was the excitement I was feeling now. I was scared to see her looking so washed out and lewd, but a little sad, too.

"Why do you keep reminding me of the other men you've had? Do you think I won't like you once I know the truth? No kidding, you seem to go out of your way to rub my nose in it . . . I mean, to make me feel I'm just another in a long string of guys you've had." Her face hadn't changed. "What do you think psyched me back in your father's room? Not just his things in there, but the way you knew about his bed."

She cackled at that, and I forgot everything else I wanted to say. Her bed wasn't very wide, but I tried for the maximum distance apart.

"What do you think, I do it with my father?" Her eyes were wicked with delight. "You're right, Gordon, that was a stupid remark. I can't get over how sensitive you are. I should have more respect for your feelings." Her face was warm now. No one could have looked kinder.

"Something's going on in you that I don't understand," I told her. "There's some kind of pain in you, some deep hurt. Don't be afraid to tell me the truth, Jan. I can take it. Are you a nympho?"

She laughed out loud, but it was a merry laugh and musical. "Golly, I hope not! No, Gordon. I'm not a 'nympho.' Haven't you been with a woman who responds to you? Do they just lie there and let *you* do everything?"

"Of course they respond. Their eyelids get heavy, their eyes are blurry, they start panting and moaning. But there was never anyone like you, not right away. I had to work them up to it."

"You're amazed at how fast I get hot."

"It doesn't worry me. I'm in love with you. As long as I'm enough man to satisfy you, we should get along all right. I couldn't take it if you were playing around with other men, though—even if it was just cockteasing. I never knew it until recently, but I can be the jealous type."

She was still amused, but there was an edge in her voice when she told me, "I'm not a cheat. And when I'm with a man I'm not looking around. Don't ever forget that."

"Be fair. You're the one who's always bringing up all the men you've had. Right in front of your father you said, 'I've had my share of affairs.' What was I supposed to think? Sure, maybe you were only trying to shock me, maybe you were trying to check me out, but from what you say about yourself and the way you act the minute I get my arms around you, I'd have to think you're one hot tomato."

"You're right. I am a 'hot tomato.'" She was light-hearted again. "You're not the first person who's told me. There I go again. I can't help it, there have been a few men, but I was serious about them. I wasn't whoring around."

"That's hard to believe. Any guy in his right mind would jump at the chance to marry you."

"Maybe you're right. Men have been committed to me, but I would lose interest in them. I was the one who was backing out, ending relationships. Those times it didn't hurt. The one time I was hurt was when the man backed out on me. Then I was sure I was involved with the guy I was going to marry, even if it would have taken some work . . . "

"That was the guy you lived with, right?"

She wasn't talking.

"Well, I'm sorry you were hurt, but maybe you want everything too fast, huh, Jan? Maybe sometime you could give a guy a chance and don't make him have to prove himself too much. How do you account for falling in love with all these guys and wanting to back out right away?"

"Those men didn't want me any more, that's why . . . They only cared about prestige. I know I'm goodlooking. Men want to possess me, but they don't want to love me. It was a fight, sometimes. People don't love their possessions. I would get the idea that more than anything they wanted to prove that they *didn't* need me. They needed to feel superior to me to keep their self-respect."

"Wow. I get it. Were they older guys?"

"Almost always. Let's not talk about them."

Fair enough. I didn't hold her experience against her as long as she was breaking men's hearts. Apparently the only man I had to worry about was in France and content to stay there.

I was enjoying talking to Jan like this, naked under the covers of her little bed. There was a frosty moon outside but her room was warm. We had all night.

Somehow I got into the story of the booze party in my dorm. She was interested at first but then her hand was exploring and the moon was still part of my life, but the school was not.

Her voice was soft and full of catches. "Let me be on top. Have you done it that way, Gordon?"

"Yes." It was true, but the girl hadn't been comfortable, and we'd stopped.

"Don't do anything. Just touch my breasts. It's going to be so good. You'll see."

"I'll bet," I said, but I wasn't sure. My cock wasn't as hard as it should have been.

She began to caress me and I relaxed by degrees. She made me feel more and more at ease by saying, "I love it," "I love you," "I love your body," in English this time. When she wasn't talking her lips were buzzing, making the sound "hmm" that people make when they're considering something, except that the sound she was making meant, "I love your body." For a long time I couldn't believe she could like a man's body so much, but somewhere along the way I did believe it, and later still I began to be proud of my body for being something she could love so much.

She'd slipped down and was infiltrating everything with her nose and her tongue and her lips. Her hair parted and I saw her watching me, making sure I could see her smiling willingness, as if there was nothing she was afraid to do. All her movements were slow and loving.

Where she'd been too fast for me the first time we embraced, now she was too slow, and the result was that I began to want her something terrible. I'd never been so sure of myself with a girl. Perhaps this was the first time I knew what it felt like to be a man.

She stopped to show me how big I was. It wasn't my own. It belonged to the man I felt I was at the moment, a man with steady eyes who had no doubt of himself or his love, no distrust of his woman.

"Now," she said, starting to come over me. She settled back by degrees, moving side to side very slightly. She was deeper than the other girl but when she was sitting straight up it was all the way in, flush.

"It gets so big when I move back. I swear I can feel it getting bigger."

Her eyes had a faraway look as if the things she were describing inside were happening in the sky.

"This is the greatest thing that's ever happened," I told her. "Look how beautiful you are."

She was moving her hips every which way, turning as she bent forward, turning slowly again as she slid back. Her breasts swung heavily, full of quick little flips. She didn't want me to slide too much inside. She knew, she knew how close I was.

Our lovemaking went on and on. Jan saw my frustration building and was proud of her creation.

"Now . . . " She raised up, inviting me to reach for her, to do it to her, and I did, and she met me. When she raised up the next time she was clutching with that muscle I'd read about, rapidly seizing and relaxing her hold. Her eyes were shining but there was nothing in them. She was watching what was going on inside. When she raised up she made herself very tight. There's no point in trying to tell how good it felt when she forced herself down.

When she saw she had me out of control she pressed

against me, rubbed against me and began to shudder, babbling about how good it was and about coming—"Come with me, let's come together our first time," and I think I was babbling, too, but I didn't call her darling or anything.

She called me "my sweet man," which sounded right at the time, but later I thought of a jockey talking. There's no doubt she was the genius and I was the dumb brute. So what, though? By some miracle she had to have me, I was what she wanted.

Her beauty had awed me, it still awes me to think of it. I couldn't deny her anything, I couldn't resist her because I couldn't deny her beauty and it was too perfect. What was this beauty, though? How was she different than the others? All of the women I'd held naked in my arms up to this time had been beautiful.

I've been exclaiming over her breasts, but smaller ones could have been just as beautiful, closer to some classical ideal. I wasn't one of those idiots who only noticed girls with big tits, and I didn't have any ideals. Jan had awed me by the way she carried herself. She knew she was beautiful and she knew I was awed, but she didn't hold back, she didn't tease me to prove I was hooked and enjoy the power she had over me. She acted proud and pleased that she had her breasts to give me. She gave me her body. That's what they say and I think that's the right way to say it.

It might seem that I was obsessed by Jan's ass, tits, etc., but I wasn't. Sheila Burke had obsessed me because no matter how wild and perverted we were I got frustrated when I was with her. She could have turned herself inside out trying to give herself to me and I would have been frustrated. I wasn't obsessed with Jan because when thoughts of her came into my mind there was a cool falling away in my chest and I felt weak in the legs but the other things I had to do which didn't include her were still sweet, even the little things.

I didn't stop asking stupid questions just because I was

in heaven. During one of our intermissions I came up with: "What was Benson like?"

Since Benson was about the best man Andover had ever produced I didn't know how to take her laughter.

"I don't think the reason you're interested is the right one. You want to know if you're a better lover than he was. No."

"What?" I sat up fast.

"See? Kidding. Alan was a frightened little boy. You might think he dropped me, but it was the other way around. When he found out I was a little older and more experienced he had trouble being the lord and master. That's what he thought he had to be to have the respect of his friends."

"B.S. They were all jealous of him, I'm sure of that. Who wouldn't want to love an experienced woman, especially someone as pretty as you? That's just the kind of affair kids brag about back at the dorm. Of course there's usually nothing serious with a townie woman because it looks bad for her."

"Maybe a fling is what we did have. We had more dates than I told you, and I think he cared a lot for me, in his way, even after we broke up. But no more Phillips boys were coming after me, and there would have been some if he'd told them I was available and that I 'went all the way.' I think he probably never told the other boys that he'd stopped seeing me, hoping they would leave me alone."

"It wasn't altruism. He didn't want the other guys to hear your opinion of him. Reputation is everything."

She saw I was right. So much for the great Benson.

I learned a lot of other things that night—facts, I mean—besides what she taught me about sex. About her mother, for example (we had a long talk in the kitchen at 3 a.m.): she came from a very old, rich family. Jan had been brought up in a mansion back in Minnesota, with servants. Her father still had some money in stocks and things, but this was about the poorest she'd ever been.

Why had she come East?

Her mother had been getting worse and her father had been drinking too much, and during the summer, while she was living at home, there had been terrible scenes. Apparently her mother was a real fruitcake, hearing voices and so forth, and her father was violent when he drank a lot. (Breaking things, but not bones.) Only when the mother had been put in a home did Jan's life return to normal.

Since her mother's family had helped Mr. McBride with their daughter's care, the divorce wasn't full of a lot of sneaky infighting. Mrs. McBride didn't even know what was going on.

About her father: he was a changed man after he returned to the East. He and his wife had both been born and raised in a town not far from Andover and he felt that the East was his home. He had stopped the heavy drinking. Except for their unhappy love affairs life had been great with her dad.

The best news from Jan had to do with my Thanksgiving recess. After what her father had told me about staying over when I wanted, or when Jan wanted me to, I thought he might let her spend Thanksgiving at my place.

Jan was sure he'd want her to go. He'd be wanting to have Thanksgiving dinner with Ruth, and Jan and Ruth didn't get along. Nothing would make him happier than having Ruth stay with him at this house over the holidays. Jan had wanted to cook Thanksgiving dinner for me, but she agreed that helping my mother was the next best thing.

About four in the morning we were in her father's bedroom sitting naked on top of the covers, listening to the Mozart horn concertos and sipping wine. I fell asleep after Jan took me on a tour of the Milky Way one more time. She remembered to set the alarm so that there was time for another launch in the morning before I had to be in church.

I felt like death when she dropped me near the campus, but the weather had cleared. The white and red and green of the school was very clear, and my life seemed so much simpler.

ELEVEN

The choirmaster was paranoid. Everybody knew it. In a few years he'd be climbing the walls with Mrs. McBride.

When someone's getting paranoid they pass through an irritable stage where they try to do something about all the things that are bothering them. When they think you're trying to trip them up they might point a finger at you and give you a knowing look. Or say, "I know what you're up to, Bancroft. Believe me, *I know!*"

Our choirmaster, Mr. Lewis, went through this stage last year when I was an upper. This year the only way he let us know that he knew what was going on was with big eyes. He never did anything to stop us. He'd fix his eyes on the troublemakers—usually my section, the second basses—and his eyes would get bigger and bigger so that he seemed to be coming toward us.

It's a terrible human trait, but when someone's going insane people tend to help him across the line. They chauffeur him to the nuthouse. The guy might only be borderline, he might still find a few things about the everyday world worthwhile, but people will try to deny him the normal things he wants, and they'll make him doubt his normal behavior, as if he should realize that only the abnormal things about himself are genuine.

I was a normal human being and I'd inherited this cruel human trait. I was ashamed of myself because deep down I probably liked Mr. Lewis better than any other master. He'd won me with his Figaro aria after a school meeting. In costume! The whole school roared with laughter when he took the stage, but as soon as he started to sing he shocked everyone into silence. No one understood a word he was saying, but his voice was loud as hell, and Mr. Lewis was dead serious. Everyone knew something important was going on, something tragic, maybe, and it was impossible to laugh.

I knew that the Figaro aria wasn't supposed to be tragic, but it *was* the way Mr. Lewis sang it. To sing opera in front of seven hundred and eight-nine guys like us was a *tragic idea*. There's a point when ridiculousness is no longer funny. That's why clowns are always sad no matter what kind of smile they've got painted on. Mr. Lewis's audience was scared to death, I tell you. One of their instructors was going mad right before their eyes, and the school had given him its blessing.

I hate to admit it, but I was the worst of Mr. Lewis's tormentors. Or one of the worst, but I'd invented more kinds of torture than anyone else. Odd, but no one had ever thought of singing wrong notes before. That's how obedient people could become, even at a place like Andover. Musicians were incredibly obedient people, it was a characteristic defect.

Oh, everyone had sense enough to sing the wrong words. This was going on in the congregation. "A Mighty Farter Is Our God . . . " After that there was a lot of straining for effect, at least in my version. " . . . Amidst a flood, with gastric juice prevailing, etc."

We had to invent our changes on the spot, that was half the fun. Rarely would one of them catch on. I think "A Mighty Farter Is Our God" was standard by my senior year, and I ought to get credit for it. From the second line on there were a host of variations.

Wrong words didn't bother Mr. Lewis so much. Everyone would be singing something different and the sound would be some kind of dark diphthong, but Mr. Lewis liked that sound. When he gave me voice lessons he tried to get me to imitate him by "covering," and I never seemed to make him happy unless I could sing everything as a cross between OH and AH (AW).

When we would sing different words he'd stop us and complain that he couldn't hear the words. He'd take the passage over and so long as one kid sang the right words, Mr. Lewis would say, "That's better," and we could go on. His hearing was tremendously acute. He could pick the right words out of a hundred different wrong ones, and as long as *his* ears were satisfied, that was good enough for the public.

Singing wrong notes drove Mr. Lewis out of his mind instantly. First he'd swat at his right ear as if a mosquito had just touched down there. Then the hall would give back that little echo it had (another of his bugaboos) and he'd jump once into the air and swat his legs when he came down (he was a barehanded conductor).

At first I was the only one putting in the wrong notes. I was subtle about it. I started by flatting the pitches, but when I did that he knew that the second basses were off and he'd bawl us all out to try to get the innocent basses to turn on the culprit. Naturally, no one ever pointed the finger, you couldn't do a thing like that and be a good man.

After a time the feud between Mr. Lewis and the second basses got boring and the first and second tenors began to look a bit too angelic. Very subtly, using falsetto if I had to, I'd put in wrong notes that sounded like they came from the tenors. Even though the tenors were on the other side of the practice hall and all the way across the chancel when we were in chapel, I would aim the wrong notes at them and think like a ventriloquist. Sure enough, it would sound as if one of them had blown the note. Before long the rest of the choir was pulling the same stunt—very discreetly, just once in a while. But with everybody doing it, once in a while was damned often.

I think all the choirmembers liked Mr. Lewis. When it came to screwing up the music, we couldn't help ourselves.

There might have been a deeper motivation than a desire to see Mr. Lewis go berserk. As much as we liked serious music—we wouldn't have joined the choir if we didn't—we couldn't see why the shits out in the congregation should hear any.

I never asked myself why I wanted to drive Mr. Lewis insane, or why the other choirmembers were so eager to help me. Clearly we all felt it was the thing to do. And I think all of us felt guilty while we watched him disintegrate.

In retrospect I think I know why we were so awful to the poor man. Unlike most of our teachers, Mr. Lewis liked us. Maybe some of the other teachers did, too, but they were masters at making us feel next to worthless. Somehow we gave the most respect to the teachers who thought the least of us and we destroyed the mind of the man who thought we were halfway decent. I had to bear most of the guilt for my class at school, too, but Mr. Lewis had been tortured for more than a decade before I got to him, and I didn't have it in me to finish the job. There'd be a shred of normality left for next years biggest shits to go to work on.

The short guys were supposed to be in front and the tall guys in back so the school could see what a big choir we had. But that was too logical to let happen.

In spite of all the drills the tallest guys always ended up in front and Mr. Lewis had given up trying to figure out how it happened. Yet the short baritones came into view after all when the basses started lying on the floor between hymns. Channing and I had started it, but it had caught on fast and now all the basses were doing it. If it spread to the baritones maybe the school would put a stop to it.

I never understood the school's attitude. Rebellious behavior at Andover was usually punished at the drop of a hat. In chapel the administration fell down on the job completely.

The collection plate was another big laugh. At the start of the year some wiseguy started making change out of the collection plate. He'd put in a dollar and taken back seventy-five cents. Then inspiration struck and guys began to swipe the money. Pretty soon so many guys were swiping money that the plate would be empty when it came back from the pews. The religious fanatic would still put in his quarter, and there were holy wars when some other guy would make sure it didn't get through. Actual fighting in the pews. The fanatic just wanted his money back, but what kind of idiot would put anything on the plate in the first place? I thought I had the answer: the type who thought God was always watching. They expected us to sing for such imbeciles?

Still, I think the biggest blasphemy was lying down on the Lord. The sight must have demoralized the believers out front. After the opening hymn a big black mass near the altar fell out and created a sickening, sad bald spot. Then, when another hymn came along, like magic all the black was back, rising out of nowhere with a great clanking of chairs. (We sat on metal folding chairs because there weren't enough stalls to go around.)

Mr. Lewis never said anything about us. The guy who checked attendance from up by the organ pipes had nothing to do with us, either. He had enough trouble checking who was where out front. (Catholics and Jews went to church in town so the ranks were ragged on Sunday.) Somehow there was no one to force us to sit up. Oh, the chaplain, the boss, never gave us a thought. I'd swear the only skill he'd learned to equip him for life was how to read. He was a droning drone—one of God's creatures, maybe, but not much of one.

Channing and I were lying under our chairs after the opening hymn when his nose started to twitch.

"What is that?"

"Sorry. Been having sex all night."

"Here I am in the House of the Lord of a Sunday morning and the stench of sin is enough to gag me. Where did you find this hag, crawling on the street?"

"We met in a hardware store."

"Something wrong with her plumbing?" Channing was

about the fastest guy in school when it came to a stinging remark. Since he always looked as if he had just stepped out of a bath or onto a yacht, gutter talk was his specialty.

"Come on, give. An Abbot wench?"

He knew it was Jan.

"A student in college once."

"What a tale of woe. The laggard and the college dropout having trysts in back alleys. Bring her around the dorm. We've got a spare room. She's not a screamer, is she?"

It was time to stand and sing another Thanksgiving hymn.

"We gather together to ask for more dressing . . . "

I felt all worn out by the time we were back on the floor. Channing wouldn't leave me alone.

"You know it's not some whore. My girlfriend."

"You mean . . . she'll not be a virgin when you wed?"

"I don't want to hear any more shit about her."

The look in my eyes shut him up. A good man would have been appreciating him, but I was sick of all the shit and stink. There ought to have been some way we could talk about women without bringing in the dirt. But there wasn't. If anyone ever spoke *about* women with the same sweet words he spoke *to* them he'd have been laughed out of school.

I guess the purpose in being a good man was to practice having a tough life. If you were a good man, after dumping a plate of spaghetti in someone's face over dinner you waited for him to dump his in yours. Then the milk, the juice, the dessert. If you wanted to be good men you walked out of commons covered with food and you didn't look at each other and you went hungry. A good man was someone who made other people suffer, and was willing to take as good as he gave. As a code it helped us to understand each other and work and play together without bloodshed.

It was an effective code but it didn't deal with the reality of what we were and what we felt. Because the truth was we were a miserable bunch of bastards. We felt the lack of a family life and the warmth of home, and most of us keenly felt the lack of girls our age and their special warmth. By calling them every rotten name and referring to them as nothing but a hole we were able to live with our lack.

If you wanted to be honest about what a good man was, well, he was pathetic. But to see him that way you'd have to graduate. Not to be a good man at P.A. was to let on that you weren't miserable, that all the deprivations and hardships we shared didn't get you down.

Channing let me off. He had a book with him. I snoozed while he read. After the anthem he started in on me again, at first just chiding me for letting "a cunt" put the whammy on me. I insisted I wasn't under any spell.

"It's the guys around here that are living in dreamland, Channing. I might be overboard because of Jan, too romantic for you, but what's going on with her is real. The other girls we had were for sport."

"Speak for yourself."

"Didn't you ever feel disgusted about the woman afterward, and ashamed of yourself for all the bullshit you had to tell her to get her to give in? This is different. I'm never going to get enough of her."

"Oh, spare me. What you need is a hot shower, a strong cologne and a good night's sleep."

He saw me looking at him with tired contempt.

"I'm sick of playing games with you," he said. "I know what you're going through." I felt his wrestler's grip on my arm. "I'm envious as hell. I've got a bad reputation in my home town. All the girls I'm writing don't really know me. I couldn't get one to come up here if I tried. I've thought of playing around with the townies, but it would be what you said. High school girls are so incredibly stupid, and it does make me feel like a bastard to have to lie so much to get in their pants. It was a miracle you could find someone you care about. How old is she anyway?"

"Twenty-two in January, but don't let it get around. She

might be pissed at me for telling her age. She doesn't want people to think she's robbing the cradle."

"Twenty-one isn't old. It would be perfect, except all the women that age want to get married. First it's a degree they're worried about, then it's a pedigree. What a dismal scenario. Where is she going to college?"

"She was an A student at Bradford."

"Why didn't she finish if she was making A's?"

"She wanted to travel. She's lived in Europe. I told you that before."

"Smart girl. She sounds like someone even I could be interested in."

"You wouldn't be her type. You're not tall enough."

"What do you mean? I'm six feet. Is she an Amazon?"

"No, no. Five-ten and a half. But with heels she's as tall as I am."

"Well, that lets me out. But maybe not. I've never been with a woman that tall, it might be interesting."

I let the thought get to me and couldn't say anything.

"Come on, Bancroft, I'm serious. Give me her number in case the school gives you the boot."

"What makes you think I'd stop seeing her? Anyway, I'm not going to get kicked out. I'm going to do my best not to, put it that way."

"Then stop staying away from dorm all night, even if it means she'll have to use her own finger."

I didn't have to check, I knew he'd be giving me a sly smile, and I knew just as well that Channing would be the last person to rat on me. He'd provided the alibis before when I needed them.

"Tell you what, Chris, if Sanborn ever does come up looking for me, and I'm not in the dorm, I'll have Barton say I'm up with you, and you say you're not sure—you get the picture—I might be in Thomson's room, or Farnham's, or whatever. Maybe he'll give up. What a weak spot, huh? I can do the makeup work and I can go the rest of the term without cutting a class. Barton never takes a cut and he'll make sure I'm up and at 'em. But I can't give up my Saturday nights with Jan."

"I'll cover for you, Gordie, but take a word of advice. Don't make it every week. It already came up at the bullsession late last night. 'Where's Bancroft?' 'Out fucking the townie.' Too many people already know, and it would only take one enemy . . . "

"Nobody would dare rat on me."

"They might if they could do it anonymously. It would be nothing for Sanborn to check all the rooms. Even if he thought you were innocent, he might want to be sure." He paused. "So it's true what Barton says. You've turned over a new leaf."

"That's right. I'm going to see if any good comes out of working hard. I don't know why I'm doing it, really. Maybe it would give me some satisfaction to let them know what kind of student I could have been if I'd wanted to try."

"Mighty flimsy motivation."

"Not if your teachers don't think much of you to start with. They've always respected you, Channing. Not just your ability, but your desire to succeed. When the bastards started listening to my father and making me see a psychiatrist and giving me pep talks every time I turned around, I just gave up."

"You didn't have to see a psychiatrist last year, did you?"

"Sure, and be in a dorm with Dr. Hughes. He thought he was a psychiatrist, all right. How do you feel about this or that, that's all I ever heard."

"Well, I'll try not to worry too much about you, Bancroft. There's certainly nothing wrong with your attitude."

After chapel Channing walked all the way to commons with me and changed his mind. He didn't like the menu. He'd go down to the Andover Inn with some of his rich friends. He asked if I wanted to come along, but I had to turn him down. He couldn't offer to buy me Sunday dinner because that would mean he knew I didn't have money.

165

Every Andover boy was presumed to have money except the boys on scholarship. You knew who these people were because they worked in the commons doing all the kitchen and cleaning jobs. They were made to wear white coats so everyone would know who they were, and they would have had as much prestige if they went around dressed in black and white stripes dragging a ball and chain. It came as no surprise that Gill took money from perverts not to be one of them.

The Sunday midday meal was supposed to be the big treat of the week. They skimped on Sunday supper by giving you "mystery mounds" in order to put a few nuts and raisins on your tray, or maybe a slice of pumpkin pie or some other petroleum byproduct. I guess this meal was meant to reward us for sitting through the Sunday service. It was one of the few times we were served the kind of thing we ate at home. Roast chicken, roast beef. But when you're turning out eight hundred portions of anything it's mighty hard to keep that homey touch. If my wife ever put such shit in front of me I'd dump the plate right in her face.

The dish that had turned Channing around was leg of lamb. This was a gray-blue slab of something with a dab of mint jelly beside it. The only time you could find anything green in that kitchen was when they dished up mint jelly. Next to the lamb would be some gray peas. Next to that some powdered potatoes with something that looked like *café au lait* splashed on it. There'd be more of this *café au lait* stuff in your soupbowl setting off a bit of carrot, a few grains of barley. The same color motif was carried over to the frosting on the cake which passed for dessert. The frosting was honest: 95% sugar, 4% grease and 1% coloring. The frosting was fine, but you couldn't live on it.

I found an empty table and tried to eat as fast as I could. The next thing I knew I had half the linemen on the football team sitting next to me. I knew what they had come for. Thomson had been spreading the word.

"Well, Bancroft, does she gobble the gook the way they

say?" Porter speaking. His neck was bigger around than his head, but that was true of a lot of them. I waited till they were all eating.

"You want some dirt, don't you? Something to quote."

Knowing their game didn't make it any less pathetic.

"We wondered if you were big enough to be walking around in Alan Benson's shoes." This was one of the biggest guys in the school, and size meant everything to him.

"Palpably not, Browning, but I seem to be the person she wants, all the same. Hard to figure, isn't it? How could a woman smart and beautiful enough to snow an Alan Benson fall for someone like me? Maybe because she got fed up with football players who were always in a huddle trying to think up dirty shit to say about her. I don't care what you say or what you think. Where you guys are concerned I've graduated."

These pricks had so much prestige they didn't have to catch on right away when you were downing them. They played together and laughed together, but usually only one or two of them did the talking and decided when it was time to laugh. The best thing they did together was stay silent. They could sit silent for a hell of a long time looking straight at you and feeling at ease. Intimidation was their stock in trade, but they only tried it when they were in a group. Alone, many of them were nothing but softhearted slobs.

"We know where she lives, Bancroft," said Porter. "Some of the guys used to know her. We might like to pay her a visit, talk over old times."

"Gee, fellas, that sounds like a good idea, but you can count me out. When I visit, I go alone, you know. She expects me to. And since not one of you has seen her in two years, I hope you'll phone her first and make sure you're welcome. It might frighten her to see a bunch of guys who look like you just come walking up to her door out of the blue."

"What's that supposed to mean?" said two of them in unison.

"You're kind of scary-looking, that's all. Big as you are, with such mean faces. You'd be well-behaved, no doubt. The honor of the school, and all that. Isn't that what you're fighting for in those big games?"

"If you're being sarcastic, Bancroft, I'd watch it." A new voice. Forget who it was. The same old voice. They were speaking as one, but I knew that a lot of them were privately ashamed of the bullying.

"I wasn't being sarcastic. If you'd like to know her better, I've been giving you good advice. I'll tell you another thing. Don't say you're friends of Alan Benson. She doesn't think much of Al."

"She got something against football players?" The voices of these Neanderthals were always hoarse. It was all the "hut, hut" business, and the yelling encouragement in cold air.

"Not that I know of, but she would have if she knew what you guys are putting me through. You come over here and move in on me all at once and start asking me about a woman you don't know, start asking me about dirty stuff she doesn't even know the word for, much less how to do. I'll let you in on a little secret. She might have wanted to go to bed with Benson, but it never happened. Benson couldn't get it up."

Nothing intimidating about their silence now. They were blinking at each other, at a loss to decide who was going to lead the counterattack.

"So you want to see her? Pay her a visit? Go ahead! She'll open the door and tell you to beat it. And you'll go, because you don't want to get kicked out of school. And that's the same reason you're not going to get revenge on me. I've got the worst record of anyone in school. I don't think one of you all-American boys wants to risk his college career over an insult from Gordon Bancroft. But if anyone does, go ahead, try to kick my ass. I say try, because you'd better want to kill me. I've got nothing to lose, and I'll cut your fuckin' throat."

There were smiles at these big words. I couldn't help feeling these guys were starting to like me.

"Fuckin' A I will! Is there anything else you want to know before I dump my tray?"

"Yeah," said Porter. "How come you got all the luck? There isn't a guy on the team who wouldn't give his right arm to go with that girl. She's a knockout."

I sat there with my elbows just inside my tray and my head in my hands and thought about that.

"I know, it's weird," I said, finally. "The things that count so much in this school don't mean a thing out there. I can't get over it myself. She called Alan Benson a 'frightened little boy.' Don't take offense, I'm not comparing him to you just because he played football. I saw him play. He was great. I couldn't believe someone saying a thing like that about him."

"I can." A new voice. "I used to scrimmage against him. He was a mean prick, but he hated to get hit. He used to want me to go easy on him."

"What do you think, idiot," said Porter, "he'd want to miss an important game because of something a dumb lower did to him in practice?"

"Gentlemen," I said, getting up with my tray.

"Take it easy, Bancroft," they mumbled, or the equivalent. In spite of myself it felt good to be accepted.

They weren't such bad guys, I was telling myself on the way back to the dorm. They'd have been good friends if I'd grown up with them, and they might have been my buddies in the army. Andover had turned them into shits, but that was true of all of us. When people found out what behavior was expected of them, and found that they could cough it up, they didn't waste a lot of time trying to be different. Everyone I knew here was shooting for the same goal. Conformity was bound to be a problem.

But not for me. No longer. I was shooting for something different. I wanted to be a person that Jan could love, whatever that person had to be. If she wanted me to quit school and come to live with her, I would do it—I wouldn't think twice. If she wanted me to stay in school I'd do the best I could. (I'd have to do my best in any case.)

I didn't feel any pressure. I wouldn't be fighting the work, I could handle it. "Do it for yourself!" That was all they ever told me. But I couldn't "do it for myself" and I couldn't "do it for my parents." I loved my parents, but it had always been much too hard to make them happy.

I felt I could do anything for Jan. She would only have to ask. If she wanted me to provide for her, I was ready. If it was too soon, then I would think of school as a way for me to become a better provider.

I no longer felt like a son. My father's hold was slipping.

I was becoming someone who thought like a father.

TWELVE

I took Channing's advice and stayed in the dorm the next Saturday night. But I'd already done something much more dangerous. I'd stayed with Jan on a school night, Wednesday, after another game which we'd won 3-2 thanks to our forwards.

I'd played hard but I'd been up against some slippery guys who made me look bad a few times. Jan and her dad didn't seem to notice my blunders. If anything they'd been more thrilled than usual because the game had been a contest and we had won it.

On Saturday I had an away game and I was bushed by the time we got back. The game didn't take it out of me so much (an easy win), it was the bus ride back. Sitting quietly all of us got stiff. We never sang.

I called Jan and explained. I'd told her my fears before. She'd been ready for the worst.

She agreed that I shouldn't risk anything since we were going to be together over the whole Thanksgiving recess— four days. Four days in a row!

It didn't seem like much of a vacation, but four days with Jan would entail an incredible number of contacts between us, thousands of kisses, countless moments and incidents. I remembered that long first night I spent with her as a kind of vacation. I had felt like a different person when I returned to the school routine.

Five nights together! The Thanksgiving recess was four and a half days because when we got off on Wednesday afternoon there weren't any games scheduled and all of us were free until Monday morning. Some poor bastards had to hang around the school the whole time because they couldn't afford to take a trip across country for such a short holiday. But all the New Englanders could enjoy the Thanksgiving recess as long as they had a family.

It would have been tough darts if a New England guy couldn't go home for Thanksgiving. New England was what Thanksgiving was all about, in my opinion.

The last two weeks before the holidays I did more work than I'd done my entire upper year. I stopped lifting weights at night. Instead I did calisthenics like crazy during the time allotted for sports. While I was doing my sit-ups and push-ups I was memorizing irregular verbs.

The guys in the dorm thought I was crazy and I caught some looking at each other to see if I was to be shunned, behavior I remembered from my first days at the school, two years ago. Even my friends looked upset when they came across me mumbling to myself and I was getting hand signals that meant, "It's your life." I had a book open on the floor of the chancel now and Channing had followed suit.

Thanks to Channing some of the other second basses might have already been wondering if reading a book between hymns was the new "in" thing to do.

Barton still gave me pep talks in the morning before I shouldered my responsibilities and tottered off to the Main Quad. He fed me school news by the shovelful. He scoured the campus to find people who had something good to say about me and then tried to talk to my teachers. He did everything he could to encourage me and acted as a one-man publicity department by telling anyone who would listen what a great guy I was.

Judging by the response to me in commons, Barton was doing a lousy job. People were looking at me out of the corners of their eyes as if they thought I was about to spring.

The fact that I was going to a psychiatrist once a week was beginning to make sense to them. For the first time in my school career boys were being polite to me. It was a bad sign, but I didn't have time to worry about impending disasters. All I cared about was my standing in class.

I may have been foaming at the mouth, but I was moving up in the pack. My teachers were calling on me every day. They made a fuss about the correctness of my answers, their brilliance and thoroughness, in order to humiliate the rest of the class. "If Bancroft can do it . . . " Thanks to me even the hardworking members of my class were perceived to be loafers. At the start of classes I was greeted with as much affection as a doctor coming with bad news.

I went to Dr. Bellini on Tuesday with a pile of books under my arm and took about five minutes out of my busy schedule to give him a rundown of my activities and plans. Then, since his office was so comfortable, I wondered if he would mind studying with me for the next forty-five minutes.

I knew I had him over a barrel. He wanted to earn his money, and he may have wanted to hear some juicy stuff about Jan, but for years he'd been saying, "Do a little work!" till he was blue in the face. It would put his sincerity in doubt if he denied me the chance to.

When I'd seen Jan on Wednesday after our 3-2 win I'd had two books along, but she didn't gripe about it. She'd already told me she approved of the way I'd chosen to finish out the school year. She was delighted that the other boys and the teachers were getting to see how bright I was even if Harvard or Yale would never know. And she was pleased that she could be the cause of such a change in me. "Thrilled."

Since I'd also told Mr. McBride about my hard work I had to explain why I had to work so hard, and this was the first he had heard of all my troubles at school. He wasn't any less friendly toward me, but I could tell he was looking at me in a new light and giving some thought to my future.

He'd probably thought I was a cinch to be going to Harvard or Yale or Princeton or someplace like most of the Andover guys, and that his daughter was hooked up with someone who was making the right connections and might go far in life.

I gave him a lame account of the virtues of a state university for someone like me. I needed to consolidate what I'd learned at P.A., I told him, instead of going on to more difficult stuff right away. I needed time to "stabilize my foundation."

None of my careful plans roused him to encouragement. There was merit in everything I wanted to do, according to him, but I couldn't shake the impression that he was disappointed in me.

For all I knew he had problems of his own. Ruth might have been giving him a hard time. He was moody just like his daughter—Jan admitted it. He was so much better now than he had been back in Minnesota that she tended to think of him as a happy man regardless of how a stranger might take him.

I agreed that he seemed to be happy with his life, pleased about us, even happy with his work, since he had said as much, but I had the feeling that something was gnawing at him.

Jan didn't want to think what. After all she'd been through, who could blame her?

There was a big difference in the way Jan and I made love on Wednesday night. With her father in the house—sleeping right down the hall, for godssakes—I couldn't see where we were going to whoop it up and march her little bed around the way we had the last time. There weren't any love words because they would have sounded dirty.

Maybe I was cramping her style. "Dirty" felt right with her at times. I could even imagine her telling her father about the stuff we did which had a hint of perversion about it. According to her, Mr. McBride was a lapsed Catholic, but the lapse had taken place a couple of generations ago. He didn't think much of morality such as it had been when he was growing up, and he was as comfortable with French-type immorality as she was.

It scared me to realize she was being considerate of my feelings, if that's what it was. Anyway, our sex was different. She was doing her duty, letting me have her body because I expected it. Of course, having someone as beautiful as Jan naked in bed with me in her father's house went far beyond any expectation I'd ever had of life away from home, or life as a man of the world.

Since it was impossible for us to cut loose I drifted with her in a sumptuous boredom that made me think of the poetry of Baudelaire. Sex with someone like Jan could never be completely boring, but tonight, even when she was putting something into it, I thought of her as an older woman who was amused.

I came, but it only felt great momentarily. She never came at all. I always wanted our loving to be spectacular and I was worried that I'd let her down, but she told me that our sex had been some of the best she'd ever had.

I hated it when she made comparisons like that because I thought the only proper comparison was with the other times we'd been together, but I was used to her sounding like a whore whether she was one or not.

We had a quiet talk in bed before I had to hit the books and she put my mind at ease about something that had been bothering me plenty. She was putting in a diaphragm before I came to see her and would take it along whenever we went somewhere in case there might be a chance to screw.

I didn't need to see it. I knew all about birth control, and the diaphragm in particular, because my mother used one.

It was true, my mother did, but I had no idea how a piece of rubber as shallow as a dish was going to be a safeguard against somebody's big dick spewing sperm all over the place.

It was a policy with me to let women break the ice

about birth control. If there was a problem about it, I was sure to hear from them. As long as they thought they knew what they were doing, let them practice birth control any way they wanted.

Actually, if I'd thought Jan would be willing to keep my baby, I'd have tried my damnedest to get something past that catcher's mitt of hers. It was the thought of knocking up someone I didn't know that scared the hell out of me—one of the girls from last summer, for instance. I hated rubbers and didn't even trust them that much, but that was the thing to do back in Dudbury, and the girls even knew how to put them on you.

I'd been sure that Jan was protected somehow because the subject hadn't come up the first time we were together. Everything had been so natural that it would have killed me if I'd had to go into my wallet and fish out the only Trojan I ever got from a girl, one with a damaged wrapper that I was keeping for sentimental reasons.

After a week plus working like Sisyphus there had finally been a small reward. Sanborn caught me coming in for my fifteen-minute cram session before chow and had me into his office. He revealed that ever since I became the first student in P.A. history to be on probation twice (not to mention one general warning and six postings) there had been weekly reports about me from all my teachers. Until now, getting those reports had been the low moment of the week for Sanborn, but everything had changed. The reports, his mood, and . . . now he believed it . . . me. He couldn't have been any happier if I had been his own son.

The thought of having Sanborn for a father was enough to make me laugh out loud, but I kept my composure. I had to live up to my new image.

Sanborn was going to write to my parents quoting from all the glowing reports about me and adding some remarks of his own about what a delightful young man I was to have around the dorm. He would post this letter today—special delivery—so that it would reach my parents before I showed up for turkey.

Sending such a letter was Sanborn's duty—he'd have written another glum one if the reports had been the usual—so I didn't think of it as a reward, but that special delivery stamp was above and beyond the call of duty and I would have kissed him for it if he had looked or acted a bit more European.

When Wednesday noon rolled around I was jumping out of my skin. I'd packed a small bag and dumped in some books just in case I felt like working over the next four days. However, the orgy of study was over for the moment and I acted like my old self around the guys.

As for them, my being a straight arrow for a couple of weeks was hard to remember against my long record of misdeeds. Anyway, everyone was one of the guys when it came time to leave and star athletes were chatting with weenies out in front of the dorms where their bags were piled.

The same thing was happening over in front of the main entrance to the gym where there was a turnaround. The line of cabs extended to the main road to Boston, and in order to find two or three guys to split the cost of a cab some of the biggest men in school were suddenly on a first-name basis with guys they'd never noticed before (except in the address book).

Naturally, Jan was coming for me at the dorm. I didn't want some asshole trying to mooch a ride in the half-seat she had in back, and I didn't want any of the guys on the football team to get a look at her or there was sure to be a high-speed chase on the way into Boston and beyond.

Sanborn was out in front of the house saying goodbye to us while his pregnant wife was watching and swaying from side to side. Since the Healy was close to the ground and the top was always on these days Sanborn couldn't get a good look at her, but the idiots from my dorm swarmed over her car before we could pull away. I knew she'd knock them dead because she was only wearing a sweater on top.

Did she wonder what all those guys had heard about her to make them so curious? Some knew quite a bit, that was the sad truth, and it wasn't my doing. (Suspiciously, Thomson was nowhere to be seen.)

I kept my head down till we got onto the highway, and Jan thought that was funny. I told her that I was trying to avoid harassment from the guys who remembered her, but she was sure that no one remembered her and wanted me to stop being silly.

I didn't relax until we were on the Massachusetts Turnpike.

Relax isn't the right word, though. I was riding high. It was easy to picture us this way in the future.

Oh, I was behind the wheel now. It had been her idea to pull over and let me drive. In the future I'd be driving her like this when we were off on a vacation to Vermont, or down to Bucks County, Pennsylvania, maybe, where I had some connections. I'd own the car, though, and there wouldn't be anybody waiting for us and wondering "where can they be" and there wouldn't be anybody at home waiting for us to come back. We'd choose where we wanted to be from day to day and we would belong wherever we were at the moment, that would be our place.

There was no one wondering "where can they be" at the moment because I hadn't told my parents that I was bringing Jan. And I didn't tell Jan that I hadn't told my parents until we were getting near the Connecticut border.

"But Gordon, you said you'd made all the arrangements. I don't think dad would have wanted me to go if he'd known I wasn't expected. How could you do such a thing?"

"Try to bear with me, Jan. I had a good reason. If I had told them ahead of time that I was bringing you, they'd have called the whole thing off. Well, that's not exactly true, because there are going to be a lot of guests besides you."

"Oh, no. I was hoping for an intimate dinner."

"You'll have plenty of time to get intimate with them. They'll let us stay."

"Are you sure? What'll we do if they don't?"

"We'll stay in a motel somewhere. Don't worry, I know my way around town. We could even go to New York for the weekend. I've got some friends and even a great-uncle who's got a fantastic spread in the Village. He'd put us up. He's kind of a lush and he'd love to be hospitable to me now that the rest of the family is giving him the cold shoulder."

"Listen, I've got some money with me. A hotel might be better."

"I could borrow some dough from Tom. He's still got all the money he made last summer. If I promise to pay him interest he'll give me the whole bundle. I'd rather not do it, though. My folks will come through, you'll see. They've got to, there's a precedent. My mother let me and this girl Sheila Burke sleep out on the porch last summer. It's a sleeping porch, we've got twin beds out there. Well, we went to bed in different beds, but I was in hers when my mother came in ringing her bell to tell us breakfast was ready. Sounds crazy, but it's kind of cute as long as you're not getting up for school like Tom is when that bell starts ringing. Anyway, when she saw me and Sheila there like that she just smiled."

"Was this one of the girls you had sex with?"

"Oh, we weren't doing anything at the time. We did a lot of things, though. Still, from what I hear, I'm about the only guy in town who didn't go all the way with Sheila."

"Hmm. Well, if your parents would let you sleep with a girl like that . . ."

"Oh, she didn't become a whore till we broke up."

"She was trying to make you jealous, I suppose."

"Maybe she was, but all she did was make me feel sorry for her."

"That's something in your favor. Look, Gordon, if your parents don't want me to stay, I'm not going to feel right having Thanksgiving dinner in your home. I'd rather go out with you someplace. Maybe we could team up with some of the people you know in New York."

I told her to wait and see. I was pretty sure Sanborn's

letter was going to make a big difference in my mother's morale, and my father would have to admit that I wasn't as worthless as he had thought. My father might be persuaded that all was not lost for me if I told him that I planned to transfer to Harvard and room with Barton during my sophomore year there. I could have told my dad about these plans in a letter, but I was saving the news for Thanksgiving. Also, I was counting on Jan to put my father in a good mood.

"You're my ace in the hole. A girlfriend as pretty as you will put him on his best behavior. Stick close and I won't even have to listen to any lectures."

I started to choke as we got closer to Dudbury, so I talked Jan into stopping and buying some beer. I had two and she drank one herself. The beer calmed my nerves and I was actually looking forward to seeing my parents when we pulled up late that afternoon.

While Jan was still in the background my mother embraced me on the doorstep. I thought someone had died, but no, there was my father coming up to shake my hand gravely (it was the first handshake in more than a year) and then Tom, who threw an arm around my neck.

My father looked as if he'd just been kicked in the balls. My mother followed his eyes. My brother pushed past to see.

I pushed past all of them to run interference as Jan approached.

"Mom, dad, Tom, this is Janet McBride. She's my girlfriend. It's because of her that I've been able to get some work done this term. She's my inspiration."

My father had her right arm, my mother her left.

My mother wanted to drag her into the kitchen where they could get to know each other while dad and I talked.

My father wanted to drag her into the living room and feast his eyes while I kept my mother occupied. I did need to tell mom how her financial support was finally paying off.

We all ended up in the living room with my mother trotting back and forth with hors d'oeuvres and my father with drinks. I was only allowed to drink beer at home, but my father completely forgot about the rule when Jan asked for sweet vermouth and he gave me sherry. It was easy to imagine that I'd been gone a long time and had fought a war or something as I sat in the living room of the old house with a sherry in my hand watching Jan dazzle my parents.

I was wondering why I'd been worried whether my parents would let her stay. They'd have given her their own big bed if only I weren't going to be sleeping with her.

I pushed boldly on: "Before we start telling stories and getting lit I think we'd better get a few things straight about our plans. Jan and I sleep together, and her father lets us sleep together at her place."

I looked blandly over to my father. Nothing but a wistful smile there. Could he have been envious? The thought that he could envy me made me remember how much I used to love him and I started to get tears in my eyes.

"If you want us for Thanksgiving you're going to have to let us stay together," I said in the hardest voice I could find.

"But where are we going to put you, dear?" said my mother, all sweetness and worry.

"They can have my room and I'll sleep in the guest room," said Tom, helpfully.

"There are twin beds in that room. It's where I used to sleep with Tom," I told Jan. "I don't think that's what we want." I faced down the folks. "We'll stay in the guest room."

"But that bed is only a one and a half," said mom.

"We don't need much room. We're used to sleeping in each other's arms."

I heard my brother say "wow" under his breath.

"I don't see anything wrong with that arrangement as long as Janet will be comfortable," my father put in, trying to look as if he had more important things on his mind.

"Oh, boy, then I get to have girls overnight when *I'm* a senior."

181

My father looked at Tom as if he were a dog that had just shit the rug.

"Good," I said. "I'm glad that's settled. Now we can get to the important stuff. What's for dinner, mom?"

While my mother was telling me what she had planned, Jan stood and moved to her side. My father and brother were watching so closely she could have been carrying a bomb.

"Why don't you let me help you get things ready, Mrs. Bancroft? I'd like to learn my way around your kitchen so I can help you on the big day."

"I'd love you to help, dear, but you've got to call me Peggy."

When the ladies were gone the rest of us came down out of the clouds.

Tom fired the first shot. My father was staring at the chair Jan had left, watching the crater she'd made as it slowly disappeared.

"Jesus, Gordie, where did you find her? What a knockout. And the way she dresses you can tell there's nothing cheap about her, in spite of her figure."

"I've failed you, son . . . "

This was usually the beginning of a list of things that were wrong with me that my father could have prevented by sending me to a military school when I was 8 years old.

"I can see that clearly now. You must have something wonderful in you to interest a girl like that, and I've been blind to it. I refused to see. I should have been encouraging you, and instead I've been carping about stupid things you did when you were going through a phase."

"Gee, thanks, dad, it makes me feel good to know that you still care about me a little."

"Care about you! Do you see what an ungrateful bastard you are? Care about you? I've sweat blood over you, boy! The amount of worry you've given me over the past year has taken ten years off my life. Before you went away to school I thought of myself as a young man. Forty-three I was, and I was thinking how lucky I was to have a son at a school like Andover, with a chance to go from there to a famous old New England university, a chance I never had, with a certain career after that, a life that wouldn't wear him down the way mine has me. Yes, I thought my worries were over. You know, you were always the only one that worried me, Gordon. Your brother may not have your talents, but he's the steady type like your mother. He'll find a place in this world without even trying. Now look at me at forty-five!"

His voice was up so high it would take him an hour to wind down.

"You don't look a bit different to me now than you did two years ago, dad. Tell him it's the truth, Tom."

"It's the truth, dad."

"Then you're both liars. But I forgive you, Tom. I know you'll say anything Gordon tells you to. I'm a WRECK! My hair is falling out! My face is full of wrinkles! My doctor tells me I've got an ulcer. Thank God we caught it in time or I might have bled to death. Tell me what you think about this, Gordon. Are young men supposed to turn into old men between the ages of forty-three and forty-five? Is that happening to any other men you know?"

"I don't know that many men your age, but I don't think it's unheard of. Once I read about a guy who went to bed with black hair and woke up all white. Kinda makes you wonder what his dreams were like. No, I tell you, this really did happen: Humphrey Bogart's hair started falling out by the handful overnight. One of my girlfriends last summer read it in a movie magazine. If it can happen to Humphrey Bogart . . . "

"You've changed? Is that what they expect me to believe? Ha! Your mother believes it. I don't blame her, poor thing, she hangs onto every good word that's ever been said about you, and believe me that doesn't give her much to hang onto, Mr. Andover Boy. She's been crying her eyes out every night."

"C'mon, dad," said Tom, "she doesn't cry every night. Once in a while, maybe."

"Are you calling your own father a liar?"

"No, but I can hear everything that's going on in there."

"I tell you she's been crying her eyes out, and well she might. So you've been making an effort for a whole week, your housemaster tells us. Isn't that nice of you. Of course it doesn't mean a damn thing any more because you'll be lucky to pass, and your fall term grades are all that matter for Harvard and Yale."

"You'd be surprised. I might pull higher grades than you think. I know I'm going to rack my final exams. I'm going for a hundred and high honors is only an 88."

"Will that put the hairs back in my head? Will your mother's smile ever be beautiful again?"

"What are you talking about? Are you accusing me of ruining mom's *smile?*"

"Yes! I am! Peggy used to have a beautiful broad smile, and now it's nothing but a timid little one. She can't even *force* a smile. Her cheeks start quivering. You tell me that's not her nerves. The next thing you know she'll be having one of those nervous breakdowns you hear about. We all know what *that* means."

"I can sympathize with you, dad, but did you ever stop to think about all the starving people in India?"

My mother made an appearance at that point and there was no trace of any kind of smile. Jan followed looking worried.

"John, I won't have it. We can hear you out in the kitchen. We agreed that we weren't going to discuss Gordon's problems over Thanksgiving. I'm ashamed to have Janet hear you talk that way."

"Forget it, ma. He'll never lay off me. It's force of habit. Now he's accusing me of ruining your looks."

"Gordon, that goes for you, too. I want this to be a happy time for us all."

My father was biting his lip and thinking. She had him on the run.

"We can always jump in the car and get the hell out of here. I don't want to spoil your fun. Jesus, all I did was arrive . . ."

"I'm not going to let anything be spoiled. I think Janet's a lovely girl and I want our friends to meet her."

"I do, too," said my father in a surprisingly soft, low voice. "I'm sorry I flew off the handle. It just drives me crazy when he tells me I haven't cared about him. You know what we've been through."

"We've been very concerned about Gordon for the last two years," my mother said to Jan. "If you care for him I'm sure you can understand what it must be like to live so far away, where it's so difficult to show him our support . . ."

I snorted. I couldn't help it. My father raised his eyebrows and gave my mother his "I told you so" look.

Jan's voice surprised me. Firm. "I don't see what's wrong with a family argument. My father and I argue all the time. I like him to know how I feel and he wants me to know his feelings, too. It takes an argument sometimes for me to see how much he loves me."

"Well, it's not like that around here," I said bitterly. "All you'll see is how close we can come to killing each other."

"That isn't true, Gordon," said my mother. "I wish you'd stop trying to provoke your father."

"I know what he's trying to do," said the big man. "I won't give him the satisfaction. I'm content to let him go his merry way. He thinks he doesn't need any guidance from his parents. He doesn't want to listen. He'll hang himself sooner or later."

"See what I mean, Jan? He couldn't finish me with his fists, he tried that already, so he wants to see if he can goad me into suicide. Why don't you knock it off, dad, the way mom says. A fat lot I can do to change my record while I'm down here on a four-day recess. But I brought some books,

I'll have you know, and I was grinding the last two weeks to catch up."

"I know, and we're proud of you, dear."

"Two weeks," said my father with sarcastic appreciation.

I went out to the kitchen with Jan and left my mother to cope with the old man. I picked up the sherry bottle on the way and the dusty bottle of sweet vermouth.

"What do you think, Jan? Should we try to stick it out? Shit, I shouldn't have brought you."

"Don't say that. Your mother's sweet. It's wonderful to know her. And your father will come around. Try to be more cheerful. You're very antagonistic toward him."

"I'll say I am. He starts spouting that shit as soon as I come through the door. He thinks he's going bald, so it's my fault. He's getting an ulcer—that's my fault, too. Pity my poor brother if I make the honor roll and he has to be the scapegoat. I know I let my father down up there, but Jesus Christ, am I the only thing he's got going for him? It's like a horserace and he's got his life's savings on me. He's convinced I'm going to be a winner . . . against all the odds. That's the trouble, see. He's only concerned about evidence when it proves him right."

"Doesn't his work keep him busy?"

"He's making army training films lately. It's been quite a comedown for him. Mostly he just sits on his ass and dreams his Ivy-League dreams."

"You're awfully hard on him."

"I've got a right to be. But that's OK. I'm with my mother. We'll bury the hatchet for a couple of days. One thing, Jan—you've got to promise me. Don't lose faith in me on the strength of what my father says. I know I've got it in me to do something great someday. I don't know what it is yet, I don't even know what kind of career I want. School has got me all twisted around. But when I find out what I want to do, I'll give it everything I've got."

She put her arms around me and kissed me hard on the

mouth. We were still in each other's arms when my mother walked in. Not a word. She just went about her business with a timid smile on her face, humming faintly. What a great mother I had. And what a girl to kiss me like that in front of her.

THIRTEEN

When it was time for the big dinner at about 3 o'clock on Thursday afternoon Jan had eaten with us Bancrofts twice already and she was beginning to feel like one of the family.

Dinner the night before had been solemn thanks to the sour expression on my father's face and all the self-conscious chewing. My mother didn't help any by asking Jan all the questions she could think of and depriving my father of the chance to ask the same questions when he was in a better mood. Brunch had been a big success because everyone was excited about what was about to come, and the people who were supposed to come, people who'd been my parents' best friends since the early days of their marriage and now lived as much as a hundred miles away.

It hadn't occurred to me until now, but this would be the first Thanksgiving in quite a while that I wouldn't get to feel up Susan Osborn. It was getting to be as traditional as mincemeat.

Jan had won my parents over and my father was even beginning to tolerate my presence in the house, but Jan and I had had some problems with the guest room.

At least the room was downstairs and had its own bath. (My brother and my parents slept in two enormous bedrooms under the dormers on the second floor, at opposite ends of the house.) Our bed really was too small, smaller even than Jan's. I'd slept on it a few times long ago when my mother had kicked me out of my bedroom for fighting with Tom, so I felt at home without being comfortable.

Now I was the one who didn't care how much noise we made and Jan was inhibited. She was convinced the walls were thin when she could hear my parents and my brother moving around. I told her that the carpets upstairs would deaden any sound from below, but she wouldn't buy it. She claimed to know a lot about how houses were built, and how could I argue with an architect's daughter?, but I didn't think our house was flimsy. I'd been beating hell out of it for years, or Tom and I had. At one time or another we'd slammed into all the walls, and I'd even tried to put my fist through them, but not since I weighed about fifty pounds less than I did now.

Making love to Jan so as not to make a sound frustrated me plenty. I'd been full of her all day. I'd never been with her so long at a stretch without the chance to relieve my tension. "Relieve my tension"—isn't that nice. Without the chance to make love to her in some way. I never looked at Jan the way I looked at a buddy, just listening to what she had to say and thinking of something to say in reply. I looked at all of her, and I could never look at all of her without wanting her clothes off and my hands on her sleek back and her softness pressed against me.

I'm not saying that fucking was all she was good for. She had a lot to say. But I heard everything she had to say through a haze of desire. It was like talking through music. After wanting her all day, when the chance came to have her clothes off, to have her against me, I didn't care that much about my surroundings.

Yes, it was a change in me. The first time we were together I'd turned down the chance to have her on a big hard bed in order to be with her on a small soft one with frills that meant she was a good girl and what was happening was romantic. Now I wouldn't have minded taking her in the back alleys that appealed to Channing.

The different places in the world were the same to me. Her presence was my environment. Outside of her influence the world was old and peeling. Even where it glittered the luxury of it was sterile next to the luxury of her breasts, her limbs, and the deep, warm, wet insides of her. (The word luxury didn't go far enough to describe the welcome she gave me there, delicate and precise like the way she embraced me in the focus of her shining eyes.)

We started out gently, on our sides. I felt like a Roman eating grapes. The idleness of our movements made me think of soft bellies and boredom. Right at the start we were far from the clutches of decency. I teased her the way I knew she liked me to do by pulling it all the way out, then sliding it around in front for a moment before I gave a little push to get back inside.

She wouldn't budge. Not a whimper. She was touching me tenderly and in the faint light from the window I could see her eyes were open, watching me. They were her dead eyes, not the shining eyes that thrilled me.

I could hate her when she was passive like this or too gentle when she stroked me. She seemed so much older then. A woman who could say "dear boy." Her caresses were already saying it.

Reaching for the response I remembered I forced my way. Then she was pushing, trying to get me out. I rolled on top and let my weight press down where we were joined. She got her arms between us and said, "What's got into you?" in a strangled voice. Her eyes were fierce and I froze. For a long time the only movement was my erection slipping away. Then she began to cry and I came to my senses and rolled off. I wanted to sob with her but I was so stunned that the tears wouldn't come.

I knew I should commiserate but I was afraid to stroke her gently or even hold her because she might think I wanted to have sex. Naturally, the way it did whenever I was tied up in knots, my mouth went ahead and made things worse.

"I couldn't help myself, forgive me," I was saying. "I'm sorry."

None of it rang true. She knew I was writhing. It was like telling the judge, "Nice to see you! Good to be back!"

She said she wanted to sleep. I could tell that she didn't want my body to touch her.

I lay awake half the night, forced to sleep on my side, but the main reason I couldn't sleep was that I'd made her cry. The only time I'd spent a worse night was camping out in the rain when Tom and I couldn't keep the water out of our tent. No, on second thought this night was worse. I'd been angry out there in the wet woods, but I hadn't feared for my life. Tonight I was listening to my heartbeat and wondering if hearts could really break. And I had to think to breathe. I thought that maybe I didn't deserve to live, and I knew that if I lost Jan, I wouldn't want to anyway.

From our first words in the morning she led me to believe that everything was all right. *She* apologized to *me* for last night! According to her, she hadn't been fair to me.

The next thing I knew she was kneeling by the bed making love to me with her mouth. I was leaning back on my elbows with my feet on the floor. It took me a while to get over the embarrassment of feeling too much like a king. As much as I was enjoying the way she was making me feel, I knew I'd never be able to come. It would be vile to come in her mouth, or right in her face if she got her mouth away in time. Then I realized that she was doing different things to me. It was like a rain of fire.

Somebody was walking around upstairs, or staggering. The way the heels came down I knew it was my father going for his morning piss. His feet were bad enough, but I hoped she wouldn't have to listen to him pee for five minutes straight the way I'd been forced to all my life.

She never broke stride. A whore would've had to charge a thousand dollars for something like this.

Suddenly my arms, my chest and legs were stiffening. All my blood was rushing to the center of me. I erupted all over the place but she didn't try to get out of the way. Any movement would have meant revulsion, but there wasn't the trace of one. She stayed motionless so long I couldn't help but feel she was grateful to have reached my seedy center.

Could there be any doubt that this was the most generous woman on earth? The kindest, the most giving, the most pleasing?

She rested while I took a shower. My Andover friends might never know what a woman could be. The girls they wanted were a bunch of teases, but they'd marry them eventually. When the men couldn't be teased anymore, the girls would cheat, and when no one wanted them enough to make cheating possible they'd spend the rest of their lives under an umbrella at some country club trying to drink themselves to death.

What an idiot I had been to think that Andover guys who did everything right would lead a privileged life. What an idiot my father had been to think so, and Gill's father, and all the rest of the fathers and sons who believed that our school was a preparation for anything but misery.

Jan was worth more than a social life, a life of prestige, a life of accomplishment (when everything you were supposed to accomplish was at the expense of life). Jan gave me another life. She filled me with a joy of being which was much more rewarding than a pride in my accomplishments. I didn't have to do anything to have her love, there was nothing to prove. She wanted me as I was, and I had nothing to offer her yet but myself. No money, no job, no prestige.

To be wanted the way Jan wanted me enabled me to trust the future and fall in love with life. Knowing that she wanted me in that way made everything else that was beautiful in the world a superabundance, and what was ugly didn't matter.

Our guests started arriving about noon. The Osborns, the Potters, the Hansens and the Rosenbaums (who for a little while would be the only Jews in town). The Rosenbaums had a horny kid my brother's age (David) who was fun in many ways, but useless at Thanksgiving and New Year's because he didn't like to get drunk. The Hansens were older than the rest of the crowd and had always been childless. The Potters had three children: two tall blonde daughters a year apart (the oldest one a year younger than me—Tom's age—and the youngest two years younger still). They also had a son whose voice was beginning to change. He was a good kid, more fun than either of his sisters, so that it was no problem including him in our activities. Last year he got drunk and puked on the Osborn's rug.

The only person my age was Susan Osborn, an only child. She was actually a half year older than me and was already attending college (Smith). Since I've mentioned the Osborns' rug I should explain that each year the Thanksgiving dinner was at the Osborns', the Potters' or at our house, depending on whose turn it was. The Hansens and the Rosenbaums were city-dwellers and I guess my parents and their friends thought that the special atmosphere of Thanksgiving would suffer if there was a guy with binoculars watching them celebrate and the smell of roach-spray.

Susan Osborn and I had been made for each other. We would have dated and fallen in love and ended up married to each other if only the Osborns hadn't lived so far away. We'd grown up hating the same things about our parents and we both had a passion for telling the truth about how we felt. While our parents were sitting in smokefilled rooms boozing and laughing we had been hidden in a warm part of the basement diddling around.

There had never been time for kissing and romantic shit. We'd have kissed and petted like crazy if we'd had more time together. But we trusted each other, and examining each other's bodies was an extension of the frankness of our conversations. There wasn't any shame. We touched, tasted, explored. We weren't aroused so orgasm never came into it. I'd no more have thought of screwing Susan Osborn than screwing her mother.

That's not right. Screwing her mother was all I ever thought of. Her mother was built along the same lines as Susan, and the sly way she looked at me got me hard a lot quicker than anything Susan had done with her sharp little fingers when my pants were down. Still, given the opportunity, I don't think I'd have been able to go through with it. I'd thought of her too long as a mother to start thinking of her as a woman, and even if I could, what was the point of destroying a friendship I prized? (No mother could keep *that* secret.)

Surely Susan came prepared to lord it over me now that she was a college girl—and going to one of the Seven Sisters, no less. I saw the sight of Jan jolt her. When she realized that Jan belonged to me I think she wanted to go somewhere else for turkey.

In the back of her mind she must have banked on being my wife someday. She had to get past all the sleazy adolescent stuff, but when it was time to settle down, I'd be there. And now maybe I wouldn't be.

I'd felt the same about her. Until I'd met Jan she was the only woman I could imagine having for a wife. Sheila Burke? I knew what torture that would be. She'd kept my interest by denying me. She had to. She had nothing to give.

"I know this is dumb," I whispered to Jan when I saw her disappointment, "but let's make the best of it. Later we'll all be in the living room and you'll get a chance to shine."

"When I saw so many kids arrive I wondered how your mother was going to do it. It's all right. They're such wonderful people. So different."

"They met when they lived in an apartment house in Bronxville. There are about another dozen who are still part of 'the Bronxville crowd,' but they're scattered around. Yeah, they're a great bunch. Their kids are OK, too. That's one thing I'm proud of about my parents: their friends."

It's depressing to describe what was on the table that afternoon. I know I'll never eat that way again. Besides the turkey and my mother's great stuffing there was an oyster casserole, creamed onions, yams drenched in butter, potatoes in giblet gravy and green beans with mushroom sauce to go along with homemade nutbread, mounds of cranberry sauce and candied crabapples (from our tree) carefully followed by small bites of mince and pumpkin pie and when there was no room for anything more we let ice cream melt down our throats.

This was one time of year that the kids were allowed to drink all they wanted. Except for Ricky Potter (who remembered last year) and Davy Rosenbaum, we all got smashed.

The younger kids had adjourned to the basement where there was pingpong and darts and my brother's record player, while Jan and Susan and I stayed upstairs inventing complete sentences with the grownups.

After a while the novelty of Jan began to wear off and the folks wanted to talk about old times or the economy.

We excused ourselves and with Susan went to check on the younger crowd.

There were cases of beer below and lots of wine (even a bottle of champagne) because we were free to rob the basement refrigerator (where my father kept his beer).

Jan was having as much fun as the rest of us. She didn't try to act like a babysitter. The one time I thought there might be trouble was when she caught me and Susan Osborn together.

The booze had really gotten to me and I'd felt an urge to squeeze Susan's tits to see how they were doing. She was drunk enough to let me, finally, and she gave me a good grope in exchange.

If Jan was annoyed by any of this horseplay she didn't show it, and she never said anything afterward. However, in view of what I found out about her eventually, I have to wonder what she was thinking, besides being ashamed of me and seeing what a kid I could be.

From sometime that night till the time I woke up in the morning I was on automatic pilot. I don't even remember getting into bed with Jan, but my clothes were off, so I assume she undressed me.

I tried to remember all I had had. Four or five sherries. A little sauterne with the turkey. At least ten quarts of beer downstairs—probably more, because I didn't stop being thirsty just because my conscious mind had conked out. My hangover was indescribable, so I won't try.

Everyone else in the house appeared to be under the weather except my mother, of course. She would drink a fifth of Scotch and run around her kitchen in the morning whistling *Little Brown Jug.*

No one ate breakfast (no one could have), but we all got together for a lunch of turkey soup and turkey sandwiches (with lettuce and lots of mayonnaise and pepper) which was another tradition, or at least my mother hoped that it was. My father, Tom, Jan and I were talking in monosyllables, if we talked at all, but my mother was summarizing everything she'd been keeping quiet for the last few years.

It was torture. You'd think she was on the payroll of AA or something.

That afternoon I went around the neighborhood to see some of the kids I'd grown up with and to look for a basketball game. Jan wanted to come, even though I told her there'd be nothing but guys. She never backed out of anything because she was a girl.

I found a game at Charley Wynn's place.

"All right, you guys, put your tongues back in your mouths, this is my girlfriend Jan McBride, and she wants to play."

Everyone was so glad to see me back in town.

Jan could even play a little basketball. With her tits bouncing every time she moved, no one else could. It was a lot of fun embarrassing everyone, but it was a far cry from basketball, and some of these guys were basketball addicts, and would have been priests if there had been a basketball priesthood.

In half an hour we decided to head for home, or I helped

her decide. I'd had what I came for, a good sweat, and Jan had got one whether she came for it or not. My hangover was behind me and so was hers.

Later that afternoon Jan got me alone to tell me she wanted to leave. She wanted me to take her to a hotel in New York for two nights, and then, after we had loafed through upperstate New York and western Massachusetts on the way back to school, to a country inn.

I'd been planning on doing some studying, and I was finally beginning to feel welcome in my home, so maybe she sensed I wasn't that keen on decamping.

Then she told me that the real reason she wanted to go was that she wanted to make love to me in a place that was our own, a place we had paid for, like the apartment we would share someday. She had close to two hundred dollars on her and wanted to pay for everything herself.

My parents were shocked that we were pulling out. They had wanted to "get to know Jan better." I told them the truth for once: we were in love, we wanted privacy. It would be wonderful to see New York together. It would be our first taste of what the future would be like when we were on our own—away from our parents and not yet parents ourselves.

My parents were glassyeyed. They were probably thinking how different their lives might have been if they hadn't decided to have children. Jan kissed my mother goodbye and hugged my father, scrunching her tits into him for five seconds while he told her "come back and see us." It didn't occur to my father that the sight of Jan would mean that I wasn't far behind. She was clouding his judgment.

We were in a great mood after we made our escape and laughing as we flew down the Merritt Parkway in the dark blue of early night.

Ripe for a splurge we checked into a dowdy but cozy old hotel near the Museum of Natural History where I thought the chances would be good for thick walls.

We were at each other as soon as the bellhop cleared out. Hard to say what it was like this time. For once *both* of

197

us were fierce and fast. I would have expected even New Yorkers to take some notice of the noise.

Two hours later we emerged to look for a restaurant. There had been room service at the hotel, but it was my feeling (without any experience to back it up) that we'd just get a lot of mediocre food at a high price, and she said she thought so, too (and she had had some experience, having been a rich girl most of her life).

I took her to a Chinese restaurant I knew—a good one with softlit booths and gleaming white napery. It turned out that we were both crazy about Chinese food, and she knew how to order. Before long we had enough in front of us to keep us busy for two hours.

I ate Chinese food slowly and washed it down with beer. I liked to live in Chinese restaurants for a while, especially in New York, where they kept late hours and the waiters yelled a lot.

Jan must have known what a thrill it was to eat with her away from a family table. Not counting Callahan's drugstore (how could I) the closest we'd been to a restaurant had been a parking lot. In spite of Mr. McBride's occasional prompting we'd never gone anywhere together but upstairs to bed.

Could that have been why he seemed to like me less these days? He thought I was too cheap to spend money on his daughter? Or didn't have any money to spend?

Tonight was no time for such thoughts. Jan was all smiles. Even our Chinese waiter seemed to react to her radiance (and didn't Orientals think white women were devils?). When I wanted to live it up this was all the luxury I would ever need.

We spent the next day seeing the sights I ought to have known so well. My parents had taken me to see them often enough, but I'd never paid any attention until now. Being Jan's guide was like a *déjà vu* experience. Nothing new: it was normal for me not to know how to do something until I was teaching someone else.

The way I felt about New York changed because of Jan.

All the people we came up against when we needed something—waiters and cabdrivers and people behind counters
who had something we wanted, even if it was only information—were smiling and helpful. I'd been to New York with
Sheila Burke plenty of times and she was one of the prettiest
girls in Dudbury, but nobody paid any attention to us (even
when I wanted to pay. My wallet was immaterial, too.). The
way I saw it, Jan had conquered New York, at least all the
parts of it we got to see.

Saturday night I took Jan to my favorite restaurant and
drinking place, the Old Brewhouse up on East 54th by
Third. It was here that I'd been served my first drink in New
York when I was two years under age, the summer between
my lower and upper years. I was still carrying the same
forged ID, a Connecticut driver's license that was fading to
pink, sweat-softened and disintegrating at the edges. Legal
documents were more authentic-looking when they were
falling apart, I thought. Hoped. I'd spent hours weathering
my forgery.

At the Old Brewhouse the summer before last I'd been
served without having to show any ID and I'd got gloriously
drunk with my friends from school without distressing the
old German waiters who lumbered into our back room and
acted unsurprised each time we ordered more to drink and
brought the drinks wearing a faint smile, exuding a decency
peculiar to old ponderous waiters who'd been stooping all
their lives, presiding over other people's good times.

I went to the Brewhouse at least once every time I was
in New York and I was known to the waiters, and to the old
violinist and the pianoplayer who cranked out schmaltzy
music with the same ruddy resignation that the barman dis-
played while he cranked out endless foaming mugs of beer.

Last summer I'd gone to the Brewhouse three times
with Sheila Burke, and I'd brought another girl on the sly.
I'd met friends from school there on two occasions and once
I'd even gone with a guy from Dudbury who'd been a close
childhood friend. Now I was on a first-name basis with two

of the waiters and I was accepted up front with the people who looked like they belonged.

Being accepted meant everything to me, Jan must have known it. At the Brewhouse I could be served whatever I wanted to eat or drink without comment, I could get beered up and sing tired old showtunes to a lame accompaniment and not be ejected or silenced or even made to feel like an asshole by one of the old waiters. These were the best times of my life, and if the world outside had been a tenth as accepting of me as the waiters at the Brewhouse I'd have ended up in the bureaucracy some day with a lot of fat friends, a bare desk and a blank brain, dedicated to the betterment of mankind.

The Brewhouse was a strange place to take a girl, I guess. The walls were covered with pictures of prizefighters. The ancient oak tables had been carved by drunken Neanderthals. Beer wasn't a lady's drink in the first place, what with all the belching and running back and forth to the john. Yet there were always a lot of redfaced women at the Brewhouse, even some younger, unbloated ones, and once I'd seen two women eating the limburger cheese.

This cheese was the best in the world and it was a standing order whenever I appeared. Maybe it was unusual for someone as young as I to like limburger so much. Well, sure it was unusual not to order anything else, but the waiters weren't surprised any more and they were getting used to my orders for stout instead of German beer.

I'd ordered my usual split of Guinness to be mixed with a full bottle of Ballantine's India Ale, and Jan had ordered the India alone, so she was surprised when a slab of limburger arrived covered with raw onions. There was a crock of dark mustard and another of horseradish already on the table.

"What *is* that?"

I told her while I was bestowing the mustard and horseradish.

"I love limburger, but I've never seen it sliced off a loaf like that. I want some, too!"

I gave her a taste.

The waiter went for more limburger looking pleased.

"Now there can't be any doubt that you're the right woman for me," I rhapsodized.

"Even if I didn't like it I'd have to eat some before I could kiss you. But really, I love it. With onions, too, and the other stuff. Not mustard and horseradish together, I'm afraid. There's a cheese that comes from Alsace that's like this. The French call it *münster*, but it's nothing like the *münster* here."

"I know, and this limburger isn't anything like the limburger here. Maybe it comes from Germany, but I like to think it's homemade."

"That might be a hard business to go into at home."

"I wouldn't mind. I'm such a fanatic about this cheese that I'd like to have some on our wedding night. Sure, it's a longshot that we'll be married in New York, but think what a way that would be to go into married life, with all our welldressed friends giving us lots of room . . . "

Her cheese arrived while I was slicing her a taste of mine. The cheese *was* extraordinary. Each slice was in the form of a large irregular oval that fit the slice of black bread it was on. The cheese was moist and creamy, the light brown smear on it sizzled in your mouth, and it stank like hell. The cheese was perfect with beer, and not only to the taste. Eating a stinky cheese was a way of saying to hell with the rest of mankind, and so was beerdrinking the way I slopped it up. I'd had my share the night before in the Chinese restaurant and I'd been soused the night before that, so there were a lot of dry places in my body that were crying to get wet again.

I blew most of the money I'd borrowed from Tom at the Brewhouse, and that made me feel good considering what Jan was spending for our hotel.

Well-primed, and with the creaky violin and the piano

behind me, I sang *Some Enchanted Evening*. I cracked on the high E-natural at the end, but everyone applauded any-way . . . except Jan.

I can clearly remember singing for Jan so I couldn't have bombed. My friends had told me I was awful when I was dead drunk, but that was no more discouraging than be-ing told your car doesn't handle well with a flat tire. I'd been staring at Jan while I sang and I'd been sure that her eyes were full of love. True, I saw what I wanted in people's eyes when I was drunk.

"You didn't like it."

"Oh, yes. You have a nice voice. It's funny I never heard you, or asked to."

"Just as well, I haven't got enough ego to sing for you when I'm sober."

"I don't know, it made me sad to hear you, too. Don't worry, I'm having a great time. I must be crazy. I get scared when I'm so happy. I'm laughing and suddenly there's this big chunk of nothing and I see us sitting here and I watch things keep happening that'll be beautiful memories some day, one thing after another. Beautiful days together. Why can't we go on from here? How can you go back to school while I go on looking for a job and living with my father? I'm drunk. It's been a riot. Let's have some more."

I'm sure I complied and we had a riotous time, but I'll never know because the rest of what was in store for us that night could only be reconstructed as a series of likelihoods. Vague regrets were all I had left, and a relentless clash of cymbals.

We left the hotel early on Sunday morning so we would have all day to drive through the country and choose the place where we wanted to spend the night. We found it in the Berkshires after following endless country roads we didn't know that always brought us to a numbered highway that we could find on Jan's not-very-detailed map.

There were plenty of guests at the inn we chose and it

didn't have the "rustic charm" my parents were always looking for—in fact it was just a large hotel in a rural setting—but at least the clerk didn't try to satisfy himself that I wasn't Jan's husband.

Jan was much too beautiful to kick out of a hotel. My brother had been right about her. She looked great in her clothes and they were beautiful clothes to begin with.

We had a simple dinner by candlelight holding hands a lot. Just when we were tired of sitting and wondering what to do, music started in an adjoining room.

I'd thought someone was throwing a party because all the folks I'd seen going in had been middleaged and dressed the same—coat and tie. I was dressed that way myself, hoping to look like another tired traveler with my rumpled coat and slacks, but I couldn't be inconspicuous next to Jan.

If someone tried to drag me out I was going to say we were on our honeymoon. Jan had a ring on that she'd brought from home. All the money she'd brought was further proof of how much she'd wanted to have a great time in hotels with me.

As soon as the music started she asked if I wanted to dance.

"How do you know that's not a private party?"

"It's not."

"What if we've got to pay to get in? We've got to pay for the room tomorrow and have enough left over for gas."

"It's just two dollars a couple."

"Have you been to this place before?"

"It's all on the sign outside. Where have *you* been?"

"Not paying attention. I guess I was too worried about getting past the desk. Being able to stay with you out here in the country is enough of a blessing. If they think they made a mistake giving us a room, dancing around all night with these old geezers would just be rubbing it in."

"Forget it, then. We'll get to dance together someday."

"I wouldn't mind if we could drink, but that's really pushing it."

The legal age was twenty-one now and I was sure to be carded.

"You're right. We could use the rest. We'll put this supper on our bill and go upstairs."

"The hell we will. What's two bucks? That band's pretty good, it sounds like that Lester Lanin guy who's always playing formal dances in Dudbury. We can drink, too. I'll latch onto some older guy and get him to buy for us. We'll say we're on our honeymoon. What do you bet we won't even have to pay?"

"All of a sudden I'm not the least bit tired."

She was on her feet towing me.

Dancing with Jan I forgot all the techniques I'd learned, the steps—I forgot myself. It must have been obvious that we were in love. Before long everyone was buying drinks for the "young honeymooners" and the guy at the set-up bar was looking the other way.

I never felt the drinks, I was drunk with Jan. It never crossed my mind to sing her a love song with the band behind me. My ego was doing fine. Here I was in a room full of bigshots and Jan was dancing with *me*, dancing closer than the legitimate wives. At times I felt the band was playing with us in mind. The leader winked whenever I caught his eye.

The booze kept flowing and everyone was half gone before the night was. Men were cutting in a lot to talk to my "bride." I knew that some of the wives wanted to get their hands on me but they all looked like crones after Jan and I was forced to get into passionate arguments with drunken men, sticking up for things I didn't care about, while I tried to catch her eye.

She was being polite, she kept looking at the guy she was with, but she was holding him away. Finally one guy tried to get close. She was pushing so hard she appeared to be holding him up.

I went to her as soon as the music stopped and she wanted to go. A trumpet brayed and the drums rolled as we made our exit, waving. The dancers were despondent. Drunk and lost.

Our love needed no proof now, nothing needed to be done. There was proof every time we stopped to think or look around. The world looked different, and our love had been the cause. The past was dimmer, the present more vivid, and our love assured us of future happiness.

We said very little getting ready for bed and waited for sleep in trusting silence.

I'd set the alarm on the clock Jan had brought and left word at the desk for an early call because I had to be getting back to school. Technically I was supposed to be back in the dorm on Sunday night, but nothing was said if boys made breakfast on Monday morning.

So it was that we were checking out of the inn in front of a bleary-eyed night auditor at four a.m. It was unnerving to think that if we had car trouble, I'd get a cut for breakfast, chapel, 8 o'clock class, and so on. One more cut was enough to put me on posting, and one more posting was enough to get me expelled.

Under some pressure I drove carefully and avoided the rest of the cars on the road (there might have been drunks coming home). We made it to Andover with an hour to spare and hugged and kissed a long time on a quiet town street near the dorm where we could smell coffee brewing.

When I saw her car getting smaller and taking a distant corner I felt lost. I didn't belong here. I belonged on the road with her, in our various homes.

Approaching the dorm I heard the shouts of the guys and was ashamed to be one of them. A window went up.

"Hey, Bancroft! He's back, you guys. He's been at it all night again."

FOURTEEN

Before I plunged into my studies I wrote my parents a long letter. (A long letter to my parents was two pages; a long one to Jan would run twenty.) I told them not to write back because I wouldn't be answering any more letters this term. They could expect a note from me a week before Christmas vacation to let them know my plans. For news about me they could rely on Sanborn's weekly reports, where they were sure to hear quotes from my teachers and anybody else who had an interest in me. I didn't want to sound like an ungrateful son, I told them, but I was budgeting my time for the last four weeks of the term and I didn't want any messages from outside the academic world to interrupt my concentration.

My second day back I went to see Dr. Bellini with another pile of books. At a glance I knew this was the last time we'd see each other.

"Gordon, I wonder if you resent coming all the way down here and taking time away from your studies?"

"No. It's great to see you. True, I've got a lot of work to do . . ."

"What do you say we talk for a few minutes and you can spend the rest of the time in the library."

"Fine. Are you letting me go for good, then?"

"Yes, much as I like to see you. There's no need for us to keep working. I never felt there was anything wrong with your mind and I think you know your problems didn't stem from some weakness in character. You've got a lot of character. You were having problems of motivation, and I think a feeling of rejection was responsible. That's why I wanted you to talk about your father."

"It was great to be able to tell someone the truth about my father. I think it did me a lot of good."

"I'd like to think so, but we both know that you didn't do a lick of work until you met your girlfriend."

"Want to hear what happened over the holidays?"

"If you want to take the time."

That was the phoniest thing Bellini had ever said to me. He was half out of his mind to hear about Jan. Psychiatrists had a right to expect some juicy stuff. Hearing the secrets of the boudoir was their big payoff for choosing psychiatry. Priests might have had the same motives in choosing their profession, but I'd vowed to keep quiet about them until I was dead certain what went on in confessionals. Anyway, in telling Bellini about Jan and me, I went overboard by going back to the time we'd made love all night on her father's bed. I was giving him details that I thought he'd appreciate, but then I realized that he would know the school rules well enough to get me in trouble. He had to know that it was illegal to sleep over at a girl's house while school was in session. I tried to head him off.

"I hope you appreciate how honest I'm being and I won't get in any trouble for telling you about the things I've been doing with Jan."

He gave me a look that meant we were talking man to man for the moment.

"The things you've been doing with her are fine. You're lucky to have found her. Just don't get expelled on her account. Try to use good sense and see her during vacation." He stopped looking me in the eye. "But maybe that would be too long to wait. I can't say I blame you. Be careful, Gordon."

He stood. I could tell it upset him to have to say good-bye. Seeing him this way, I became emotional myself.

"I wish you the best in everything you do," he said. "I'd love to know what becomes of you in the next few years. I know it's too much to expect that you'd drop me a line."

In the emotion of the moment I didn't see where that was such an unusual thing to expect, but by the time I was approaching the library I was already glad that my meetings with Bellini were a thing of the past. No longer would I have to tell my inquisitive classmates what a nice guy he was.

Truth was, he was far from being a jerk, but I didn't have much respect for his profession. Nothing would come of the notes he took while I was turning myself inside out. If I made a few honors grades nobody would care anymore what Bellini had to say. I wouldn't have been nearly so nice to the guy if the school hadn't been forcing me to see him, and I was damned nice considering how much I had to suffer from the kids who knew about my visits. No, I would always like Dr. Bellini, but I was well rid of him.

After grinding the way I had before Thanksgiving for a few days I decided to try a lower gear. Barton was probably responsible for my change of heart. When I saw him cranking up his publicity campaign all over again I knew I had to find a new role. I would study just as hard, but I'd try not to be so obvious about it.

Such a type was nothing new. Plenty of guys were ready to play pranks with you or kill a few hours in a bull-session, but they were grinding on the side. Channing and Hobbs were lifting weights all night, true, but who was to say what was going through their minds? Channing was reputed to have a photographic memory, so it would have been easy for him to photograph his assignments and spend the rest of the night lifting weights and looking through the pages he'd memorized.

It would be possible to slow down a bit now because I'd already made up a mountain of work and my teachers might have begun to feel stupid about all the praise they had to heap on me. I didn't give a damn about all the nice things they had to say—these were just stock phrases—but the other guys were taking them to heart. If I didn't knock off handing in the extra work I was going to give myself the reputation of a kiss-ass.

I vowed that henceforth I would never come to class without being thoroughly prepared, but I'd quit trying to make up the work I'd let slide earlier in the term. Channing was glad to see me back in his room lifting weights, and when Sanborn found out he didn't have anything bad to say because the reports from my teachers were as enthusiastic as ever. I hadn't told any of the teachers about my study plans because there hadn't been any need. They were relieved to have fewer papers from me to read, and they might have been relieved as well that one of their students wasn't going to break down from overwork.

My popularity was finally on the rise.

The quickest way to tell that you were in favor was at commons. The football team was sitting down with me. I had never presumed to take an empty seat at a table full of football players, and I didn't now, but whenever a seat would open up beside me it seemed as if some big man or other was sitting down. At first I thought I was going to be grilled about Jan some more, or that certain players were going to try to get to know her better through me, but that wasn't the case. Her name never came up, and there weren't any specific questions. I was hearing "How's your girlfriend?" or "How are you and your girlfriend getting along" from everybody in school, but my stock answer was a turned-down smile and a couple of nods to mean "Everything's fine."

The fact that the football players who knew Jan's name never used it could only have meant that they respected me. Sure, I was big, but I didn't play football. The thought that they would accept me as one of their own was every bit as odd as the laxity of the school in permitting prone basses in the chancel.

Jeff Putnam

Now that I was becoming good friends with the football players, guys who'd been in my dorm two years ago were reminding me how close we had been. Barton was so proud of me it was getting embarrassing to walk around campus with him. Even Channing, who might have been the smartest guy in school, was showing me more respect than he had in the days when I'd been nothing but a troublemaker. Still, there was one countercurrent in my swelling popularity. One guy who seemed to think I wasn't such a good man after all. Gill.

I was sure he was avoiding me in commons because I had put him to the test. Since he was on crutches, he had a scholarship guy carrying his tray for him. Being Gill he wasn't about to let that poor guy follow him around while he decided where he wanted to sit, so he'd take the nearest table when he passed from the kitchen into the senior dining hall.

When I noticed that Gill wasn't very far behind me in line one day, I decided to take a table right in front of the kitchen entrance, where there were plenty of empty seats, just to see if Gill would sit with me.

I managed to lure one football player to my side, but when Gill came out with his flunky he walked right by me. Even the football player noticed the cut and said something about Gill being a "hard case" these days.

I made up my mind then and there to pay Gill a visit. I thought I might be able to catch him in before study hours because he wasn't the type to hang around the snack bar or in the room in the basement of the refectory where there were pool tables and smoking was allowed and you could find every dip in the school.

I barged in the way I always did and he gave me a mean look. The papers had been cleaned up, but the room was so bare it looked like a prison cell.

"Get out of here, Bancroft. I've got work to do."

His mean look stayed the same, and I realized that I

210

wasn't seeing an expression on his face, I was seeing his face.

"What's eating you, Gill? I saw the way you cut me at commons today. We were practically best friends once. Has someone been telling you shit about me?"

He snorted. "The whole school's been talking about you. You're some kind of celebrity. That's the way they reward a big mouth around here."

"What are you talking about?"

"I'm talking about the way you've told the whole school about that girlfriend of yours."

"Hey, I don't talk about the things we do like some guys. Thomson, Porter and them, they might be talking about her, but I don't care what people think. With a love like ours . . ."

"Janet McBride might care what people think."

"Who told you her name?"

"What are you talking about? The whole football team knows her name."

"Dammit, that wasn't my fault. I didn't tell you her name when I came here the last time, did I? Sure, I know, you're the type of guy who would never ask. But the only people who knew her last name were Barton and that bastard Thomson. And it wasn't as if I even told them. Both of them saw this letter I got from her. Barton would never tell anybody her name, though. It was Thomson who spilled the beans to the football team. Anyway, they're not giving me any shit about her these days."

"No, I've seen them getting cozy with you. It's sickening."

"Come off it, Gill. Those guys are supposed to be your friends. They've got more prestige than anybody."

"They put out more shit than anybody. There are only a half dozen guys on that team that I'd be willing to call men. They know what I think of 'em. Let 'em have their little clique. I sat with them when I was a lower and we were the only men on the varsity. I don't have to tell you I was the only lower who played on the varsity lacrosse team—who started, I mean. If they hadn't segregated the classes I'd have been eating with my friends over in the senior dining room. But that's beside the point. Playing football and lacrosse I got friendly with Alan Benson, and that's how I got to go out with Janet McBride."

"No!"

"After he broke up with her in the spring I saw her twice."

I had my hands on the side of my head. "Wait! Go slow. You're shaking me up with this, Gill. *You* dated Janet McBride when you were a *lower?*"

"No lie."

"What happened?"

"I'm not going to tell you anything. I wouldn't tell you even if you'd already stopped seeing her."

"Let's go over this one more time. First of all, she told me that she was the one who told Benson to walk, not the other way around."

"Could be. Anyway, I'm not going to call her a liar."

"There's one more thing. Don't you think she was kind of old for you?"

"Old? She told me she was Benson's age, even if she was out of school. Most of my friends in this school were seniors. The difference in our ages didn't mean anything."

"Gill, you've got to answer me this. Did she go out with any of the other guys on the team?"

"Not that I know of. Benson pretty well monopolized her most of the year. But I saw her with someone else once during the time she was supposed to be going with Alan."

"Who?"

"An older guy. Not one of us. I've seen him before but I don't know his name. I used to think it was a big deal to get served in the taverns downtown. I had an easier time than Benson. I was walking back alone one night and I saw her on this guy's arm. They were laughing and talking. It made me suspicious the way she leaned against him. I kept on walking, though. I didn't want to be a spy."

"If she was a traitor then why are you still protecting her? Tell me what you did with her for chrissakes!"

"We didn't do anything abnormal. Does that help?"

"Yeah, after knowing what goes on over at Paul's with Lynn."

He looked away from me and stared at his blank wall for a while. I had the feeling he might tell me something if I gave him time.

"I went to bed with her once," he said at last in a small voice. His voice made me think how hard it must have been for him to drag a cast around for so long. Strangely, what he was telling me about Jan didn't affect me at all.

"She was the best I ever had. But I guess I must have done something wrong. She sent me a note saying she didn't want to see me any more. I took it hard for a day or two, but what the hell. She was a rich bitch. She might have thought I was beneath her. You're the only one who could find out the truth, but don't bother. I don't care what she thought of me. If she still remembers."

The truth began to dawn on me.

"Jesus, Gill, is the reason you've been cutting me lately because you're jealous?"

The meanness had gone out of his eyes, but he didn't say anything.

"I thought something was fishy when you started giving me all that high morality. 'Mustn't talk about girls.' What a load of shit. You've been jealous because she sees something in me."

He stared a while longer before speaking. "I wouldn't call it jealousy. I think I'm pissed off at how much you can get away with. Call it a chip on my shoulder, say whatever you want about me, but I resent the way you've suddenly become the big man on campus thanks to that girl."

"Well, then you're right. We can't be friends. A friend

would be glad of the good things that are happening to me. I thought you were a bigger man than that."

He was still staring in front of him. I waited a long time for him to tell me he was sorry, but the words never came, and I left.

As the upshot of my talk with Gill it was brought home to me what a precarious position Thomson had put me in with his big mouth. There was nothing wrong in talking about girls from your home town by name. You could go into great detail about what you'd done with them. There was no chance that one of the guys at school would visit your home town to see a girl on the strength of what you'd said about her. Talking about an Abbot girl or a townie was something else again. A lot of guys did it, but that was because Andover men in general didn't take their relationships with women all that seriously.

I was up in Channing's room lifting weights and wondering if I'd ever be strong enough to mess up Thomson's face when he came right into the room and put on his friendly voice.

"Hey, Gawdon, when we gonna have anothah pahty?"

"Thomson, you're never getting another drop of my booze. And there aren't going to be any more parties. What I've got down there is going to last me the rest of the year, and if you need a drink so bad, go out and get your own."

I left then because I couldn't stand the feeling that I was a coward for not punching him out then and there. Closing the door, I heard him asking Channing what he'd done to me, and I heard Channing say that Thomson could probably figure out why I was pissed off if he thought about it long enough.

Channing was so smart that he already knew. Anyway, I'm sure he knew it had something to do with Janet McBride. In spite of my hard work and all the changes in my attitude, Channing knew that Janet McBride was all I cared about.

As for Janet, Gill's revelations had hurt and for a day or

two I was tempted to tell her what I knew, but then I began to think that the fact she'd been with a friend of mine wasn't such a big deal. As far as I could tell she'd been with a lot of men both here and abroad, and who was to know how many admirers she'd left behind in Minnesota? That was the way she was, that was her nature, she was a hotblooded woman—I couldn't hate her for it.

One thing did worry me, and that was what Gill had told me about seeing her with an older guy when she was supposed to be going with Benson. If Jan ever cheated on me, I didn't think I'd have the strength to leave her, but I might have had the strength for a gesture like killing us both. It was scary to acknowledge feelings like that, but they were there, and I acknowledged them at the time just as frankly as I'm doing now.

I thought I could ask her about her time with Benson and sound casual.

"Did you ever go out with someone else while you were seeing Alan Benson?"

Her head moved back no more than a click, but I caught it.

"No! Why? Are those boys at school still talking about me?"

"Sometimes they do. One guy was saying he saw you with an older guy downtown on a schoolnight."

"I don't know who said that, but he's a liar."

"Don't let it upset you, Jan. I take everything they say in stride. A lot of them are jealous of me, you know."

We were having this talk after a Saturday game and a lot was different that day. For one thing we'd lost 2-1 to the Yale Frosh. Another difference was that Mr. McBride hadn't been to the game. Jan had said he had work to do, but he'd been reading a novel in the living room when we came in. He'd asked me about the game, but before I told him all that I wanted to say, he'd excused himself and gone upstairs.

"I can't help but feel you're suspicious about me, and I wish you wouldn't be." I started to object, but she raised a hand. "I know there's a lot I haven't told you, and I'm sure if we stay together long enough you'll hear it all."

"Hear about the different guys?" I chuckled to soften the statement. "I mean, if there have been that many. You always give me the impression that there have been. Frankly, the way you make love is . . . you know, so great . . . you must have had to learn some things." She was smiling so I hadn't lost her. "I love you so much, I don't think I could ever be jealous. That's what worries me about cheating. What's to stop you if you know I won't blow my top?"

Her smiled broadened.

Mr. McBride came down in fresh clothes and told us goodnight. He didn't say anything about where he was going or when he'd be in which was like a slap in the face for some reason.

"I get the strangest feeling about him these days," I told her when I heard his car. "He's not that friendly to me anymore. I don't expect him to come to all my games, but not coming is in line with the other stuff I've noticed. He just doesn't sit and talk to me the way he used to."

She looked concerned. "I haven't noticed anything. Well, maybe I have. A lot of it has to do with the way things have been going with Ruth."

"You think so?"

"Even if his feelings about you *have* changed, he's not getting in our way."

"Yeah, that's a relief. Listen, I was on to something . . . When are you going to tell me what happened to you in France? Or do you think maybe I'm not jaded enough to understand?"

"I'd tell you everything if I was sure it wouldn't change your opinion of me."

"Nothing could do that now. I wouldn't care if you actually sold your ass." Not a glimmer in response. At least she hadn't sunk that low.

"What did you want to hear about in particular?"

"Tell me about the guy you lived with."

"I wouldn't before and I won't now. It's a painful subject."

"We weren't this close before. Wouldn't it be easier?"

"His name was André. I met him on the slopes at Chamonix. I think I was drawn to him at first because he was so cute. He had a very round face, and curly hair like some Swedish friends of ours in Minnesota. He didn't look French at all, and he was almost as big as you are."

"The hell with his pedigree. Give me the part that will hurt."

"You want to know what he was like in bed?"

"Sure, for starters."

"It was different. I loved him. I guess I enjoy sex more with you."

"See why it's nice to hear you tell me about other men?"

"Well, what else do you want to know?"

"Wasn't he the one who taught you things?"

"I don't know how much he taught me, but it was while I was with André that I found out how much I liked sex in all its forms."

"What do you mean, 'in all it's forms?' Perverted stuff?"

This was where she shocked me. I should have seen it coming because a blush was starting, and she hadn't blushed in a long time.

"You might think the things we did were perverted, but I never felt that way while I was with André. It was the way he lived, it was the way his friends behaved, and I just went along. We had sex with other couples."

"You mean, orgies?"

My eyes were popping out of my head. Her cheeks got redder. But she'd made up her mind to go through with her story. She was testing me. It was something I hated about her: she was always inviting me to hang myself.

"I wouldn't call them orgies. Everyone would be nude in the evening and we'd drink some wine and make love."

"You mean, all mixed up? Together?"

"Yes. Some of them were bisexual."

There was nothing teasing about the way she told me. Her face was so red and her voice so timid she had to be ashamed, but that didn't stop me.

"You did it, too? You actually played with more than *one*? With a *woman*?"

"I don't want to talk about it any more. I was afraid you'd act this way."

"What way? What did you expect? Look, I could handle all the stuff about other guys, I can see where that would be normal . . . one by one. Maybe it's childish of me, but the thought of you being with a group makes me angry as hell."

"How can you be angry about things that happened before I knew you?"

"Where was all this stuff happening, anyway—in Paris?"

"No, in a small city called Annecy. Such a beautiful place. There were small canals and swans on the lake."

"Jesus, I can't believe the French would behave like that in the provinces. I thought those people were still going around in wooden shoes . . . "

She smiled over my pain and my heart went out to her.

"I'm sorry, Jan, I'm being an idiot. The point is you left all that and came home to good old New England where people don't like to be naked in the bathtub."

"I left because André got tired of me. I thought we had a special relationship based on more than just sex, but it didn't turn out that way. When I could see that it was annoying him to have me around, I left. It took all my strength. Maybe you won't understand this, but I'd been enjoying the life we had. It was an approving atmosphere. I wasn't ashamed of what I found out about myself . . . "

She gave me a searching look that became distant.

"Life with André was too intense to last, I know that now, and I'm glad. I meant what I said to you that time about a home. I could have accepted a home that wasn't conventional, but I know I could never have raised children around André and his friends, and that was the deep thing between us that was never right. Still, I expected him to marry me, and I thought I could change him if he did. For a while I even thought I could persuade him to come to the States and live with me here . . . Or maybe closer to New York, down where you are."

"That would be a laugh. A guy like that in Dudbury. The town fathers would nail his balls to the meeting hall."

We were both laughing at the thought of André among the bluestockings.

Jan had rocked me with her stories about life in France. It hurt to realize that what she'd told me in her bed that first night, that she was serious about her relationships, was nothing but another lie.

When André was back in oblivion she had another surprise. She'd found a job. She'd told me before that she'd been looking, but in the back of my mind I'd thought she wasn't serious.

She brought up the news about the job when I tried to talk my way out of staying the night. I wanted to make love for a couple of hours and have her drive me back before the Saturday curfew. I was scared as hell these days of getting nabbed for breaking some stupid rule and seeing all my hard work go down the drain.

Then she dropped the bomb. From now on, Saturday nights would be my only chance to stay. Monday she started work from nine to six. She couldn't come to any more Wednesday games. She'd be working for a planner over in Lowell who was a friend of her father's. There'd be a bit of a commute and she feared she'd be too worn out to see me on weekdays.

She would be after she saw me, I agreed. I told her there were no more Wednesday games on my schedule. Those days I'd been planning to spend the whole afternoon with her away from the school.

She looked disappointed for my benefit. There were still

two Saturday home games left to play. I hoped she'd come and be with me after . . .

Again we argued about me staying over. She couldn't get me to stay, but I promised I would next week. In spite of her disappointment she was loving to me upstairs.

The guy she was going to work for was named Peabody and I had a hard time working up a jealous rage over a guy with a name like that. Still, he was divorced, and I thought his operation bore looking into.

On my free time Wednesday afternoon I took a bus over to Lowell, looked up Peabody's address in the phone book, and dropped in on his office, ostensibly to see how Jan was doing on her new job, but in reality to get a good look at this Peabody.

The first thing I didn't like about Peabody's operation was the size of it. There didn't appear to be more than a dozen employees. I had been hoping for a bleak sort of place with hundreds of nameless employees wandering around in a daze.

Jan was a centerpiece in the outer office, her bosom a burst of color in her chair. She was as out of place as . . . you name it, Beethoven at the Senior Prom.

She was the secretary and receptionist, but Peabody had her doodling little trees and people on his plans for a shopping center. Jan looked glad to see me even though she must have known that I was spying on her. She was about to take me back to meet her boss when he came into the reception area.

It was hard to get an idea of this guy's sex appeal because women had such goofy taste. He was a guy in his early forties, I guessed, but he might have been younger, there wasn't any belly on him at all. He had the body of an athlete, but he jumped around a lot and made violent gestures like someone who'd been harried all his life. I thought there was a chance planning was work he didn't like. Maybe that didn't make sense, but something was eating him.

Afterward when I thought about how he looked I was

struck by a resemblance to someone I knew. Then with a jolt I realized that it wasn't someone I knew, but someone I'd imagined. André!

At first I thought, "Oh-oh. This guy has a round face and curly hair (over his ears, where he still had a lot). That's the type Jan likes."

Then I began to have darker thoughts. Jan had lied before. What if she'd attributed to André all those qualities of Peabody's just so I'd think her debauches had taken place in France? Maybe she'd been involved with this Peabody for years. He was her father's good friend, wasn't he? There were plenty of excuses for them to get together.

After some thought I decided that André and her experiences with him had been authentic. She had no reason to want to shock me, and I could see the effort her honesty had been. Even so I promised myself to ask Gill if the older guy he'd seen Jan with that night two years ago had had a round face and curly hair. But Gill and I were avoiding each other. Anyway, jealousy with me was an emotion that made me suffer violently for a while, but it wasn't something I could carry around with me for long.

FIFTEEN

When I saw Jan the next Saturday night her father left no doubt he was cutting me. We didn't talk and leaving he just looked at me after I'd said goodbye.

I wanted an answer this time.

"All right. He doesn't approve."

"What have I done? Since the days when we were buddy-buddy I've been doing everything right!"

"Maybe so, but it doesn't sit well with him that you have a bad record, especially when he thinks I might live with you while you're going to some state college next year."

"Well, that's it. If your father feels that way about me, I can't stay over, and we're doomed if I can't stay here Saturday night."

"What are you talking about? Weren't you afraid to?"

"Too often, yes. But now that you're working and knowing your hot pants you'll take up with some other guy if I don't get to sleep over at least one night . . ."

"I won't either! How can you think that about me?"

She was madder than I'd ever seen her. We appeared to be having our first fight. I kept it going because I was angry that she seemed content not to spend the night with me on Saturdays.

"Don't worry, I have a lot of respect for your feelings. I remember what happened right here our first night."

222

"You think if I don't see you every week I'll throw myself at the first guy that comes along."

"If you want to know the truth: yes."

"Get out!" She started to cry. "Go on, leave. We'll see each other some other time. I want to be alone tonight."

I knelt in front of her and put a gentle hand on her knee. She slapped it away and showed me an angry face that made her look much younger—all red and wet with tears, with slime dripping out of her nose.

I got next to her on the sofa and took her hard into my arms. I felt as I did after a cross-country race. For a few moments I was the only thing standing still and the rest of the world was going its way. She fell silent after a time and rested against me.

Later we had a long talk. The change in her father had to be explained. A lot of things came out that I didn't expect from what I knew of her old man. He was more like my father than I would have thought. Obsessed. Andover had been his first choice when he applied to a prep school all those years ago and the idiot had been bitter that he hadn't made the grade. So had his own father, who'd also been obsessed with my school, having been raised near the place.

The thing that terrified these fathers most was that someone like me would make the same mistakes and take the paths that led to them. That was how much they had hated their lives.

"It still amazes me that he thought I could be the right person for you." I had a terrible premonition. "I hope you won't hold it against me that you've got to ignore him now."

"I'm not saying that anything has changed with us, but we can't forget my father entirely."

"What do you mean? I have to!"

"I can't. I've got to consider him. For instance, I'm going to insist that I keep seeing you, but I'm not always going to tell him it was you I was with."

"This is so crazy. Why do you have to be the perfect daughter? Why do I have to be the perfect Andover man?"

"Because his wife was a nut and he was never popular in school."

"Incredible. the whole system of fatherhood must be screwed up. Aren't we interesting the way we are?"

"To me you're a lot more than interesting . . . " She took my hand and rocked back and forth with it. "Maybe that's the point," she went on softly. "It was reacting to fathers like ours that made us interesting. It might be a good thing that there are a lot of fathers with definite ideas about what their children should be doing in school and what kind of life they should have."

"Come on. Not when the schools go right along."

She ignored me. "There will always be some kids like you and me who will go against their fathers and even their schools. That's how we're the same, Gordon. I made it hell for my dad. I wanted everything my own way. Maybe all I've got to show for it is a lot of painful experience. He might see it that way. The way I see it, I've had a lot of pain—but a lot of experience."

"He must have thought Al Benson was perfect for you."

"Right. And he thought you were another Alan. I never told him that you were in trouble. And I didn't look down on you for not doing your work because I understood your problems at home."

"I know. I was afraid you'd think less of me for grinding."

"Don't be silly. You don't have to have my approval no matter what you want to do."

"You'd make a great parent . . . "

"I think I learned what a father should be, or could be, from my dad."

I hadn't expected to be taken seriously. I waited for her to find the words.

"Loving. And patient. Wiser than us about what we're going to face in life, but willing to let us make a few mistakes."

"That's great, Jan. And still you can love your father so much."

"I know how much he loves me. I couldn't hurt him. I always hated to hurt him, even when he was trying so hard to rein me in."

"Funny, but hearing you say that I realize how much I love my own father in spite of all his faults. I have trouble believing that he loves me."

"You told me all he did to keep you in school."

"He just wants me to get into a big-name college."

"Of course he does! He wants the best of everything for you. He loves you!"

"But his idea of the best and mine are nothing like the same. Sure as hell I'm never going to spend a lot of time in classrooms even if it's going to cause me pain the rest of my life and my father the rest of his . . . So who's the realist? Who knows better who I am than I?"

"I don't know. Sometimes I think my father really does know who I am, and loves the person I am even if I'm different from him. He's just afraid . . . Remember, my dad wasn't much at the start, just like yours. He had to fight hard before he had it made. I don't blame him for thinking his is the only way."

Her words caused me to see my father in a new light. He may not have been as successful as Mr. McBride, but I was suddenly proud of him for trying so hard. Maybe if I hadn't been giving him such a pain . . .

"Jan! What have I done to him?"

I got teary-eyed at this point and let her comfort me like a mother. Perhaps I was only broken up for a few minutes, but it was enough time to change how I felt about my life. I saw everything I'd done up to now as selfish, insensitive or stupid, and I felt I'd accomplished damned near nothing.

No. Wait. I had Jan. But as much as I loved her, it was little comfort to realize that *all* I had was Jan.

"What does it mean then that we've been bucking the system or refusing to play the game?" I asked her later.

"Maybe we've just been screwing ourselves and making the people who love us unhappy."

She thought for a moment. "But how can the so-called system be right if it makes us *feel* all wrong? Take your school. You could be thrown out on my account. My father and Ruth and all his friends who know about us think that I'm selfish to put the rest of your life in danger, but I still don't *feel* it's wrong."

"I know."

"It scares me to go up against so many people, but only when we're apart and I think about us. When we're together I'm sure of myself and calm."

"I've got to see you more, that's all. Wait till Christmas vacation."

"I've been thinking about it. How wonderful it will be to wake up together with a whole day ahead of us, and a night in each other's arms."

I forgot my fears. She loved me.

I didn't stay late that night and I was depressed as hell when I got back to the dorm. As usual Barton came out of his room before I made it to the liquor cabinet.

"You know, for once I don't think booze would help. Thinking about this problem is more important than putting it out of mind. I've got to come up with a plan."

Barton was all over me to find out what had gone wrong. I told him the whole story this time. We both saw nothing but trouble ahead for me. Since nothing I could do would change Mr. McBride's opinion of me, Jan would be faced with constant pressure from her father to let me go, and a need to lie and be furtive just to keep the peace in her home. The only way I could keep her, we agree, was by per-suading her to leave her father and live on her own.

"She's already been on her own in France," Jim re-minded me.

"Yeah, and she's going to be twenty-two next month.

Unless she's lying to me again. Every time we have a long talk she comes out a year older."

"She might already want to have her own place."

"I wonder if Peabody's paying her enough to rent something. Dammit, all they've got in this part of the state are mansions. Anyway, even if we could find a slum I wouldn't expect her to live there on my account."

"Maybe she could take a room in somebody's house. A lot of students live that way."

My look told Jim what I thought of him lumping Jan with students.

"She couldn't live in anyone's house. We wouldn't be free to do as we liked in the night. She screams."

Barton kept silent while I pondered on.

"Why do the women scream like that? What is it you do?"

"Barton, you might not be the right person to help me out of this mess. Why don't you go back to your room and read about model airplanes or have a few snorts and go to bed."

"No, you've got me curious. I know what they sound like. How can they want something that hurts that much? I know they hate being raped, innuendo to the contrary . . . "

"I only do things she likes, and they're all the same normal things that even you will be doing someday."

He thought for a minute, looking flustered, and then decided he *would* leave me to sweat things out for myself.

"I think you're in over your head, Gordie," he told me at his door. "Sometimes it might be better to let things get sorted out by themselves."

I didn't pay much attention to him, but I ended up taking his advice. I was helpless to get Jan to move out of her father's house (as I had thought I would be) but things did get sorted out.

I wrote Jan a string of love letters over the next week to make up for not meeting her on Wednesday and I called her twice at work to make sure her voice was the same. She was busy, but her voice was sweet, and on Thursday she told me she'd got one of my letters, so at least her father wasn't intercepting them. I was sure he wanted to throw them away, and opportunity wasn't lacking with Jan at work all day.

In spite of the blanket of affection I was putting around her, or call it a snow job, I wasn't myself when I saw her on Saturday. Not being good enough for her father had stripped me of a lot of confidence. Not seeing Jan for a week had made her new to me, more imposing, and it panicked me to think she would have to be reconquered. That would be like reconquering Mt. Everest because it was still there. I'd never be able to stop wondering if I'd merely been lucky the first time.

Jan wasn't at ease either because she could never let me feel anything solo. When she finally asked why I was being so cold to her I didn't have the guts to say that I wasn't sure of myself any more, but I came up with a plausible explanation.

"I guess it worries me that you're working around so many men and they've all got so much more to offer than I have. Do they take you to lunch?"

Perhaps this had been an unconscious fear of mine ever since I knew about her job.

"Sure. But I'm not attracted to anyone at the office, Gordon, I swear it."

Embracing me she reassured me further and before long we were Gordon and Jan again, laughing and teasing. Sex was always as fresh for us as a step into new snow. As our bodies grew hot we forgot the cold, the dark, the doubts. I didn't care where we were going, I just wanted to keep on with her as my companion.

Timing. That was the key to success for someone on the right track to start with. To someone with my opportunities.

If the point was to learn histories and literatures, to learn the structure of a frog, or how the French language was put together—well, I learned those things. But I didn't learn them when I was supposed to. I'd flunked a lot of quizzes before I got down to business, and my grades would reflect that, so that my final grades would not reflect my knowledge at the time, but the state of my knowledge from day to day throughout the term. In other words, honors or high honors students were the guys who were on top of their work from day to day and not guys like me who would grind at the last minute and to the surprise of everyone make a brilliant showing under fire.

I had a vague idea that there were systems in Europe that were different from ours—where it was possible to come through with flying colors after taking it easy all term. Rumors about these paradises wafted about our campus, but they were easy to put out of mind. Because of timing once again we'd be graduating without the chance to have bene-fited from these humane conditions. And few of us thought of going to college abroad. Andover had always been a proving ground for Harvard, Yale and Princeton, and Ivy-League fathers wanted Ivy-League sons.

A last-minute grind like me might have been a star stu-dent in Europe. And being able to produce at the last minute would be a useful quality later in life. I could imagine ex-ecutives having suddenly to face a big problem and organize all their resources to deal with it. The plodder would freeze, but a clutch player would meet the challenge and survive.

Giving the correct answer to problems I'd only recently and briefly thought about, I wasn't myself. My memory amazed me, but nothing in it was my own. These guest ideas were gone forever once I committed them to a page in my bluebook at exam time.

Oh, not that quick. They'd linger for a time, popping up for no reason, but in a month or two they'd just be a shape in my mind, or words beginning with H or W. Still, the blue-book would remain, or someday, perhaps, a report, a pro-posal, an essay. What difference did it make to the world how much mental baggage I was carrying?

The solid-foundation people, the one-step-at-a-time types and steady accumulators that the school prized—although the vast majority—would turn out to be dull adults, I felt sure. With so many facts in their heads, whenever they were confronted with a new problem they'd want to search their minds. If you were someone who thought nothing was new, fine. You'd always have an answer and you'd feel good about it even if it wasn't right.

I thought everything was forever new. If that was childish, so be it. I felt different about it when I was burned a second time. I wanted to make fresh attempts and encounter unforeseen obstacles. Obstacles had a lot to teach. Success wouldn't have meant much without them.

There were heady moments after I'd done what my father wanted and received a trophy for pitching or a commendation for horn-playing. When Andover accepted me he was off my back for months. Somewhere along the line it occurred to me that all my ideas about success had come from my father. I could never feel successful without pleasing him, but the Gordon he thought I was or could be and the Gordon I knew I was and wanted to be were different people. By the end of the fall term, worlds apart.

Fear was at the bottom of my difficulties with dad. He wanted to show me the way to success by pointing out pitfalls. I'd driven him crazy by falling in all the pits, and by now he was convinced that I'd be climbing out of new ones whether he pointed them out or not.

I'd resisted my father's idea of the way I should go because I didn't like being forever fearful. I didn't want to worry about where I was going because I knew that when I got there I'd still be raring to go again.

My father wanted trophies and clippings from the newspaper and pictures on the wall. He wanted people to notice me.

I wanted to make less of a splash and learn to use my own eyes. I was curious about the people everyone was noticing, but I was just as curious about the guys like me I was sure to find at the bottom of a hole. Every day would be a bit of a climb and a bit of a fall, and when my time came I'd just be making way.

I'd seen it too often at Andover. The leaders with a pleasing manner and a winning smile never stopped smiling. Everyone esteemed the leaders, and I did, too, but I didn't want them along when I was going out on the town. One of our revered leaders once turned down an invitation to revel with us by saying, "I have a responsibility to the class." He might as well have said, "to Big Brother."

I could never see what was noble about counting on someone—knowing what he was going to do. People who believed in images and worried about their own—people like my father—viewed life as a movie that they were seeing for the umpteenth time, trying to find new meanings, looking for something they hadn't noticed before. They were glad of the chance to keep looking and didn't realize that they were merely obsessed.

I thought I knew better than my father. I'd learned that the truth was different for everyone. That the only heroes were heroes of the moment. That no one was a winner or a loser in the quiet of his room.

Most important, I was learning to be content with my father's bad opinion of me, and the school's. Changing that opinion was no longer important, as it had been when I began to make up my work. Changing my father's opinion wasn't even possible. I was studying because I wanted to. Daily assignments might have bored me, but I found it exciting to take in large amounts of material all at once. I was finally discovering my powers of mind.

SIXTEEN

We'd had some flurries of snow in November, and during the month of December there was heavy snow on two occasions, although there would always be a warm day now and then to melt it all. Andover had bad winters, but you'd never hear a complaint about them to outsiders, and there wasn't a word in the catalogue about the extreme winter cold.

In January the heavens would dump about four feet of snow on our school and not want any of it back. Allowing for the beauty of first snowfalls, the snow was a tremendous pain in the ass at Andover and the only kick I got out of it was watching the more imposing instructors picking their way around the campus with tufts of red fur over their ears and sometimes mittens instead of gloves. I never saw a snowball fight between a Classics professor and his pregnant wife, but I never stopped being on the lookout for one.

I was so fed up with Andover by the Christmas holidays that as soon as I escaped from school the first thing I was likely to do was go out and shovel snow—just to remember what a wonderful and profitable thing snow had been when I was younger.

When we were ten or eleven or twelve we *built* things in the snow, and you could even think of the paths we made as something built because we took such pride in making them black and straight.

Only babies wore mittens and earmuffs when they went snow-shoveling. I always went around with a watch cap turned down over my ears and unless it was bitter cold I didn't wear my leather gloves. I worked in snow, I didn't play in it.

Snow. There's something about it that obsesses me.

Jan looked great in her winter clothes. Not so sexy, but cuter. She was used to the subzero cold of Minnesota, so the Andover winters were fine with her. Her cheeks got so red when it was cold, her eyes were such a bright blue—I swear, the colors were loud and she wouldn't be wearing any makeup. Throw in the white teeth and she could have symbolized our country (a lot better than Uncle Sam).

Jan. God, she was beautiful when we were walking in the open country near her house, in the cold and the snow, warm with our love.

For hours that afternoon we kept apart. Our lips were too cold to kiss. We just held hands, and we were both wearing gloves, but whenever we stopped walking the look in her eyes made me feel as close to her as I ever had when she was naked in my arms. Jan. My love.

During the last weeks of school we saw each other on Saturdays and we had two Sunday afternoons. In spite of all Jan's reassurances I no longer felt like a welcome guest in her home. We still made love on Saturday evening when her father was out with Ruth.

The first Sunday afternoon we did everything we could in the Healy, but the next she drove me all the way to Lowell, and since she had a key, we made love on the soft carpet in Peabody's private office.

Even when Mr. McBride was gone I didn't feel at home in her house. The rest of the world was mine, I belonged, but I never felt like I belonged in the bosom of someone else's family, no matter how genuinely I was welcomed. I don't know why it should be so, but I'd be humiliated by the sight of old shoes, or stockings hanging in the bathroom, or a toothbrush there, or two, or three, and a shrunken bar of soap. It disturbed me to think that householders, people I looked up to, were just as messy as I was when they were at home.

Jan had some bad news that she'd been saving for one of our last meetings. I wouldn't get to spend Christmas with her. She was going to Minnesota to be with her mother and her mother's family. Because these people were rich she would be having a Christmas deluxe, but it would be painful to see her mother, downright depressing.

This year her father was going to make the trip more fun by taking her skiing at Aspen before they came home. She didn't know when she'd be home, but she'd call me as soon as she got back and we could spend the rest of the holidays together, at least a few days (Peabody was giving her two weeks off). Since she had money of her own now that she was working we could find a hotel room in Boston, or maybe another country inn where people wouldn't be too suspicious.

I was mighty let down because I'd been looking forward to Christmas and the end of the term as a chance to feast on Jan, to spend hours in bed with her, but I was consoled that we'd have some time together at least, and to judge from before, if we had a lot of sex the first couple of days we wouldn't be good for much from then on anyhow.

Final exams rolled around and when I walked into the huge hall (they used the main gym) with three sharp pencils I had a shelf full of books between my throbbing temples.

Andover was such a tough school that 88 was high honors, an A+ in other words. To get a grade in the 90s you had to know more than your instructor. I swear, at final exam time our teachers asked us questions they'd never been able to answer themselves. I wouldn't call them trick questions, but they made you use a lot of information to come up with opinions you didn't necessarily want to have.

That's confusing, but a sample question will give an idea what our exams were like. "What documentation would support the view that the British did not do all they could to win the Revolutionary War?"

I know that's a preposterous question, but if you knew your stuff you could argue convincingly that the British were *trying* to lose the Revolutionary War. These were the games we played at Phillips Academy. Woe to anyone with common sense if he got into an argument with one of us.

I was sure of a high honors on every one of my exams and thanks to solid high-honors work for half of the fall term I was looking for a standing somewhere in the second fifth of the class, or maybe even at the bottom of the first fifth, since some of the geniuses had received early acceptance to Harvard or Yale and might have been slacking off.

My father showed up with the station wagon to take me home and this time he didn't look as if he'd just run over a two-year-old rounding the last corner. He wasn't exactly smiling, but there was a good chance he was suppressing a smile. If Sanborn was telling the truth my father had been hearing every week about how I was near-perfect in class, a mainstay of the choir and the soccer team, considerate around the dorm and one of the best-liked boys in school. It would have been holding a grudge for him to be ashamed of me in front of the other kids. For once I don't think he was.

Even with my good record behind me and my parents being nice to me and my being extra-considerate of my father I got depressed as hell around the house. For a couple of days before Christmas I sat on my old bed up in what I now thought of as Tom's room reading Émile Zola, of all people. I had a copy of *Nana* in French from the school library. The margins were full of exclamation marks and crude drawings of naked women. There was only a physical resemblance between Nana and Jan, aside from the fact that they were both incredible sluts.

Jan was no goldigger. She luxuriated in her body, but she didn't seem to be aware of its power. No. She had to have been. Women spent so much time looking at themselves in the mirror. Jan had plenty of mirrors around. She remains the only woman I've known who really liked herself in them. Jan could have used her beauty to get anything she wanted, any man certainly. Why, then, was she fooling around with a senior at a prep school? A kid with no future, at that?

She couldn't help herself. Because she was honest about her feelings, when she found herself attracted to me she wasn't afraid to show how she felt. Most women, I think, would have said to themselves, "He's nice, but he's younger and probably broke," and I'd never have had an inkling that they'd been interested in me.

Jan was kinder by nature than Nana. She could never have taken a new lover to spite the old.

I still hadn't heard from her two days after Christmas when dad got a special delivery letter from Sanborn.

I knew I was doomed. Sanborn wouldn't have sent a special delivery letter to wish us a Merry Christmas, or to tell us he was the father of a baby girl (though he was, and that was one of the things he had to say). It was too soon for grades. They usually came right before New Year's and gave me an excuse to get dead drunk.

My father was pale and trembling when he began the letter but he was red by the end, and no doubt his ulcer had just been doused with acid. He threw the letter into my mother's lap where she'd just put down a magazine.

"Read that and tell me what you think of your good-for-nothing son. *That's* what you've been working for! How do you feel now? No, you wouldn't listen to me, you thought there was some good in him. He's rotten *to the core*. I knew it. I tried to tell you. Now you know."

My mother only sobbed. I wanted to hold her in my arms and comfort her, but I had to get ready to fight my father. I'd been thoughtful and pleasant to him thus far in my vacation and it was a shock to feel the old hatred welling up.

"I suppose I got thrown out of school," I said as calmly as possible.

"You're damned right you did! And they should have done it a long time ago!"

My mother was out of her chair and getting between us. She knew what was coming.

"That's not the end of it, either. I'm throwing you out of this house! I don't want you in my house! Get out! Get out of here right now!"

"John, please. Where will he go? Be reasonable."

"Out! I won't stay in the same house with that monster!"

"Listen, you asshole . . . "

It was like throwing cold water on him.

"I'll join the army. I mean it. My 18th birthday's coming up. Or you can sign me in now, since you're so anxious to get rid of me. But until I join up I'm staying right here whether you like it or not. This is my home, too. It's the only one I've got. If you cause me any more trouble, I promise you, I'll lay you out cold. Unless you want big trouble around here for the next few weeks, I'd stay out of my way and keep your big mouth shut."

"I'll call the police!"

"What are you going to have them arrest me for? Bad grades? Even if you could get them to arrest me, they wouldn't be keeping me long. I'd get out and I'd be coming for you. Try me if you think I'm bluffing."

He was convinced. "All right. There's a recruiting office in Stamford. See that you get down there today."

"Don't give me orders. I'll get down there soon enough. I've got some things to take care of first. I'm not joining up till I hear from Jan."

When the ruckus died down I had a look at Sanborn's letter.

One of the boys in the dorm (I guessed) had left a letter for Sanborn the day he went on holiday. The boy wanted to be discreet because he was afraid of retaliation from "your son" (the monster). This boy had complained that I was throwing wild booze parties in the dorm, and had steered

Sanborn to a filing cabinet in my room where big bottles of hard liquor could be found.

Sanborn had entered my room, opened the filing cabinet by force, and found a full bottle of liquor, and one half-full. (This showed how little I'd been drinking since the party. Practically nothing, in fact.)

The Discipline Committee was informed and Gordon Bancroft was immediately expelled from school. His room-mate, Barton, was put on probation. Barton had not been one of the drinkers, according to the informer, but he had known about the liquor and had been protecting Gordon.

Sanborn ended by saying he had held off sending the news of my being expelled until after Christmas so as not to spoil that day for two parents who had cared so much about their son, and tried so hard to influence his behavior . . .

P.S.: My father was to come alone to the campus to pick up my things. If I were seen anywhere on campus, the police would be called.

All of a sudden everybody wanted to hand me over to the police. What would Sanborn's complaint be? Suspected drunk and disorderly conduct sometime last October?

Too bad we hadn't killed all the bottles at the party. Too bad I hadn't dumped the rest of the stuff (but the thought of dumping something so precious never occurred to me). Too bad about a lot of things, but the timing of Sanborn's discovery was worst of all. I'd been eager to hear from the school because I was sure of good grades and my parents badly needed something to be happy about.

Jan's trip to Minnesota and Colorado was my salvation. If we'd been together for Christmas she'd have known about my getting thrown out. As it was, I wouldn't tell her. She wasn't close enough to the school to know what was going on. I'd stay with her four days, five, until I was supposed to be back in school, and then I'd explain what happened. By then she'd be so in love with me she'd trust me to find a way to go, a way to succeed, even if I had to do it as a soldier. I'd become an officer, a leader of men. I'd visit her in my uniform, marry her and live with her on the base. My head was swimming with possibilities. I kept counting the ways I had open and inventing happy endings no matter which one I chose. Thank God I still had Jan, I thought.

But the days passed and there was no word from her. There was a thaw, and I played some basketball down at Charley's. I said hello to the people at the drugstore where I used to hang out. The Italians in that drugstore and the little commercial center around it never seemed to change. The big-breasted Italian girls were already big-breasted Italian women. They might have been putting the weight on so gradually that you never noticed unless you were gone a few months at a time like us kids who went away to school.

Right before New Year's there was a blizzard and I did some snow-shoveling and made some money.

Time was running out for me and Jan.

I was tempted to give her a call. My good sense told me she was having fun in Colorado—getting laid, no doubt— and wasn't in any hurry to come home.

Feeling sheepish, I did call on New Year's Day. No answer. Nope, she still wasn't back, I thought.

The next day my father left early for Andover to return *Nana* to the library and collect my things. I was still waiting for my grades, but when the mail came at eleven there was another big shock. A thick letter from Jan.

I would have been delighted if I hadn't noticed by the postmark that the letter had come from her home. She was home, but she hadn't called!

With a sinking heart I opened the thick envelope and found inside all the love letters I'd written over the last four weeks of school when I was only able to see her on weekends.

There was a brief note in her hand.

Gordon:
I never want to see you again. Even though I'll never

forget what we had I don't want you to write or call. I'm not going to change my mind. My reasons are sound.

Goodbye, Jan

I jumped up and down yelling "No!" My mother and my brother were scared out of their minds. No doubt they were sure I was finally out of mine. I grabbed a baseball bat and went out to swing at an old tree in the backyard. When I broke the bat I continued to assault the old tree with my fists. At last the pain of my bleeding hands eclipsed the pain inside.

For a couple of days I wandered the town like a madman. I only came home to drink my father's liquor right out of the bottle. I was turning into a derelict in front of my parents' eyes.

The police picked me up wandering aimlessly in the snow on the town beach. These were both guys who knew me and they were kind enough to bring me home.

I just had a few drinks and left again. I was beginning to look such a fright, my father was worried the army wouldn't have me.

I pulled myself together enough to make a phone call. I didn't think she'd talk to me, but maybe I could find out what went wrong, a shred of evidence. Or if Jan wouldn't talk, maybe her father would tell me what was going on.

I was incoherent from pain when Mr. McBride came on the line, but he knew it was me.

"She doesn't want to talk to you, Gordon."

"What is it . . . Tell her . . . Tell me . . . Why, Misser McBride? Why, tell me."

"She wouldn't like to know that I told you, but it moves me to hear your voice like that. Much as I thought I wanted to see you hurt, I'll give in to you on this. When we got back from our skiing holiday there was a letter here accusing you of talking about your intimacies with Jan in front of your classmates. I thought this was nothing but slander from

240

some fellow who wanted to know Jan better himself, but I guess it wasn't. The letter was full of details about your relations . . . things about Jan that no one but you could have known. I'm sorry, but there you are."

It took me a while to reply. "It's not true. No one signed?"

"It was typed and unsigned. Jan has no idea who the fellow might be. Even if she knew she's told me she wouldn't tell you. You'd want revenge and that won't do. We'd like you to forget Jan and finish the year as best you can. Come to think of it, I saw the boys coming back today. You'd better get yourself together. Start thinking about your hockey games."

"They threw me out."

"How could they do that to you after all your hard work?"

I had nothing to say.

"What are you going to do now, son?"

He hadn't called me son in a long time. "I guess I'll join the army."

"I see. Well, that's a hell of a way to learn a lesson, to have all the walls come tumbling down, but I think you've got a lot on the ball and you'll make something of yourself someday."

There was nothing more to say.

I knew what I had to do. Tom was the only friend I had left. I'd borrow some money from him and borrow the hot rod he was fixing up. It wasn't much of a car, but it would get me to the school and back. I couldn't think of leaving today in the shape I was in. I'd have to set off in the morning when I'd sobered up.

As it happened, it took me a couple of days to get myself together, but it was just as well. Now I'd be going up on a Saturday when I might be able to catch her at home alone.

Every kid in the school came to a halt when he saw Tom's car, and when the kids saw me behind the wheel their eyes popped out. The whole school already knew about me being expelled. Tom's car was a '51 Ford, a two-tone job (green and blue) with an extra long aerial, a necker's knob, and mudflaps with metal stars on them that dragged along the road thanks to the fact that the car had been chopped and decked, or lowered, or some such shit. Frankly, I had no idea what my brother had done to the car, but the back end was riding mighty close to the ground.

I didn't acknowledge any of the staring boys and I ignored the waves and the shouted comments of my friends. I wasn't drunk, but I'd had a couple of beers on the way up to take the edge off, and I had four more on the seat getting warm.

I parked near the dorm.

It was afternoon. Bright and cold. There was an inch of new snow and it was still coming down.

I got past Sanborn's and took the stairs two at a time.

Barton was in. Being on probation there was no place he could go.

"Gordie . . . " He was glad to see me, I could tell, but surprised by how awful I looked.

"Do you know who ratted?"

"No. They've got me on probation."

This was the first time Barton had ever been disciplined at Andover. I'd heard about people the first time they were arrested: they could even cry.

"I know all about it. I got thrown out, so don't try to make me feel sorry for you. What do you think, was it Thomson?"

"Gordie, really, I don't know."

There was someone else. It upset me to think it could be him, but . . . "Did Gill come back? Have you seen him yet?"

"Sure, I saw him today. He's still got the cast on. Maybe a smaller one."

"I hope he's not the guy behind this."

"You think it might be Gill? Next you'll think it was me!"

My look told him "never."

"All I know is that I'm going to be thrown out if Sanborn catches you in here with me. We've all been told to report it to him right away if you ever come around."

"Jesus, what a bunch of babies they are, the people at this school."

"How is your girlfriend taking it, you being thrown out?"

"I haven't got a girlfriend. Someone wrote her a letter telling about all the dirty things I've been saying about her in front of the 'whole school.' I know Thomson is behind this. He knew her address. He's the one who told the guys on the team about me and her, not Gill."

"But her address is in the phone book, isn't it? A lot of people know her name."

"I'm sure it's Thomson. I'm going to do him in, the son of a bitch."

"Gordie, please, don't try anything. We'll all be in more trouble. That's all you'll accomplish. Thomson is tough. He'll put up a hell of a fight."

"He'd better, because if he doesn't I'm going to kill him."

"You're crazy. Don't make me stop you. I don't want to have to go to Sanborn. Sleep it off and go on home. You'll regret it if you don't."

"I'm not drunk. And don't try to stop me with your fists, Jim. Please don't let there be blood between us after everything that's happened. I want you to make it through, to make it to Harvard next year. When I'm in the army or someplace I want to be able to think of you and know that you're getting by in life. That you're doing well."

Barton claimed that he was the only guy left in the dorm, or just about. He'd heard Thomson leave, he'd left with some others, and he knew where Thomson was: at the Cage, the enclosed arena where the winter track team worked out, to watch the time trials. Thomson was out for winter track this year—putting the shot and throwing the hammer.

Barton suggested I "sleep it off" on my old bed, and see how I felt about Thomson three or four hours from now. Anyway, if I still wanted to confront him, he might be back in the dorm by then.

I went along.

About seven o'clock I stepped into the hall and the guys who were chatting outside their rooms fell silent. No one made a dash to tell Sanborn, I was glad to see.

I walked up the stairs with Barton behind me. He was going to protect Thomson or me if there was trouble (whoever was getting the worst of it). I think he was counting on having to protect me.

I heard Thomson's voice inside his room. He wasn't alone. I knocked.

He opened after a moment.

"Whah, Gawdon, good to see ya."

He had his hand out as he stepped into the hall.

I hit him with all my might. I hit him with my whole life, right on the end of his chin.

He couldn't even put his arms out, going down.

I knew by the way it felt that I'd broken his jaw. Somehow I didn't have the heart to kick him in the balls or put my heel in his face. Someone was holding me back just in case.

Big Porter emerged from Thomson's room to see what had happened to his friend. I could tell by his face that he was delighted, but he changed his expression right away.

"You want to try to put me down with a sucker punch, Bancroft?"

"If these guys'll let go of me, you'll get yours."

"You're a bigger dummy than I thought."

At that moment Channing came down the hall and told Porter to back off in a loud voice.

"Jesus, Channing, don't tell me there's another idiot in this dorm who wants to get his ass kicked."

"You're not going to kick my ass, don't worry. But I'll

sure as hell kick yours if you make a move against my friend."

"Look, Channing . . . " He was going to say, "I've got no quarrel with you," but Channing cut him off.

"Help Thomson get back in his room."

"Don't anyone lay a hand on me. I'll take care of mahsel'. Fuckah broke mah jaw."

Thomson got to his knees. Then his feet. He was weaving. Rhythmically, in pain.

"Why don't you head down to the infirmary," said Channing in a quiet voice.

"Like as I will," said Thomson, stumbling into his room.

Porter made way, then followed him inside. Their voices were loud and unintelligible. It sounded like a scuffle.

Thomson emerged with a hunting knife in his right hand. By this time the guys had let me go and I raised my arms to take him on. Channing stepped in front of me.

"Back off, Gordon."

I did, and pushed the crowd behind me back as well.

"This bastard is going to get what's coming to him once and for all."

I had found out from Barton that Channing had been put on probation for letting me drink in his room. As if I were the only one who had . . .

Thomson wouldn't back down. He knew how to use a knife. He had it low, blade high, but when he leapt at Channing a strange thing happened. Strange, because no one could have anticipated Channing's movements. With his left hand Channing had Thomson's wrist next to the butt of the knife. In the same split second Channing had Thomson's shirtfront with his other hand. Dropping onto his back he brought his feet up into Thomson's middle and propelled him right over our heads, clear down the hall.

He hit with a sickening thud and slid to the foot of the wall. That was the end of Thomson. The knife had come out of his hands. I saw his chest move, so he was breathing, but something else was surely broken. He'd had enough.

"Stay where you are, gentlemen, the police are on their way." Sanborn's voice.

"That's tough for them. So am I."

He was standing at the head of the stairs.

"I don't think so, Gordon. You belong in custody."

"Fat chance. You could try to hold me, sir, but a lot of people are going to get hurt. Go on, say the word. I'm sure you can find enough guys to do your bidding. Is that what it takes to make you feel good? Speaking of feeling good, how did you like that booze of mine you confiscated? I don't hold that against you, but I think it stinks to throw a guy out of school for taking a drink. French people would laugh at you. I laugh at you. I'll be having orgies in France while you're still here grading papers and threatening boys with a lousy future if they won't do as they're told."

Channing stepped in again. Channing was always stepping in, it seemed.

"Why don't you just let Gordon go, sir? He's had his revenge. He won't be back. It's over."

"I'll let him go, but I want him to know that he hasn't had his revenge. He's hurt an innocent man."

He'd noticed the wreckage at the end of the hall that was Thomson.

"I want him to know how useless it is to try to solve things by violence. He should have looked to himself if he wanted to grow. He broke the rules and he had to leave our school. It's as simple as that. I'm sorry to see him go. He may not believe me, but I am. He was a good boy. All of you are good boys—good men. But you can't make your own rules. You can't now, you can't when you go to college, and you can't when you go to work someday to earn a living. Rules are what keep peace in the world, and until Mr. Bancroft appreciates that fact he's going to fail and he's going to suffer."

I shook Channing's hand. Barton's. Sanborn made way for me as I started down the stairs. Then I turned to him.

"You're full of shit, you know. There's another world. A free man listens to his heart. Love makes the rules. And they're different from day to day. Scary, huh?"

I put on my winter clothes in my old room, then I walked down the last flight of stairs and out into the icy night feeling weak and sad.

I came up to my brother's ridiculous car and kept walking. I was reproaching myself for all that had happened. I *had* hit Thomson with a sucker punch. And I shouldn't have let Channing do my dirty work, even if it meant that Thomson was going to cut me up. Would I have been such a big man against Gill?

Gill had to be the traitor. He'd known about my booze and he knew plenty of intimate details about Jan. I could see him wanting to hurt Jan and me in one swipe, to get even. But it couldn't have been Gill because he was the best of the good men.

I've never been sure who it was because I've wanted to be unsure, because I wanted to remember the Gill I'd respected. I needed to look up to him the way some people needed to put their wives on a pedestal or thought one of their kids was a genius.

Was it cowardice that had made me want to believe in Gill's innocence? If so, what kind of soldier would I be? I'd have to fight all my own battles from now on.

Sanborn had been right. Violence was a dumb way to solve anything. Even if Thomson *had* been the informer, I didn't like the thought of him lying there in the hall. I wished there were some way to help him. At least the football season was over. Having his jaw wired wouldn't keep Thomson out of events like the shotput and the hammerthrow.

I wondered if Channing would get in worse trouble. Guys on probation couldn't get away with anything. No,

Channing would survive. Thomson had pulled a knife. There were plenty of witnesses.

What would happen to Thomson when Sanborn found out he'd pulled a knife?

And Barton . . . Would Jim be in trouble for letting me stay in his room? That had been a dumb move on my part, going into our old room right in front of Sanborn. Barton had a right to hate me for that, but what else could I have done? Supposing the cops were really on the way? I had to clear out.

Groups of boys were on the way to the Saturday night movie which was shown where we had school meetings on the Main Quad. I stayed out of hailing distance and drifted along the snowy paths between class buildings, alone. It was still snowing. No breeze was taking the flakes. The lights along the path reached up with a yellow and blue glow to the ivy-covered buildings. Some of the leaves were keeping the snow. The brick was faded where it showed through the ivy.

These were the original buildings. These five or six were the school two hundred years ago. When these bricks had been laid Andover had been an idea, not a tradition. The simple beauty of the school, the old buildings and trees, spoke of the kind of men who had dreamt of educating American boys—earnest, upright, stern. Since those times the courses, the rules, the way of life had changed, but the beauty of the old campus had remained. It was what I would never forget about my school. But I'd be moving on, looking for beauty somewhere else. The beauty at hand would always be everything to me.

I sat on an empty stone planter under a portico and thought of Jan. We were alike in so many ways. She had gone against accepted morality and I'd gone against my school. Jan wanted a home, a family, things that would be impossible without morality. I wanted to learn, I wanted to understand the lesson that Andover had to teach, I wanted to be prepared for adult life.

Buildings like this might exist for me again someday

and my hard work over the last weeks of the term had convinced me that I could be a good student if I wanted. And I
was sure that Jan would make a wonderful wife and mother
even though she'd gone to France when she was young and
had orgies and liked it all. Just as I couldn't understand how
Jan could do such a thing, Sanborn and my father and all the
other people who were judging me couldn't understand why
I would "throw my life away" for an evening cocktail.

I had trouble understanding why myself. Oh, I didn't
have to be Bellini to come up with excuses. A father who
wouldn't respect me for not striking out the side time after
time. A need to be important to my classmates when I'd
concluded that I'd never be anything but an average student
at the school. Who knows, maybe my wildness was merely a
plea for attention. (But why then had I been so desperate to
be left alone?)

The plain truth was I'd never felt so alive as when I was
"throwing my life away." When you're in love the life you
throw away is never wasted. That was the meaning of a cup
always full.

I went back to Tom's car and drank some beer. I'd left
the door open, but nobody had stolen any. Where were all
the good men? Well, I myself wasn't a good man any
longer. I was a raw kid with a lot to learn. It would be a big
advantage to know that about myself. I wouldn't be kidding
myself that a little world like Andover was all that counted.

It must have been eight o'clock. Maybe later. Mr.
McBride would have gone to Boston. It was time to start if I
wanted to catch Jan alone. I hoped she wasn't going out. I
needed time to convince her, she'd been living too long with
those lies about me. I hoped she was alone at home. I had to
see her again whatever I found.

I drove to Jan's remembering all the times I'd come this
way in her father's car and her own. It was different now
with the snow falling. Hard to remember all the turns.

I parked on the town road near their mailbox. Her driveway was icy in spots that were hard to see in the dark and I

had better footing in the field. For the first time I could see a pattern in the way the young evergreens had been planted. They were like sentries leading up to the house, and I was somehow less afraid of what I was about to do for having these dark and silent shapes in the field beside me.

Only one light was on. Upstairs on the side of the house away from the driveway. Her father's bedroom. A tree outside was green with the light and the falling snow showed brighter.

I crossed the little garden, picking my way through the dormant roses.

I could hear music now. Mozart. A concerto I didn't know. It sounded like a clarinet, but I wasn't yet to the side of the house where I could hear distinctly.

Then I hard her voice, her laughter. The man's voice didn't carry, but there was a man in her father's room with her, there could be no other explanation for her presence there, the laughter and the music.

I circled the lawn as far as I could get from the house so as to emerge beside the tree on the side the light touched.

The snow crunched under my heavy boots. I stepped carefully, stopping to check the window for movement. Hoping to see a shape I recognized. Dreading to.

Jan came to the window. Her father's dresser was there, and I could just see the top of a bottle over the sill. She came to pour wine.

She was naked—to the waist at least. Her breasts were orange in the light.

I couldn't understand what she was saying because of the music. She looked out of the window, but nothing she saw changed her face.

She had picked up two glasses, but before she could turn to serve, a man had come behind her and reached around to fondle her breasts.

She started to laugh and spilled wine.

It was Dr. Bellini.

I'm sure I went blank at the sight of him, saw red or something, but the things I'm about to say were already real to me. Felt things waiting for the right words. Ever since I'd hit Thomson these feelings had been coming up quietly.

I'd never know who it was who tipped off Sanborn about my stash. It could have been Thomson after all and Sanborn had lied to protect him. It could have been anyone on the football team who remembered Jan and knew something about the parties in our dorm. It could have been Gill. It could have been Channing. It could have been Barton, who was terrified that *another* informer would put an end to everything he'd worked for. Sure, it was suspicious that Channing and Barton were only on probation when it was pretty clear that they were in on my cardinal sins from the beginning.

What if one kid ratted to Sanborn and another one wrote to Jan?

Was I going to go through life thinking bad things about people in general just because one or two SOBs had it in for me? No, I preferred to think I hadn't been betrayed by someone I thought was a friend, and I still think of the guys I've named as friends, and always will whether I see them again or not, and that includes Thomson, who probably seemed meaner than he really was to kids like Barton and me who didn't know Southerners all that well.

As for Bellini, who must have been single (I'd never asked, he'd never said), I could have figured any number of reasons that he and Jan had come together. Maybe she needed to see a psychiatrist—if only to deal with the fears that she'd need one someday the way her mother did.

Bellini could have written Jan the letter about me, having been informed by the school that I had to go! He could have been aroused by all I'd told him about Jan and, knowing she'd be upset that I was getting the axe, stepped in to calm her, or was kidding himself that that's all he wanted to do . . .

I didn't think this of Dr. Bellini. Once again, I just

didn't feel such things could be true. Bellini couldn't have been a shit all along, nor Jan the kind of idiot who'd let a guy like that manipulate her.

Gill had told me he'd recognized the man he saw with Jan that night but hadn't known who it was. Well, sure, that was the doctor. He kept out of sight when he was at the school, or just walked around when the guys were in class, because he didn't want to embarrass the ones who knew him. More proof of how he had cared about our feelings.

He must have cared about mine. Imagine how hard it would have been to hear all the things I was doing with a woman he loved, and how she was responding. Imagine letting me go on breaking the rules to be with her!

He would have been perfectly within his rights to be seeing Jan—someone who'd told me more than once how she liked older men. I knew for a fact that Bellini had stuck up for me all year and had done less than any other man in authority to get me expelled. Considering what I'd done to him emotionally, more than anyone else I knew at P.A. he deserved to be called a good man—as the rest of the world used the term, though, and not us kids half crazy from all our deprivations.

Dr. Bellini had been and would continue to be, in my mind at least, a kind of friend. What happened next under Jan's window simply came from me. I still don't know why because it wasn't in line with what I felt about her.

I stormed into the light beneath the window and called as loud as I could: "Whore! Whore!"

The neighbors were a mile away. I gave no thought to their hearing me. I was screaming to the hills, the silent trees, the white sky. My entire being was screaming.

She must have dropped the glasses. Looking down, her face was in silhouette and couldn't speak to me. The light glowed in her hair, on her shoulders, on the underside of her breasts where they spilled away.

She brought her hands to her forehead and screamed "No!"

She wasn't trying to deny being a whore, she'd been scared by the sight of me there, and I must have looked a sight with so much pain on my face.

She raised the window and leaned over her father's bureau so that her face came into the cold and the snow touched her hair.

Her voice was a wail. "I'm sorry! I loved you, Gordon! Forgive me! I didn't think you'd ever come back!"

I was gone. When I rounded the corner of the house her voice was quickly faint. Then a window went up and her voice was plain as it followed me across the lawn, the garden and the field. I never turned back, I never stopped. The tears were ice on my face, my heart was stone. She said the same thing over and over in the same wailing tone: that she still loved me, that she was sorry, that she never thought I'd come back, that I should forgive her, and I think she also said, "You're killing me," "This is killing me."

I had no pity. I would have had if I'd been a better man. Or more a man and less a boy. I couldn't hear the loss in her cries. I wasn't big enough in my own eyes to understand her need. The sound of the woman I loved in such great pain didn't move me.

It was my big mistake. I should have heard, I should have gone to her, I should have fought to have her back.

Instead I lost her. Jan. My love.